12:23

By the same author

THE LAST OF DEEDS
LOVE IN HISTORY
RESURRECTION MAN
THE BLUE TANGO
THE ULTRAS

12:23

Paris, 31st August 1997

EOIN McNAMEE

faber and faber

First published in 2007
by Faber and Faber Limited
3 Queen Square London WC1N 3AU

Typeset by Faber and Faber Limited
Printed in England by Mackays of Chatham, plc

A CIP record for this book
is available from the British Library

ISBN 978–0–571–22341–1
ISBN 0–571–22341–9

2 4 6 8 10 9 7 5 3 1

One

Harper liked French airports. He noticed the way the French applied themselves to the architecture of airports, the way they took responsibility for the lyric matter of flying. There were different ways of thinking about things, an awareness of emergent technologies. There were tunnels, plazas, bridges of lightweight alloys which seemed to possess metaphysical qualities. Outside the airport buildings there were featureless spaces, sun-blasted, reeking of jet fuel.

He took the slow train into the city. It stopped at all the suburban stations. It was dusk and night hung over Paris. The train was half full. The passengers were men wearing plain denim clothing. They seemed to have come from arcane areas of manufacturing. The garment district. The meat district. There were North Africans, Turks. Migrant workers. Even those who only travelled a few stops gave the impression of great journeys stoically undertaken.

Bennett had said to find a cheap hotel. Somewhere anonymous. Bennett wanted him to get a cheap room in a seedy hotel in the streets around a railway station. A room with paper-thin walls and flimsy curtains. Hôtel du Gare. He understood why Bennett wanted this for him. The tawdry atmospherics. It was important that he acquire a sense of lives in decline. The heroin users. The Eastern European prostitutes. The hard-eyed cops. Men with pockmarked faces and gloomy existential outlooks.

He had booked into the Hôtel Quimper beside the Gare du Nord. The receptionist handed him an envelope.

'It came this morning,' she said. She was a dark-haired woman in

1

her early forties with fine dark hair on her arms and on her upper lip. There seemed to be a lewdness to the woman, the way she pursed her thin-lipped mouth, as though on the verge of describing an obscene act.

'Who brought it?' he asked.

'A courier,' she said. She was sorting mail, bending over slightly so that he could see the space where her prominent ribs met her breasts, the complex shadows.

When he got to his room he sat on the bed. He opened the envelope and took out a file. The file was made of heavy brown cardboard, the kind of file that brought an air of the ration book to everything it contained, an air of the hoarded. The front was stamped UK Eyes Only. It looked like something retrieved from a Stasi vault, reeking of betrayal. He took out both photographs and placed them on the small table in front of the window. There was a faint smell of developing fluid, an odour of the lab, of mildly toxic emulsions. Each photograph had a sheet of flimsy paper attached, covered with characters, the document typewritten rather than run off a printer. The characters were flawed, uneven. There seemed to be elements of early printing. Black traces indicating that a copy had been taken with carbon paper. There was meaning in everything that came from Bennett he reminded himself. First was the fact that this had been typewritten to avoid any trace of it in the system. Deniability was being built in from the start. But it seemed to be more than that. The indications were that he would be moving onto a new level of covert activity, something demanding a different set of criteria. The carbon gave the paper an inky, encrypted feel.

He took a felt-tip pen from his briefcase and wrote the men's names across the bottom of each photograph. Andanson, James. Paul, Henri.

The accompanying text gave a bare account of each man. DOB. Height. Current occupation.

Henri Paul was employed by Mohamed Al Fayed.

James Andanson was employed by the Sygma Photographic Agency.

The information on each man was limited to the basics. Cryptic sentences were scrawled in margins. He was to be denied the accretion of detail normal to such files, the undercurrents, the covert texture. The photographs of Andanson and Paul were long-distance and grainy. The backgrounds were indistinct. The pictures made them look like fugitive Nazis, men in shirt sleeves glimpsed in South American market towns, everything about them shrouded in hazy equivocation when what you were after was stark malice.

All the things that Bennett had given him looked unconvincing. Something about Bennett's arcane and seamy spycraft transferred to the room, made everything look as if it contained a concealed microphone, a miniature camera, a cyanide capsule. Spycraft from an era when miniaturisation seemed the key to higher knowledge. Objects were reduced, fitted into even smaller cavities. There were whole technologies of the minute, technologies with a boyish improvised feel to them. The microdot.

He got receipts for everything as instructed by Bennett. A receipt for the Metro ticket. Receipts for coffee, for the Bic razor he bought in an all-night chemist. He bought an alarm clock and taped the receipt to the base of it. This was Bennett's way of ensuring control. Everything had to be accounted for. Minor expenses were queried. You were meant to feel that your employer was niggardly, mean-spirited to the point of derangement. He thought of Howard Hughes. There is something unbalanced about the true miser, suggesting someone capable of taking extreme measures. The hoarders of old newspapers. The frugal meals. You were meant to be reminded that there was an ability to go to any lengths in the pursuit of strange goals.

Bennett had called Harper three days before. Harper hadn't heard from him for ten years. He recognised the voice immediately, the accent London, a stylised Whitechapel drawl.

'This is Michael Bennett.'

'What do you want, Bennett?'

'That's not very welcoming, John.'

'Me and you's got nothing in common any more.'

'I think we'll always have something in common. I got a job for you if you want, Harper. Discreet surveillance and low-key security. Three days in Paris, my son. A piece of cake. Six grand for three days in la fucking belle Paris.'

'Why'd you ring me?'

'Stuff gets around. I heard things were a bit tight in the ex-cop line in Belfast. I heard there are former detectives doing security work on building sites.'

'Big of you to think of me. How much did you say?'

'Six thousand pounds sterling.'

'Who is the subject of this surveillance and security?'

'Can't tell you on the phone, my old son. You've got to come to talk to me in person.'

'Last time I done a job for you, look what happened.'

'This one is safe as houses.'

'When?'

'A week's time.'

'Where?'

'Paris.'

'I never been to Paris.'

Harper was standing in a prefab on a building site in North Belfast wearing a security guard's uniform. It was raining. His life a purgatory of chainlink fenced sites, out in the mud with Alsatians straining on leashes. Harper in a van with a lightning-flash logo on the side of it going from location to location, on night patrol in a hinterland of gritty hereafters.

'I'm your man,' Harper said, 'I'm your fucking man.'

Ritz Hotel
28th August

Harper had gone to bed early on the evening of the 27th and had risen at 4 a.m. He went to the Place Vendôme. He liked to arrive at a target very early in the morning. The time of delivery trucks, early morning shift changes. Even in August in Paris he felt the pre-dawn chill as he left the hotel. In the Place Vendôme a street-cleaning truck left water running down the gutters. The Ritz looked quiet. He could see a lit chandelier in the foyer, among the deep-sunk shadow. Somehow, despite the dawn, the interior seemed to be still in full accord with the night, full of lavish glooms. A limousine was parked at the kerb and he watched as the driver held the door for a group of pinched-looking businessmen with pale after-hours complexions, who seemed adrift and fretful at finding themselves exposed to the day.

Harper circled the hotel until he found the staff entrance. The night staff had started to leave, lighting cigarettes as they pushed through the door. Busboys, cleaners, chambermaids with coats on over their uniforms. An older man who looked like a waiter. He thought that he would follow someone home to work on his surveillance technique. The thing he liked about tailing someone was that it added an extra dimension to the subject. He liked to think of himself as bringing ambiguity and drama to people's lives. That morning he followed one of the chambermaids home. She was a thin girl with her hair tied back, a straight-backed gait. He walked twenty yards behind her, keeping with her as she went down the stairs into the Metro, taking the stairs two at a time. On the Metro she sat down in the middle of the carriage. Harper stood at the end. From time to time his glance swept over her, taking in detail. Her fingernails bitten to the quick. The black slip showing from beneath her skirt. The stubble on her legs under her tights. He started to see deliberation in the signs of carelessness and sexual disinterest. As if she was deliberately working towards a slovenly allure.

The train emerged into the daylight, the tracks running between apartment blocks, every flat surface covered in graffiti, and a simmering feel to the empty spaces between the blocks, groups of youths on the streets even at this time in the morning, a landscape which looked as if insurrection had already swept through, leaving a sullen and war-hardened populace in its wake. The girl got off at the first station. He got off too. The train pulled away until they were the only people left on the platform. He avoided looking at her, but he could hear her heels going towards the exit. He knew he couldn't follow her any further. The exercise was starting to take on the characteristics of a French art film. A middle-aged man, a girl walking alone in bleak urban space. Self-conscious, slightly overexposed, charged with a cerebral eroticism.

He returned to the Place Vendôme on the next train. The train had started to fill with early morning workers. There were more

5

people on the platforms as the train re-entered the city. Men with raincoats folded over their arms. Harper thought Alain Delon. This was a city of pure-white shirts, of lightweight grey suits. He noticed the way the women sat straight-backed with an emphasis on posture. The way they sat with their knees together and their lower legs and feet angled back. Nothing was left to chance in the matter of posture. Harper had read that French women massaged their breasts every day in order to maintain muscle tone. For some reason it left him uncomfortable, this act, the grooming and toning drained of sensual content. This was Paris then, he thought, the teeming arrondissements.

Paris, Route Périphérique
28th August, 9 a.m.

Furst booked into a Novotel on the Périphérique. He liked the idea of inhabiting a prefabricated steel and resin pod. He thought that there was a chilly synthetic glamour to be had. He wanted to inhabit a space devoid of any human element. The single chair was made of hard, textured plastic. The bedclothes were made of crisp, synthetic fabrics. The hotel possessed a sub-utopian allure.

After he had registered he went up to his room He closed the room door and locked it carefully. He took half an hour to unpack his bag. He lined up toiletries in the tiny bathroom. He counted each item that he took from his bag. This was important. He issued orders to himself in matters of hygiene and clothing. These took the form of ordinances, canonical in their detail, as to the length of time in the shower. As to the quantity of shaving foam from the can.

After he had showered he turned on a porn channel. Let the fake whore-moans, the vocabulary of vixens and sluts wash over him. He realised that he had found himself in a completely desexualised space, a room that could not succumb to the tumult of abasement on screen.

He walked to the Ritz in mid-afternoon. The Place Vendôme was busy. There were several black limousines in front of the hotel. Men walking past in short-sleeve shirts, in cotton shorts. Parisians left

6

the city in August, he had read, when the heat and humidity became too much. They left the city and huge traffic jams formed on the autoroutes and the radial hubs of Auxerre and Le Mans. Darkly gleaming transhumance, the air full of tar melt. He sat outside the Duc d'Orléans as the noon approached and the heat increased to a hallucinatory glare. An American Company scientist had told him that researchers had carried out experiments in the 1960s with substances such as mescaline, fly agaric, that they had travelled to remote tundra areas to sit cross-legged on the ground talking to shamans, small men with leathery skin and expressions of cosmic knowingness. They had returned with plant materials that you smoked, chewed, inhaled over boiling water, crumbled into food, pasted on to the skin. They had broken the substances down into their constituent parts and examined them with electron microscopes until they understood enough to develop hallucinogenics as a tool to disorientate interrogation subjects. This was the sixties, the man seemed to be saying. There was an obligation to innovate with reference to ancient ways of life.

Since the scientist had retired several years ago he had found himself troubled by dreams about these experiments, about the composition of the substances they had examined. He would wake up in the middle of the night with chemical blueprints of these substances in his head, eerie compounds with complex molecular structures, spiralling off into infinity.

The sun beat down on Furst's bare head. He left the bar and stood in the middle of the Place, leaning against a tree. He could feel the skin at the back of his neck beginning to burn. He could almost feel the changes in the deep cell structure, the malign genetic shifts, but still he stood there, feeling as if there was an issue of ordeal to be addressed, that by standing in the sun he could drive himself out of consciousness. He started to understand the thinking behind the desert prophets, the grandeur of their vision, how they stood on the edge of reason, working towards an understanding that was sweeping, intuitive, connected to the godhead.

An hour later he saw a police van pull into the corner of the square. Not the gendarmerie, but the paramilitary police, the square, windowless vans harking back to archetypes of repressive

European police forces. He could not see the driver but he knew he was being watched. He could feel the flat-eyed cop stare, the look of disinterest that was in fact a signifier of this anonymous boxy van and its overtones of indefinite detention, politically motivated police violence.

He left the Place and walked east towards the river, buying water on the way. He hadn't seen Spencer but he was in no hurry to come into contact with her. He was creating a context for her, a psychic landscape into which she could later be inserted. He wanted everything in place before she appeared, walking into frame unaware of the artifice that had been imposed on her life.

Furst returned to the Ritz that night. He felt light-headed from exposure to the sun. He felt as if his retinas had been seared. The Place Vendôme seemed over-exposed, flickering, people walking with jerky movements, busy about strange tasks, bent to purposes unknown, and he thought they were like functionaries, tending to the night itself, to the matter and substance of it. It was then that he saw Belinda, standing in front of the Ritz. She lit a cigarette, the match flaring in her cupped hands, giving the portent of a signal to the gesture. The woman seemed to carry an air of political instability about with her, armed troops on the streets, martial music playing on the radio, the evacuation of embassies. It was starting again, Furst thought, in this place, in some unforeseen manner, it was starting again.

Two

Henri would drop into the Bar Laurent. They were fond of him there. They called him the Breton. He liked to pass on jokes he heard in the Ritz. He didn't pose a threat, was the explanation he gave himself. More than that though he could make them laugh. Even the butches. That was a trick he had. To tell jokes to women. When he was small he could make his mother and his aunts laugh. The secret was to be comfortable around women. The butches did not confide in him but the little femmes would come to him, all breathless confidences, and girlish asides. Most men would not have the same respect for them because they were lesbians but Henri did not care what they were. He would ask Monique to tell him what was normal in sex and she would sigh and shake her head and say nothing is normal in sex. Henri told her that he kept a copy of Paris Plan gay, a map of homosexual meeting places, which proved that he had no prejudice.

In addition Henri would look out for the girls when they were going home late at night. Against men who loitered with a hatred of women. There was a possibility of late-night knife attack. There were a range of crooks and addicts intent on robbery, assault against the person. His hometown Lorient of was a haunt of trawlermen, fishers of langoustine, and other stocky types who drank in waterfront bars. Henri knew how to handle himself. He knew these street types could see it in the way he carried himself.

In the evening Henri liked to drive to Le Bourget and park outside

9

the perimeter fencing. He liked to watch the military traffic. The taking-off and landing of F16s. Riveted to the evening light on the silver grey fuselages. Jets taking off like something flung. He had thrown the javelin at the lycée and he knew the feeling of the perfect throw, the wrist-snap at the end. The concrete apron hazed with stored heat, turbine whine. The massed decibels. He liked it when the sound made his ears hurt. As the aircraft dropped in to land you could see the pilots clearly in their tinted visors, the bulbous helmets, as though they were operating in other dimensions, dropping down through the ionosphere, gathering rarefied knowledge to themselves.

His mother said that he had acquired an interest in flying because he was born in Rue Louis Blériot. But that wasn't the case. It was the Mirage fighter he had seen in the Aero Museum when he was ten. The jet planes he saw from the ground had seemed notional, as though they existed to address the abstractions of flight. Up close they were different. There was a smell of industrial lubricants. You could see that the Plexiglas was scratched. There were dents in the aluminium wing panels, streaks of oxidation. The turbine blades were chipped in places. The Mirage had a physicality, worked over, machined. You could imagine Mach 1, out there on the edge of what mechanics could do, the controls bucking in your hands, the aileron judder. That was the reason Henri joined the air force. That was why he liked cockpits, the milieus of sweat-stained leather, the odour of hydraulic fluid. He liked to feel that the achievement of getting airborne was no easy thing, that it had to be worked up to, strained over. That gravity was not to be conquered with transcendence alone.

When he was in the hotel Henri kept on the move. He said that he couldn't do his job sitting in an office. That way you developed a nose for trouble. He liked to talk to malefactors, to understand them. The card fraudsters, the room thieves. He always had to look into their eyes. You had to be constantly aware. There were real assassins who lurked. You had to look for the paparazzi lurking with concealed cameras. You had to look for the stalker on the fire escape. He had to be vigilant against the Eastern European escorts, the Romanians, the Russian girls with their chilly émigré hauteur, the pale-faced blondes with dark shadows under their eyes who were in most demand. Henri thought that men preferred them because they had an air of the sanitorium about them, because they seemed to be death-shadowed. Henri imagined an elegant wasting away, punctuated by bouts of uncontrollable coughing.

Henri had worked that night and had stopped at the Laurent for a pastis before he went home. He told Monique that he felt uneasy. He told her that he had developed an instinct for things. He knew when there was something in the air. There was an underlying sense of events unfolding.

'You read too many books,' she said.

'The pastis doesn't taste right this morning.'

'There's nothing wrong with the pastis.'

'This horse goes into a bar . . .' Henri said.

'No. Don't,' Monique said. Henri thought he could make women laugh but his sense of humour was incompatible with the regime of the Bar Laurent. There was no place for his callow man-jokes. Monique's girls were focused on the stony governance of their state. They dressed in men's suits with pencilled-in moustaches. They wore heavy boots and shaved their heads. They clung to each other in the lonely wreckage of gender.

'You must have woman trouble,' Monique said.

'Why do you say that?'

'Your pastis always tastes bad when you've got woman trouble.'

'It looks the wrong colour.' The lighting in Monique's gave the yellow liquid a sickly hue, like some drained bodily waste-product, corpse-fluid.

'There's nothing wrong with the colour. Wear your spectacles, the colour will be fine.' Spectacles. Monique had a way of using old-fashioned words. Henri told her there was a dowager hidden somewhere in her make-up, a duchess in pearls. He got up with his drink and walked to the door. Monique watched him from the bar, a glass cloth in her hand. There was something about him that you would never really know, she thought. The way he told her one day that he had a key to the DGSE building beside the Ritz. The way he was charming, old-fashioned, then you heard what people who worked in the hotel said about him.

Max had flown in from Miami that morning. Flying in an arc up over Greenland, following the jetstream. Eighty thousand feet. You could see ice on the wings. Absolute zero. Dipping down over Gander. Max always thought of the bases down there. The Arctic tracking stations. The Arctic listening posts. You sleep for a few hours, then you were in Paris, France, swapping the swamp humidity of Miami for a heat that was dusty, European, collecting your matching Vuitton luggage from the carousel, sweeping through customs.

Max turned on his mobile when he got to the British Airways executive lounge at Orly. The first call came from Andanson. Max picked it up on the second ring. He had a habit of picking up the phone and saying nothing. It was a way of undermining the norms. It was odd how often panic set in. The caller found himself babbling into the void.

'Talk to me, Max,' Andanson said.

'Good to hear from you, James,' Max said, 'where are you?'

'I am in Nice.'

'There's a coincidence. I am in Paris. I have business to transact in this beautiful city.'

'Nothing beautiful about Paris in this heat, mate.'

Andanson knew that LaFontaine was not Max's real name. Knowing the choice of alias told you a lot about a man. Max LaFontaine. The self-dramatising nature of it. The name hinting at past preferments, of minor aristocratic lines tragically extinguished. Andanson knew that in Miami Max had presented himself as a Hungarian nobleman in exile, or as a Polish count. People believed him. He had a cruel line to his mouth. His features were fleshy and dissipated.

'I'm glad you rang me, James. I thought we might go for a drink. Somewhere fashionable.'

'Nowhere is fashionable in Paris at the end of August. You should know that, Max.'

'I don't know. Does a royal visit make a place fashionable? All those nice spa towns and casinos.'

'Spencer isn't royal any more. Anyway, nobody is sure that she's going to come to Paris or not, if it matters.'

'My information is that she will come.'

'Where'd you get it? The Breton?'

'What Breton?'

'Don't act it, Max. The Breton that works for the Ritz, for Al Fayed. Word has it he's dodgy, works for the highest bidder. Supposed to have a good bit of money stashed away and all.'

'I'll talk to you soon, my friend,' Max said. He hung up. He liked the way he had said 'my friend' at the end of the last sentence. He liked the fact that he had deployed the phrase with its mock-sinister undertone. He was aware that sometimes he came unstuck in his use of the colloquial. He missed hidden meanings in words, which annoyed him. His life in America was a search for nuance. He worked hard at other aspects of American life, but found himself seeing symptoms of decay when he knew he was supposed to see vigour. When he rented the Palm Beach house he found a small cinema in the basement. He got someone to operate the projector, Max watching 16 mm, a mogul with cigar ash on his lapel. A million dollars. That was the phrase. It made him feel like a million dollars. The velvet cinema seats were worn and napped. There were plaster mouldings of cherubs on the ceiling, vine leaves. Statues of young girls in gilt supported the lights, only one of which worked. When he sat there in the dark, black and white images flickering on the screen, he felt as if he were sitting in the ruins of a lost civilisation.

Two hours later Max was in a taxi on the Périphérique, the traffic not moving at all. Gridlock. He did not understand why traffic words were so hard and clipped. Tailback. The high concrete walls were covered in graffiti and stopped the air from circulating, so that the air was grit-filled. Suspended particulate matter. That was a phrase he had heard. Max used the time to organise the material in his briefcase.

His last night in Miami he had met a girl called Heidi in a hotel. They had both understood what the relationship would be. He liked tall long-legged Californian women, late teens, with perfect teeth, athletic and impersonal in sex. A girl bright and disconnected with small high breasts who talked in a brittle post-adolescent argot.

But when they got back to the apartment he realised that he had made a mistake. He knew it by the way she looked at the ground-to-ceiling velvet curtains, the heavy pre-war Viennese furniture with mythic carvings. She went into the bathroom. When she came out he took her into the bedroom. She sat down on the edge of the bed with her hands in her lap. Blonde, despondent. The bedroom furniture was gilded and decorative in a French style. The windows had full-length shutters on them. The house seemed to be calling out to something in the girl, to have awakened a part of her that she didn't know she possessed, a sombre, Teuton soul music.

This was the point where a girl usually produced a bindle of cocaine, chopped it out on the glass bedside table. This was the point where she would ask him, like, what do you do? And Max would reply in sweeping and grandiose generalities. That he was a consultant to the intelligence community. That he was involved in risk assessment for companies and governments that wished to undertake international trade. But she didn't ask. She stood up and took off her clothes without speaking then lay down on the bed. The lamps cast long shadows, allegorical shapes. Max started to wonder how he had found himself here, with this fair-haired girl, a pale Germanic princess, naked on his bed. He sat down and touched her ankle. Her flesh felt cold. He went into the bathroom and saw the empty packets of Paracodol, the basin filled with glittering silver-foil wrappings like a spent coinage.

Max had put the girl in an ambulance and moved forward his departure for Europe by a day.

It was after seven before the taxi turned on to the Champs-Elysées. Max leaned back in his seat. This was his favourite part of Paris. He remembered the newsreels from the war, German tanks on the Champs-Elysées, motorcycle sidecars, tracked vehicles. It was the first time he had seen Paris and the image endured, but transmuted with the years, the film fresh when he had seen it, yet somehow picking up the flickering uneven texture of old film stock, the white-out glare, so that it was not the look of triumph on the faces of the Hauptführers that stayed with him, or the Unteroffiziers with caps pushed to the back of their heads, a cigarette burning in the corner of the mouth, but the sense of the whole thing travelling into oblivion, a maw opening to receive the ghostly Panzergruppen.

He checked into his suite at the Hôtel George V. The hotel was important. Being recognised by the doorman of an internationally recognised luxury hotel was of consequence in Max's world. Overblown flower displays on Louis XIV tables. The grandiose fittings, the obsequies, the large dimly lit lobbies. These were the places of complex, barely seen brokerage. These suites were the places where treaty terms were studied, contingencies were planned for, refined appetites were sated.

                                        Novotel
                                        5.30 p.m.

Furst picked up an envelope from reception and walked down the street to a cafe where he stood at the zinc counter and ordered a coffee. He opened the envelope. Like the others it contained a photograph and a single sheet of foolscap. The photograph was of a man in his sixties with greying hair swept back over his ears. It looked like an enlarged passport photograph, taken in grey light, developed in tired chemicals, printed on cheap paper. It seemed that the man had set out to project burly confidence, but instead had ended up with a look of dank earnestness. He read the typed paper. Max LaFontaine. Aka Jean Morin. Aka Maxim de Beranger. Aka Artur Jabulowski. Aka Gerald Somner. Aka D Koeler. Thought to have been born Georg Tuchman. DOB 16 March 1930. Place of birth Munich.

Furst read on.

In 1987 he allegedly stood trial in Germany on weapons procurement charges and was found guilty. In 1991, he allegedly passed information to Reuters news agency of CIA involvement in the death of the late Prime Minister Aldo Moro of Italy. In 1990, he allegedly attended the World Socialist convention in East Berlin,

East Germany, and produced a card describing himself as a former Mossad agent. In 1989, he was allegedly convicted in Rome, Italy of impersonation of a police officer. In 1986, he was allegedly arrested by the French police for arms trafficking. In 1983, he allegedly presented himself as a professor of politics at the University of Notre Dame. In 1971, he allegedly obtained false credit by producing a forged FBI identification card.

Furst put the envelope on the bar. He had come across people like Max LaFontaine before. Men and women who operated on the fringes of the intelligence world, who seemed to have a capacity to absorb spook texture. They appeared on documentary programmes with their voices electronically disguised. They were aficionados of sweeping international conspiracies, lonely edifices of intrigue. They held meetings in hotel rooms in Geneva, New York, Brussels. They were students of multiple identity. Often they were mired in lengthy court proceedings in several jurisdictions, with parts of the evidence being heard in camera, significant portions of the transcript blacked out. There was always money, accounts held in offshore banks under an alias. Furst knew that such men were partial to complicated pyramid schemes, dubious savings schemes, and other methods of parting citizens from their money.

The fact that the file had been sent to him implied that LaFontaine was in Paris. It didn't surprise him. He knew that LaFontaine would have a feel for the outlines of an event taking shape, an intuition. Such men were readers of the minor signs and portents. LaFontaine would have some indirect interest in the affair. He would stand ready to profit in some way.

Place Vendôme
6.00 p.m.

Furst followed Henri home from the Ritz. Normally Henri drove his retro-styled black Mini home, but on occasions he walked, stopping at a kiosk to buy a copy of *Ouest-France*, stopping at the lesbian place, the Bar Laurent. Furst waited across the street, trying to see through the door of the bar, peering into the fug, the libidi-

nous miasma that seemed to lie beyond the plastic beaded curtain at
the door, watching the patrons come and go, the wounded, the
brisk and mannish, the sick-at-heart subculturists. He wondered
what drew Henri to such places. His briefing had said that on com-
mencing his National Service Henri had applied for pilot training
but his eyesight had disqualified him. Instead he had worked for the
security detail at the Rochefort air base. Henri held a Class A pilot's
licence. Furst sensed that the failure to become a fighter pilot was a
defining event, sensed that Henri might need the means to navigate
disappointment, that he might seek out those who had returned
alive but not unchanged from the icefields of unfulfilled longing.

Furst had gone freelance from the SADF in 1986. From the start he
had been useful. At first they used him to disrupt marches, to con-
vey low-level intelligence, to run minor informants, to lead teams of
thugs and others with the same repugnant aptitudes as himself, to
incite instances of riot and pogrom where it appeared that it would
be in their interest.

They brought him to the Joint Intelligence Centre at Ashford in
Kent to instruct him in agent handling, and there he mingled with
renegade policemen, informers under instruction, men being trained
as assassins. The place teemed with the protégés of loss.

They were instructed in interrogation techniques by personnel
from Langley. The six techniques. A pockmarked Argentine with an
evangelical air taught them a history of interrogation. Bastinado,
strappado, the clamped-on electrode. He told them that it was all
about purity of mind, purity of thought. You directed your subject
towards the silence within. In the middle of political chaos people
needed the certainty provided by unexplained disappearances, he
said, random abductions performed by organs of the state. They
needed to be gathered in midnight swoops, in dawn raids, to be held
in football stadiums, kneeling, afraid. They needed to know that
torture and arbitrary arrest were out there, a dark and compelling
undercurrent, a theology of despair which underpinned society,
presided over by hawk-faced men in ornate military uniforms.

Furst talked to him in the mess afterwards. The Argentinian said
that in the early days there was a spirit of cheerful amateurism

17

among his fellow interrogators. They were all in pursuit of the same goal. Equipment was scarce, there were electricity blackouts. They developed hand-cranked generators for administering shocks. There was a movement towards a return to the values of the past. Sexual mutilation was frowned upon. Courtesies were extended to the prisoners during lulls in the interrogation. The man grew wistful. He implied that there had been a better calibre of victim then, men and women of integrity, adherents to the great political creeds of their time. You rarely got that kind of person any more, he said. Too often the new ones were without conviction of any kind. There was no feeling that the betrayal of a friend or a comrade had to be wrenched from a great depth, of dignity having to be stripped away layer by layer. They did not resist the complicity offered by the interrogator. They were incapable of gratitude.

Henri left the Bar Laurent at 6.35 and walked to his apartment at the Rue Cambon. At 6.45 he left the apartment and walked to the Place de la Concorde Metro station. Furst followed him into the station. He stood at the machine beside Henri when he bought a ticket. When a train entered the station Henri got on at one end of a carriage, Furst got on at the other. It was turning into a proper surveillance, Furst thought, with all its self-conscious motifs, all the textures of deceit, the train jolting into the tunnel, a high-voltage tang in the air, and a momentary sense of true pursuit, hard and crisp and pure, that made the hairs on the back of Furst's neck stand up. He could see the reflection of Henri's face in the window opposite, his moustache giving him the look of a player in some Middle European intrigue, an artful but minor historical figure. The flickering lights, the tunnel grime. Furst reminded himself that Henri worked in security. He might already be aware of Furst. The briefing said that he maintained his contacts in the DGSE and the Renseignements Généraux. He could have been taught some tradecraft. It was quite possible that he knew that Furst was following him. That he had a tail, a shadow.

When the train stopped at the Bois de Boulogne, Henri stood to get up. Furst watched him get off then stepped through the doors just as they began to close. In contrast Henri had the air of a man on lawful business about him. He walked out of the station looking brisk and industrious, Furst coming up out of the Metro after him as though he trailed tunnel-shadow behind him.

Furst followed Henri through empty, sunlit streets until he saw the pine trees up ahead, a wood of some sort with the look of old-growth forest about it, dense and encroaching. The Bois de Boulogne, he thought. As they reached it, Furst looked under the trees – dark recesses padded out with ancient ferns and lichens. As if it were the remnant of a great forest that swept down from the Arctic Circle. As if it were a forest of antiquity, hedged about with grim and magic lore. He saw Henri turn abruptly, seeming to enter the forest itself and he hurried after him, but when he caught up with him he saw that the trees had opened out into a formal playground where women wheeled babies in old-fashioned black prams. There was a carousel, a sandpit, swings. He could hear a Viennese waltz. There were divorced fathers whose children held them by the hand, brows furrowed, looking as though they were being guided through the rules of loneliness, the exquisite hierarchies. There were women dressed in Chanel, Dior, Givenchy, fortyish, with the straight backs and full lips of the sexually unattainable, many of them accompanied by small boys, dressed in suits.

Henri crossed the playground to a blonde woman in her early thirties. He put his arm around her waist and kissed her on the cheek. Something was absent from the kiss, and the way she presented her cheek it was as if they were acknowledging each other's disappointments. Ex-girlfriend Laurence Pujul, Furst thought. There was a little girl playing in the sandpit in front of them and Henri went down on his hunkers to talk to her. The child kept on playing as Henri smiled at her. Not Henri's daughter, Furst thought. Blonde like her mother. Harper feeling the detail of Henri's life starting to accumulate now, the gritty accretions.

Three

At Heathrow Grace had stocked up on magazines. Hello! OK! with Princess Stephanie on the cover. She had a particular fondness for Stephanie, but she was drawn to both sisters. The powerboat pilots, the chauffeurs. The high-cut swimwear. The wearing of thongs. Their vulgarity was a largesse they bestowed upon the world. They understood this. They stared from the front pages of magazines wearing designer sunglasses, tan-lined, haunted. Le Retour Mélancolique de Stephanie, Paris Match said, as though melancholy had not always dogged her every step, her every bad choice, her taste in men, her small breasts bared to the pitiless Mediterranean sun. Monaco was a sunny place for shady people. There were dense and particular memories which attached themselves to minor royals. Something fierce in their faces.

Stocked up. That was a phrase of her mother's. She cut things in half, portioned fruit, sought out the reusable and durable.

Hello! carried the photograph of Spencer in a bikini with a bulge at her waist.

'A woman with children is not as trim as some,' her mother used to say. Meaning it to be understood that Grace had not given birth. Barren was the word they used. Of her loins. Though she had seen once, glimpsed on an emergency ward, a woman on a trolley, her legs spread underneath the green cover, her head turned away in rictus so that all you could see was the tautness of the neck muscles, the knotted cordage under the skin. That was what produced the sag at the abdomen, the stretched pelvic sinews, the mortal torsion.

20

If Spencer got pregnant then the father would be an Arab, her mother said, given to cruelties against women, intimate violations. They call him Dodi but his real name is Emad which has the sound of the burning desert about it.

He drinks whisky and soda, Grace told her. He is a film producer in America. Unspeakable things, her mother said. They kidnap your children and bring them back to their desert dwellings to be raised by in-laws. You read about it. Children raised in comfort and attending secondary schools and suddenly they are married to a man old enough to be their father.

Though to be fair to her she didn't complain about the home with its kidney dishes and adult incontinence pads and day rooms and the tears of the old and the bleak parsimonies of retirement-home owners. On the seafront at Margate.

Grace would wake from dreams of the elderly, tottering after her, odorous, damp eyes filled with hate, wielding a ghastly paraphernalia of support bandages, flesh-coloured hearing aids.

From the airport shuttle she scrutinised the airport radar systems. Since Menwith Hill she was aware of communication equipment. CB aerials, microwave transmitters concealed in lift shafts, satellite discs. It was the way you assessed a building's place in things. The way you saw more on police stations and army bases, foreign embassies. The clusters and arrays. The frail assemblages. The antennae were always assembled from cutting-edge alloys. The deployment of dark technologies. She knew the way it worked, the meshes and grids, geodesic domes deployed across windswept hillsides. These antennae were the way they made their presence felt, working their way outwards from the secret ranges, the tunnelled-out places. When she had received her posting to Menwith Hill she liked the sound of the name. It made her think of standing stones, the henges and tors. There was an awareness of ley lines, planetary alignments. In the early 1960s her mother had started to collect all the literature on the subject. She started bringing Grace to festivals. There were photographs of her mother in the mud at Stonehenge and Glastonbury, wearing beads and a long flowing skirt. Already too old to be there, but the younger people seemed to gather around her. There was room for the elder in their mysticism. There was scope for the toothless and mumbling crone. Her mother had performed tarot readings in their front room at Margate and talked about travelling on the great roads, the dusty thousand-mile trails. She wished to expose herself to all aspects of enlightenment.

That was what Grace had expected when she started to work at the communications facility at Menwith Hill. To stand looking up at a low hill in a fading December light, of winter solstice, open to awe, ancient lights. She had not expected the miles of fencing, the low anonymous buildings, the bristling installations. A gate with British guards that you had to pass through, then a further inner ring of fencing manned by curt Americans, marines she thought. She had not expected the sense of massive installation, the signs prohibiting photography. In the distance she could see men in one-piece white suits walking between low-slung buildings. The hooded suits made them walk bent forward, as if a wind blew between the buildings, a zephyr, eerie and localised.

She had booked through an offer in the Daily Mail. Paris, city of romance, flight only. She wanted to stand in the Tuileries, the Luxembourg, all the fragrant jardins. Bennett had booked her into the Hôtel Quimper. As she waited in the foyer a cadaverous man with black hair slicked back and burning eyes propositioned her. He touched her wrist and his hand radiated a feverish, doomed heat, as though mortality would be an issue in the encounter on offer.

She had an hour before she met with Harper. She took the Metro to the Bois de Boulogne. It was a place that she had always wanted to see. There were women of her own age and younger walking with boys in shorts with ironed creases and girls in belted dresses. There was the laughter of children. There was the pride of parents, shot through with wistfulness. She thought that the scenes in front of her had been devised for her alone, forty-five, childless. That she had come here to be instructed in formal regret, to acquire the disciplines of the childless and solitary.

Grace waited for Harper in an English pub in Pigalle. It was Harper's choice. There were tankards hanging over the bar, fake medieval devices on the wall. The barman had dagger tattoos on both forearms and a Newcastle accent. The customers were made up of French bikers in studded leather jackets, pale girls with multiple piercings, and two Serbian skinheads with skull rings and knife pouches on their belts. The atmosphere was companionable, she thought. There was a recognition of a shared taste for fraudulent baronial glooms, of needs that could only be met by overblown post-medieval symbolism. She was certain that a collection of Nazi memorabilia was not far away.

She saw him come in and stand at the door looking for her. He looked much older now, she thought, the wear showing in his face, the moral erosion. His face was deeply lined. The eyes were slightly bagged, dark, sunken, and his skin was pale. He looked like a figure from an Elizabethan drama, a plotter, a scourge of heretics. Grace wondered if Harper still smoked, if he still drank. She wondered if aspects of violent death were still native to him. He did not look like a man who lived with a woman, she thought. There would be no room for that now. He had liked a sense of subterfuge when he was with a woman. Of a thing taken without consent. In bed she remembered that he liked to see a bereft look. He liked to hear a note of loss when a woman cried out.

She sensed movement from him and she looked up. He had seen her. He had turned her way. A dark lingering stare. As though he planned larceny. Once you get in with that lot, you never get out, her mother had said. He saw her and came over. He sat down beside her.

'Well, Grace,' he said, 'hard to know what to talk about after twenty years.'

'Twenty-two,' she said, and regretted it. It marked her out as a hankerer after old fondnesses, a middle-aged hoarder of regret.

He had met her in Belfast when she was working in the policy information unit based at Thiepval outside Lisburn. He had met her in the mess. When Harper had acquired the demeanour he had been looking for, somehow incorporating the Luger in the shoulder holster he carried into his walk, his plainclothes swagger, invested with enough thuggishness to make it interesting. Not having to work at it any more. He saw her at the bar. She was long-haired, hippyish. She was carrying an Indian bag over her shoulder with little mirrors stitched into it. That was his first impression. Of things that were beaded, hand-stitched, patched, aromatic with oils of the subcontinent. She was smoking Drum, rolling the cigarettes on the bar.

'There's only two places they roll cigarettes as thin as that,' he said.

'Prison and the army,' she said, without looking at him. She had picked up languid from haunted hippy chicks at Glastonbury, at the Isle of Wight.

'Pretty smart,' he said, 'I hope tobacco is all you have in there.'

'Pure shag,' she said.

He had kept the files relating to Glenn and to other matters in the spare bedroom, in a brown cardboard storage box, indexed by date. He told himself that the files were insurance in case anything happened to him. But he knew that wasn't the reason he kept them. At night he took them out and read through them. Marked UK Eyes Only. The Winter of Discontent. Ulster December 1974. Nottingham 1984. The Ulster file contained no written instructions. Everything was deniable. There were yellowed newspaper cuttings. There were Humint photographs of suspects, witnesses, known players. Fifteen years of mayhem.

One night she had stayed at his flat in Lisburn. He had left the photograph of Glenn out by mistake and Grace had found it. She wanted to know who it was. He knew by her look that she suspected a hidden life somewhere, a son she hadn't been told about perhaps. She thought she sensed the presence of regret in his life and was ready to embark on a process of halting revelation.

'He was a rent boy.'

'What is that?'

24

'A boy who sells sex for money.' He could see the way she read-justed her perception of the whole thing. She placed the photograph on the table and bent over Glenn's face then backed away uncertainly as though the boy's face had stirred troubling race-memories.

'What happened to him?'

'He's dead.'

'What happened to him?'

'He was murdered.' She looked down at the boy's face again and he wondered what dark affinities the boy stirred within her that she questioned him.

Harper took the photograph off her and put it back into the file. She never mentioned it again.

She ordered a double gin and tonic for herself while she talked. She told him that when she had left Belfast in 1988 she had worked at the Menwith Hill station as a technical officer, Level 2 clearance, with responsibility for clerical matters. Probably transcribing intercepts, Harper thought. Menwith Hill was Echelon which had global reach. Data was pulled in from satellite intercepts, from seabed cable intercepts, from transnational networks, all the hum and babble drawn down into the nondescript buildings clustered among the geodesic domes. These were the buildings that were there to tell you that you had no secrets. It was important that they were bland and featureless. Their message was sombre. They were tapping your phone line. They had set up surveillance on your computer traffic. They monitored the frequencies. They were in the systems.

In 1992 she had left Menwith Hill. Discharged from the service following a disciplinary hearing was the phrase that she used. He wondered what she had done to merit a phrase of such dark and authoritarian purport. He thought it might be the drinking. The majority of the staff at Menwith Hill were American. There would be patriots there, men of severe and puritanical demeanour. Harper could see what might have happened to Grace. The mornings of shakily applied lipstick and other grooming lapses. How you grappled with recollection, wishing it to yield up only incidents of euphoria, hoping that the night before had not been sullied by bouts of uncontrolled weeping, of falling on exiting a bar, of surrendering to unwanted sexual attention. These were the small, retrospective bounties that you wished upon your drunk self. That your clothes were not torn or sullied, that your handbag was not lost, that consolation would be somehow available as you embarked on a bleak morning.

Harper knew the kind of men that were attracted to these postings. Big-boned, rangy and silent. These were men from the western provinces, the corn belts, and dust bowls, the feed lots and rail heads. They had experience in the field of desolation, and they would be stern and without mercy for anyone who resembled a weak point in the spiritual fabric of things.

'Where do you live now?' he said.

'Margate.'

'What did you do when you left?'

'Just secretarial work. Then Bennett called me.'

'You trust him?'

'My mother's in a nursing home in Margate. I need the money to keep her there. What have you been doing since those days?'

Her mother, he thought, the reason she left Belfast and went home. The reason she gave him anyway. Her phone going unanswered one day, the extension turned off. A handwritten note delivered to Special Branch HQ.

'Security work,' he said, 'that kind of thing. When I got thrown out of the police it got hard to get work. I spent time in hospital drying out. There's a big hole in the employment record. Do you know what you're doing here?'

'Some surveillance job. You?'

'Bennett told me it was somebody important.'

'Bennett likes to talk big. No hints?'

'You know the way he is. He says he's not at liberty to reveal that detail.'

'Not at liberty my arse.'

'The service let him go. He's out on his own.'

'He says he's got a bit of money.'

'He doesn't look it.'

'He never did. Always looked like an undertaker.'

'He wants me to go and work for him full-time.'

'You going to?'

'I don't know. He gives me the creeps sometimes.'

She kept ordering Tanquerays. She liked the way the barman poured. He treated each drink with the exacting wonder reserved for something you had just invented. She wondered if Harper had pulled her file before meeting her that evening. It was the kind of thing he would do. Examine the file of an ex-lover. The DOB, details of education, contacts, station, level of clearance. The onset of irreversible disappointment, the atrophy of character. She could feel the effects of the gin.

'Slow down on the drink,' he said. They both knew that it was the wrong thing to say.

'I think there's going to be an assassination.'

'You think so?'

'There'll be a man in a crowd, a man of Middle Eastern appearance with over-tinted dark glasses, a revolver concealed on his person. No? A sweating youth with a handgun and misguided political views who will be gunned down in full view of the world's press?'

'How many of those have you had?'

'This is number five. If not the preceding then a CIA trained hitman, an icy sportsman with multiple false identities and a rifle with a collapsible stock.'

'That's enough,' Harper said quietly. 'I'll get you a taxi.'

She could see herself in the mirror behind the bar. Her lipstick was too red. Her reflection flirted with paradigms of manic gaiety. She was working towards the point of conspiratorial whispers, of laughter with a hysterical edge. Harper got her to her feet and took her outside. She considered resistance, girlish flirtatiousness inappropriate to a woman of her age, lapsing into exaggerated sullenness upon rejection. It was one of the things she liked about being drunk. The access to a range of limited but nevertheless theatrical emotions. She had visited the late-night phone calls, rambling and incoherent. She had been to the extreme range of things. The hysterics. The storming off. The lingering threat of self-

27

harm, waking with an open paracetamol bottle beside the bed.

But as Harper eased her into the taxi she felt herself descending into a mood of icy candour.

The taxi pulled off. She could see Harper watching her from the pavement.

'I know what you did,' she said to herself, 'I know what you and Bennett did to that boy to stop him testifying.'

Hôtel George V
28th August, 12.05 a.m.

Max had taken a suite at the George V. He spent the evening watching the news. CNN. Sky News. He felt it incumbent upon himself to keep abreast of international affairs. He read The Economist, Newsweek. He was recognised as an expert in insurance matters. He kept an eye on Lloyd's List. He knew that great traditions were followed there. If a ship insured by Lloyd's sank then a bell was tolled. If you watched the insurance markets you knew what was going on in the world. Insurance was where the alarms were first raised, panics were triggered, premiums soared and plummeted. There were pipeline fires in Azerbaijan. Javanese pirates with automatic weapons prowled the eastern sea lanes. Lawlessness and turmoil abounded. People needed the news to put structure to it. The gravel-voiced men. The women in business suits. It was their function to embody values, to lower their voices gravely.

He ordered dinner from room service. He had telephoned Andanson's agency who told him that Andanson was in Sardinia but was expected back in France that evening. He was worried about Andanson. The last time he had met him he had behaved strangely. He told Max that he was checking under his car every morning for explosive devices, and that he was being followed. He was taking medicine which you placed under your tongue. Max had composed his features in an expression of grave concern. Andanson had many political contacts in high places, he said, but none of them were returning his calls. He hinted at shadowy involvements, sinister individuals lurking in the background. He made late-night telephone calls from windswept toll plazas, bleak concrete underpasses. There was a mystery about these locations, the kind of stark late-twentieth-century locale that a haunted man could take solace in. Max had seen it happen before. A man alone, plotted against, beset by shadowy foes. Max told people that he had taken similar calls from Roberto Calvi in the months before he had been found hanged under Blackfriars Bridge. There were other similarities. Andanson had started to complain of chest pains, a tightness in the abdomen. He had begun to allude to occult forces.

Max was not sceptical about the paranormal. He had participated in a seance with an Appalachian widow in Florida. He had sat over a Ouija board with the teenage daughter of a yacht broker in Key West. People were born again. They spoke in tongues. You did not deny them their accommodations with the mystic.

But the thing with Andanson worried him. Andanson did in fact have political connections that went all the way to the Elysée. You had to ask yourself questions. Why did a paparazzi photographer have connections to the government? Why was Andanson's friend, former Prime Minister Bérégovoy, found in a Nevers canal with a bullet in his head in 1993? There were other violent deaths. Bernard Buffet. Lola Ferrari. Dalida. Claude François. Andanson had been their photographer.

That night as Max lay in the dark, not sleeping, thinking about Andanson, an image of a photographer came to him which seemed to be a memory although he could not place it. A photographer stooping to an old box camera, a black satin cloth draped over his head. In one hand he holds up a stand on which is placed the powdered magnesium necessary to create a flash. There is an atmosphere of macabre processes. The sitters are women in crinolines. Men in high collars and moustaches and the sombre, vigilant expressions of the long dead.

He was woken by the telephone. He sat up and turned on the light. He was used to late-night phone calls. He was accustomed to operating across time zones. In his office in Florida he had a bank of clocks giving the time in Riyadh, the time in Geneva. He knew that people traded in the currencies of foreboding. As he expected, it was Andanson.

'James,' Max said, 'when are you coming to Paris?'

'I'm on my way, Max,' Andanson said. 'Guess what I done today.'

'What did you do, James?' Max said, keeping his tone avuncular, humouring Andanson. He thought that Andanson sounded on the fitful edge of madness. He thought he could see Andanson's face as it was at that moment. The involuntary tics, the glitter in the eye.

'I rented a chopper. A fucking helicopter. Flew over the Jonikal and Al Fayed's place. Got great snaps. I got Spencer in the old one-piece. I got her in the pool. You can see the papers. Lovers relax by pool.'

'Well done.'

'Well done. Well done. You're an old rogue, Max, but I love you. You got wind of what's going on yet?'

'Various rumours are reaching my ears.'

'There's mischief afoot, Max old son. There is mischief afoot and no mistake.'

'Are you coming to Paris?'

'Paris is where the action is. People are assembling for Paris. And Andanson will be there.'

'What kind of people, James?'

'What a spread that would be. Last moments. Star-crossed lovers.'

'What do you mean by last moments?'

'Did I say last moments? Did I use that phrase? I must have been thinking about myself. I got myself in the company of people who know all there is to know about last moments. They're fucking experts in the field of last moments.'

'What are you talking about, James?'

'Listen,' Andanson said, lowering his voice as if to impart a leery confidence, 'listen. If I turn up dead, no matter how or where, I never killed myself. You get that? No matter what they say, I am not going to kill myself.'

'Calm down, James, for goodness sake,' Max said. But he himself was not calm. Suddenly it seemed to him that there was substance to what James was saying. Max knew that there was an expertise out there in the field of suicides rigged to look like accidents. Or assassinations rigged to look like accidents. It made sense to Max. There had to be a mechanism whereby a foe could be disposed of, the awkward, the outspoken, the tainted.

'I'm a fucking dead man, Max,' Andanson said, 'I just haven't got to do the dying yet.'

Four

Andanson had left his house in Lignières on the morning of the 27th. He could have taken the plane but he liked to drive the Fiat Uno. He liked the idea of a fat man in a small car, bearish, sweating, the car a piece of rubbish thrown together in a former fascist tank factory in Turin. There was rust on the underbody. The brake linings were gone. There was four inches of play in the steering and the CV joint was shot but it had a two-litre twin-cam engine and it went like fuck. The kind of car you saw coming across the Italian border loaded with Milanese boys hoping to score a rich bird in Monte Carlo.

He carried a Nikon with Zeiss telephoto as standard, then specialist gear, camera bodies and tripods that cost an arm and a leg. You got to be ready he always said.

The fear followed him down the A7. Through the unexplained emptiness of the Lançon toll plaza at dusk. It entered the foothills of the Pyrenees with him. It lay awake with him in a historic mountain village. A spare cold wind that he thought might be the mistral blew through the shingle eaves of a small hotel chosen from the Guide Michelin. The fear rose with him in the morning. It followed him on winding mountain roads. It followed him. It followed him O Priory of Sion.

Andanson could have parked himself in the Promenade Anglaise, nabbed a suite, put the feet up. But he preferred the old town. It was one of the reasons for taking the Fiat. You could leave it on the street as not worth robbing. He liked the narrow streets, the heat, the slanty-eyed Algerian toms with scag marks on their arms.

He drove the Fiat up to Monte Carlo to see who was about, who had a yacht in the harbour, the place packed with swarthy arms dealers and their hard-as-nails blonde women wearing Gucci wrap-arounds and Prada kitten heels, Andanson thinking you might as well be selling it love, flat on your back in a crib in Nice for it's the same thing. He took a spin around the Rock, a butchers at the palace to see if anybody was home; the palace looked like a time-share in Marbella.

Into the Hôtel de Paris, the maître d' coming out to greet you, some oily Pierre or Marcel with stuff in his hair – pomade they used to call it. He sat up at the bar with a Napoleon in his hand, a few girls around though it was early; they ran the hopeful eye over him but you couldn't fool a tom, they knew the gamey fat old bloke at the bar for what he was.

An Arab arms dealer coming through the bar nodded at him. There were rumours that he kept a stable of Portuguese girls in an apartment in Beausoleil. Had hidden cameras in all the staterooms on the yacht. Get some big spender arms procurement head primed on Dom P then into the scratcher with one of the Portuguese girls. In the morning Romeo is sweating it with 8 by 10s in an envelope slipped under his bedroom door.

Andanson was ready to go back to the airport when the barman brought the phone to him, says there's a call for you, Mr Andanson, which was odd since he thought no one knew he was there.

'James,' Belinda said.

'What do you want, Belinda?' Andanson said. 'It was a nice morning in the south of France until just a second ago. I'm on the verge of hanging up here. I'm on the very edge of slamming the phone down, I kid you not.'

'We need to know if you are going to do as you were asked.'

'What happens if I say no?'

'We need your help, James,' Belinda said.

'I don't know.'

'It is a simple thing to ask.'

'This is true. But I'm busy right now.'

'You remember Paris. The sapeurs-pompiers?'

'How did you know about that?' *How did you know about the fear?*

'Will you do this for us?'

'Are you threatening me?'

'We'll be in touch,' she said. She hung up.

Early in his career Andanson had worked with the Paris fire brigade. With the sapeurs-pompiers. His job was to attend fire scenes and to photograph the aftermath. Immigrants huddled in stairwells. Drunks who had set fire to themselves. Industrial conflagrations. He had never been able to get them out of his mind. Following him through the years, rustling in the corpse shadows, the burned ones followed him, the halt and disfigured. He didn't understand how Belinda knew about it. He didn't know how she had found out about the fear. He needed this like a hole in the head. His BP was off the scale. His complexion was described in his medical notes as florid. The fear was getting worse.

At noon he picked up a flight from Nice to Sardinia. He chartered a half-decker. Andanson hated the sea. He suffered from seasickness, dyspepsia that left him popping Rennies, a bottle of Bisodol rolling around in the footwell of the Fiat. He could feel the gastric juices turn sour at the very thought of it. Rule Britannia and all that malarkey. Her Britannic Majesty could keep it. But the word was that Spencer and Al Fayed were going to get engaged that week and he had to be there. The skipper was young, in his twenties. He told Andanson he wasn't allowed to go any nearer than half a kilometre from the Jonikal, instructions from the police. Do what you're told old son, Andanson said. That was the thing about the police in this part of the world. You didn't fuck with them. You could scream police brutality all you liked but they'd take you into the back of one of their vans and beat seven different kinds of shit out of you. He would have to use the zoom. It didn't matter. He felt that Spencer knew he was there. That she wouldn't let him down. That she would step out on to the deck of the Jonikal in a white swimsuit cut high on the hips, pretending she didn't know that they were there. She knew the score from day one, feeding them girly looks out from under her fringe, the way she stood with the light behind her. Like fuck she didn't know what she was doing.

Andanson's boat drifted on the swell. The Mediterranean light harsher than you would imagine. The sea like some poured alloy, a tremulous foil. The noonday sun casting epic human shadows on the decks of the Jonikal. The skipper turned off the engine and let the boat drift. The temperature gauge on the side of the wheelhouse read 104. Andanson set out his gear on the engine cover. The Nikon. The lens. The tripod. He took a 36-mm Kodak film from the cool box and threaded it on to the spool and shut the back of the camera. Cold air flowed over the sides of the box, coiling on the plank decking, eerie and animate *the leafe, the bud*. Andanson took the lens off the Nikon and attached the big zoom. He leaned it on the gunwale and aimed it towards the Jonikal. There was no one on deck. They would be having lunch in the staterooms *the flowre ne more doth flourish after first decay.* They would be putting on Dolce et Gabbana swimwear high cut on the legs. They would be skilful in the practice of aromatherapy. Andanson attached the tripod to the Nikon and rested the legs on the engine cover. *They would read signs provided for them by their astrologers. They would abide by their instructions.* Andanson settled down to wait for her to come out on deck. He knew she would come. He knew she would not let him down.

Five

Hôtel Quimper
29th August, 9.00 a.m.

Harper rang Grace's room but there was no answer. He dressed and read through the files again. When he had finished he went out to meet Bennett. He doubled back a few times on his way there to see if there was a tail. It was probably unnecessary but every trade had its rituals. You had to feel the pulse in what you were doing. You had to tap into the deep clandestine lode. Then he went to meet Bennett.

Bennett was already at the Café Allegro when he arrived. He was sitting in a corner of the bar with an espresso in front of him. He was wearing a black suit and white shirt. Bringing that post-war East End thing with him. You thought razor fights, the Kray brothers. You thought children with rickets. His hair was thinning. You could see the white of his scalp through it. His skin seemed to have been stretched tight on his face. His hands moved nervously. He wasn't wearing gloves. Close up Harper saw that the eczema had spread to his forehead and face. He seemed to regard Harper through a mask of affliction.

'What do you think, Harper?' he said. 'Tell me what you think, old chum. You think I got the mark of Cain?'

'You deserve it?'

'We both fucking deserve it. We'll rot in hell. In the meantime.' Bennett stood up and stretched out his hand. Harper shook it. The skin felt papery, grafted on. Bennett winced slightly.

'The heat makes the hands worse.' Referring to his own body in the third person the way he had the first time Harper had met him.

36

Although Harper had heard other men do it since. As if they could thereby distance themselves from a torment recalled.

'So what building site are you working on now, Harper?' Bennett said. He lit a Lambert & Butler. 'Are you still stopping crooks from pilfering bags of cement?' Harper took the sneer in his voice as habitual rather than representing any new malice.

'What about you?' Harper said. 'Are you still Det?'

Det meaning detached from your normal unit or rank. Det meaning being sent to work for some shadowy agency or other in order to carry out unattributable operations. An agency based in a empty office in a 1960s block, possessing a shelf company profile, and a bare-sounding acronym. Chains of command were hazy. You were required to operate outside the apparatus. You rarely knew who was running you and everything you did was deniable. Truant operatives working outside the system.

'I'm not working for the government any more,' Bennett said, 'I'm private sector now. Doing all right as well.'

'So what's the job?' Bennett pushed a copy of Paris Match across the counter to Harper. The front cover showed Spencer in a white one-piece bathing suit. She was sitting on the diving board of the Jonikal.

'Her?' Harper said. 'Get a grip, Bennett. You got to be joking me.' Bennett put an envelope beside the paper.

'There's your joke,' he said. 'There's three thousand quid in there. Another three when you finish the job.'

'The woman's got to have her own people. Watching her like a hawk. Security services, the lot. What do they want the likes of me and you for?'

'A man approaches me. An unnamed principal. Reckons he has an investment in her. Reckons that she's not properly protected.'

'What do they want us to do?'

'Just keep an eye. Report back if we see anything dodgy. Any covert activity. That sort of thing.'

'I don't know. This is big stuff and I'm pretty rusty. Doing shift-work at a security company doesn't fit you for this kind of stuff.'

'Come on, Harper. You know how many dozy bastards there are

in the security services. Put the envelope in your pocket. It's a piece of cake.'

'What about this Henri Paul?'

'Henri Paul. Deputy director of security, Ritz Hotels, Paris. Former military policeman at Rochefort air base. Accomplished pilot. Completed Mercedes advanced driving course on an annual basis from 1989 to 1992. Also on good terms with DGSCE. Principal thinks that his contact is a man called Masson.'

'What would French Intelligence want with the likes of him?'

'Good source of low-level Humint. A lot of people stay at the Ritz.'

'How come you got the file?'

'The principal gave it to me. Reckons Henri might be a way of getting at the woman.'

'What do you think?'

'Our Henri also likes to spend time in the company of lesbians and other filthy pervs,' Bennett said.

'Does that mean anything?'

'That kind of thing always means something. In this case it means that there's more to our Henri than meets the eye. Means he can behave in a sneaky capacity.'

'Is he a homo?'

'Nothing to say so one way or the other.'

'What about this Andanson? The photographer?'

'I don't understand that. All the principal would tell me is that he has security service connections. That people have a habit of dying around him.'

'Is Andanson bogey?'

'We just got to keep an eye out for him.'

'Where is Spencer now?'

'In Sardinia. With the Arab.'

'What makes you think they'll come to Paris?'

'The Arab owns an apartment here. He also owns the Ritz. The principal says they'll come.'

'What sort of cover does she have?'

'Two bodyguards paid for by Al Fayed. One of them spent a few years in your part of the world. Former member of One Para.'

'That all? Two Tonka toys for hire. That wouldn't protect nobody. She's completely fucking exposed.'

Bennett fell silent. The thing that they had done seemed to be in the bar with them, huge and looming. Harper wondered if Bennett could feel it the way he did, in its actual presence, something that might brush against you in passing.

'What about the French? Mightn't like us being here.'

'We just keep out of their way. There's plenty of dodgy customers hanging about the shop. We won't be noticed as long as we keep our heads down. Take it right amiss, do the frogs, any sort of funny business on our behalf on their manor. They don't like it when the Yanks do it, they don't like it when the Krauts do it, and they fucking hate it when the Brits do it.'

'I got to ask you something,' Harper said.

'I'm all ears.'

'What the fuck are you doing bringing Grace in on this? She's an alco, Bennett. Was she all you could get?'

'You liked the odd drink yourself, Harper. You and old Gracie were up there with the best of them when it came to knocking it back.'

'I don't drink any more.'

'I heard. Twelve-step boy now by all accounts.'

'Whatever. Grace isn't.'

'She has qualities I like.'

'The qualities of vodka and tonic. The qualities of clean loaded out of the head.'

'You forgetting something, Harper? The memory she has? The stuff she has stored away in that head of hers?'

'She was in admin. She was a typist.'

'She's a fucking recording machine. You ask her, Harper. The booze hasn't got to the memory yet. She remembers the lot. Agents, defectors. Faces, places and dates. The woman's a bloody marvel.'

'What has this got to do with the job on hand? Is she fucking stable?'

'You never know. She sees a face, she remembers it. Like your two bad boys today. She might recall them. Besides, this is not just about

39

this job. It's about the future. If this job works out I could bring her in full-time to work on the admin.'

'I'm fucking amazed you asked her.'

'Dead easy, Harper. I told her about the job. Two days later she asks me to come along. Says she needs the money to pay for her mother's nursing home and besides she always liked the idea of being a proper spy.'

'Jesus Christ. A proper spy.'

London
1987

Harper had landed at Heathrow just after ten o'clock. The terminal building was barely visible through the rain. There had been turbulence on the flight from Belfast, stormy updraughts among the mid-Channel thunderheads, and the DC 10 rattled and banged with the pilot's voice breaking in every so often, crackly and inaudible with last-transmission static. The mood in the passenger cabin was sombre, dense with resignation which refused to dissipate when they touched down on the east runway and taxied to the stand. Harper walked across the tarmac with the other passengers, pulling up his collar against the rain, the jetwash, the midsummer tumult.

He walked to the baggage hall through badly lit corridors. Passengers on the Belfast flight were questioned by plain-clothes Special Branch men. The policemen had florid complexions and wore sports jackets that were too small for them. They exuded the brutal confidence of men with an array of special powers legislation at their disposal. Harper walked past the queue and showed them his ten-year-old warrant card. One of them took it and looked him over. The man had stubby fingers and an acne-scarred face. Harper knew that their look had to be worked for. You had to earn the right to a morally ravaged appearance.

Bennett had sent a car for him. The driver was waiting in arrivals with a cardboard sign. Harper followed him out to the car, an Escort estate, missing a hubcap. The driver was a tall man with a grey, ill-looking face wearing a Burton suit with a cigarette burn on

40

the cuff. He seemed to be an authority in the field of ashen looks. He listed the constitutional ills of the country, oil wells in Saudi drying up, interest rates, immigration. He kept coming back to immigration. He used words like swamped. He talked about alien cooking smells.

They were driving through the flat land between Heathrow and the city, almost an estuary landscape, a dank, reclaimed feel to it. There was something impressive about the scale and density of the housing, each tract of housing identical to the next, the featureless meridians that had been reached, the eerie suburbs rushing past. The motorway climbed on to a flyover between tower blocks. Buildings that were no more than ten years old surrounded by burnt-out cars, old mattresses, domestic items discarded in stairwells. Something here that the architects and planners hadn't seen on the plans, the forlorn devices of decay in the weave of the plan itself, in the paper like a watermark. The impression is of extending the boundaries of emptiness, creating new classifications of void.

As they drove into the West End Harper thought that it seemed much later. The streets seemed meagre, sparsely populated. Pedestrians crossed the street with their heads down. He kept catching sight of people in alleyways and narrow streets as they passed, tense strained faces as though they had become mired in some illicit trade. The driver talked about services on the brink of collapse, stark narratives of social catastrophe.

It was almost twelve before Harper arrived at the house in Cheyne Walk. You could feel the money. You could feel the night flooded with opulence and dread. Harper was accustomed to the forthright properties of urban conflict, but he knew there was something altogether more baleful at large in these streets, something to strike a note of consternation in a policeman's literal heart. Harper followed the gravel path which ran between clipped box hedges. The front door of the house was painted black and shone as if a lacquer had been applied. The door was open and Harper stepped inside. As he did so he found himself trying to arrange his features into a shrewd and undaunted expression, a servant of the public good in difficult times, but when he caught a glimpse of himself in a hallway mirror he saw a slouching provincial with a history of interrogation room beatings, witness intimidation.

The driver put down his suitcase in the hall and indicated that Harper should follow him. They walked past heavy pieces of Victorian furniture. There were landscapes, porcelain on low tables, heavy velvet curtains. Passing by what seemed to be a drawing-room door he saw a spray of cherry blossom in a narrow vase on the mantelpiece and smelt a woman's perfume, a smell he couldn't identify and didn't seem to belong, sandalwood, or jasmine, heavy-lidded mystery flooding from the unseen room. They passed another doorway and Harper heard the sounds of cutlery, low conversation. There were people dining in there, he thought, dressed in dinner jackets. Former cabinet ministers, he thought, industrialists, minor royals. Harper felt uncouth, lumbering. They reached the rear of the house and stepped through a small door into a dimly lit garage containing five or six cars. He read the words Corniche and Spyder. He read the words Silver Ghost. The air smelt of bespoke objects, hand-made, precision tooled. Racks of tools gleamed with oil. The driver opened the passenger door of a new Rover. Harper got in. He could not make out the face of the man in the passenger seat. The man offered him a slender hand. He was wearing fine leather gloves.

'You'll have to forgive the gloves,' the man said, 'there is eczema on the hands.'

That was the first thing that Harper noticed. The way the man talked about his own body as though it did not belong to him. The hands. As he turned his body towards him to take his hand Harper got a better look. Mid-twenties, he thought. Wearing a black Crombie and black leather boots. His hair was slicked back. He couldn't make out the face properly, but there seemed to be a badly healed scar at the corner of his left eye. He looked like the kind who carried a razor, a modish lout in Chelsea boots.

'Michael Bennett,' he said.

'What am I doing here?' Harper asked.

'Your boss didn't say? That was a bit stupid, really. But Special Branch are like that. Fuckers.'

His voice invited Harper to confirm that it was foolish, in a world awash with raucous mystery, to seek to add anything more to the sum total of what you didn't know.

'Force of habit,' Harper said.

'I suppose you're right.'

'What am I doing here, then?'

'I got a job for you.'

'What's that?' Bennett looked at his watch and started the engine of the Rover.

'First of all I want you to take a look at some people for me.'

The other driver opened the garage doors and they emerged on to a narrow laneway. As they pulled out the street light caught Bennett's face so that Harper could see it properly for the first time. Thin, waxy, backstreet imperious. They drove around the block to emerge into Cheyne Walk again. Bennett pulled in a hundred yards away from the house and killed the engine. He took twenty Dunhill from his pocket and gave one to Harper. Harper cupped a match in his hands. Bennett leaned in touching Harper's hand lightly to steady it, looking up into Harper's face as he did so. That was something else he would come to notice about Bennett. The way he touched you, putting his hand on your knee, taking your elbow, the way he would sometimes place his palm against your face and rub gently as though he considered himself heir to a range of furtive intimacies, not subject to the usual permissions.

'Look,' Bennett said. A Cortina and a Leyland minibus had pulled up in front of the Cheyne Walk house. A plainclothes got out of the Cortina and opened the back door of the minibus. Men started to get out of the minibus. Harper recognised each face as they got out. John White. Jim Gray. Johnny Adair. Burly men in check sports jackets with sideburns and drooping moustaches.

'Like a working-man's day trip to fucking Blackpool,' Bennett said.

That would be some day trip, Harper thought. That would be some diabolic charabanc with such men on board.

'Write down their names,' Bennett said. He handed Harper a notepad. Harper wrote down the names then watched as the men filed into the house. Some of them had their hands in their pockets. One of them spat into the hedge.

'How come them boys is here?' Harper asked.

'Consultations with the powers that be,' Bennett said. 'I want you to give me a rundown on all of these names as well as those men.' Bennett handed him a list of names. Harper read through them and started to talk. Who were community leaders. Who had carried out assassinations on behalf of shadowy state agencies. Who were lay pastors in backstreet gospel halls. Who were agents being run against their own organisations. Who were homosexual. Who were guilty of extortion, theft, assault, racketeering, intimidation, child molestation and affiliate crime.

'What kind of consultations?' Harper asked.

'They're worried about a court case.'

The door closed behind the men. They sat in the car for several minutes without speaking. Bennett started the car. They crossed the river at Vauxhall. It was a full tide. The river smelt of salt mud, of dumped toxins, the oily sheen of its surface film hatched with cross-currents, undertows, betraying a recondite commerce. They drove past Victoria Station and other vast echoing structures of the industrial age. They passed under rail bridges, massive girdered edifices, epic spans. He thought about the amount of bricks. He thought about the amount of steel. The scale of things made him tired so that when Bennett pulled off into a small mews he was grateful for the sense of enclosure it offered. There was a Volvo and a Jaguar parked beside the door of one of the mews houses. He followed Bennett to the front door. Bennett rang the bell and the door was opened by a small dark-skinned woman. The doorframe was low so that Harper had to duck under it, and the hallway beyond it was narrow.

'Watch your head,' the woman said, pointing to low beams on the ceiling, something dusky and far-flung in her accent.

'Follow,' she said, mounting the first step of the staircase which led from the hallway.

'Maltese bitch,' Bennett murmured, but Harper watched her body move under her black shift dress as she mounted the stairs, and found himself grateful for what it offered, the possibility of small-scale passions, of minor lusts assuaged. There was a doorway at the top of the stairs and she opened it and stood back to allow

44

them to enter. Harper eased past the Maltese woman, getting the scent of coal-tar soap from her.

'We need a job done,' Bennett said, 'we need a local we can trust.'

'Trust with what?'

'There's a young lad going to give evidence in court in three days' time.'

'So?'

'He can name names. Upset the whole show.'

'How does that work?'

'He was a rent boy. Lived in this boys' home outside Belfast. His services were being employed by the state.'

'I can imagine. Blackmail.'

'Steering people towards the right way of thinking is the way I look at it.'

'So what do you want me to do?'

'Talk to him. Convince him of the error of his ways. Get him to drop his testimony.'

'Why ask me?'

'You're a local. You speak the language.'

'I got a reputation for getting people to do what they're told is what you mean.'

'Just tell him to withdraw the testimony. Gentle as you can.'

Two nights later they embarked on the night ferry, lights under cold gantries at Stranraer, the Branch watching, the passengers stepping with reluctance on to the walkways. There were barriers, check-points, search areas. Bennett found himself looking for kill zones. Something about the place summoned the killing language he had learned in Belfast, the death argot. He had been in many places of ghostly disembarkation and they always had the same atmosphere, the same tending towards death.

Memories of that night remote and unreliable. The ship's plating rusted, salt-pitted. In the dark and cold. Harper's Mk II Escort on the car deck. Standing on the upper deck with Harper, smoking No. 6 as the ship moved through the North Channel. A corroded light fitting flickering. The bitter waves. Granted uneasy passage in tumultuous night.

There had been a scope to the nature of operations then. Whole governments could be subverted, armies enlisted. There were patterns of corruption, a range of extreme measures that could be brought to bear on state policy. There was a time when you could bring crowds on to the streets, armed vehicles into the financial district. These were the decades of destabilisation, of tottering regimes.

Bennett nudged him. He saw Glenn leaning on the rail at the stern. Thin, hunched over. Harper went down the stairs. There were cold pools of seawater on the deck plate. Despite the cold Glenn was wearing jeans and a sweatshirt. He didn't look round when Harper leant on the rail beside him.

'I'm going to do it,' he said.

'Do what, son?'

'Testify.'

'Testify to what?' Harper said. Glenn turned to him. The borstal pallor and dark knowing eyes. Harper knew then that he would give testimony. To corrupt self-absorption. To testaments of depravity whispering on darkened commons and in provincial bus station lavatories. To lying awake at night in a boys' home bed and waiting for the terror to come.

'You know what, mister.'

'Can't allow you to do that, son.'

Six

Monaco
28th August

Spencer had expressed a desire to see the tomb of Princess Grace.
Early that morning while she sleeps the Jonikal slips her moorings
and travels south along the coast before the sun rises, before the
heat. Sailing under the pedimented buildings cut into the sheer rock
at the harbour entrance, rising out of the mist like the tombs of
kings from the ancient world. Spencer dreams of astrology, of
reflexology. She dreams of spiritual guidance yet to be invented, of
holistic approaches, of modish necromancy. She dreams of submit-
ting her body to new therapies, fraudulent novelties to firm, to tone.

They enter the harbour at Monte Carlo and berth among the
other boats, the barques, the gorgeous sailcraft, and they drive her
in a 1960 black Mercedes 220SE along the seafront then turned left
to climb the Rock. They passed the building which contains the
Institut Océanagraphique in whose tanks and underwater glass
chambers swam shark and barracuda and other marine species of
barbarous aspect.

At the cathedral of St Nicholas the curate unlocked the door for her
and she entered alone and walked to the mausoleum and read the
words *Uxor principas* inscribed on the stone lid. The bodyguards
waited outside. She had heard stories about Grace. Of hair so fine
that she almost always wore a wig. That at night she swam naked
with others in the pool in the palace. The narratives of princesses
were uncovered here. Their promiscuities. Their self-harm. Their
untimely deaths. The light shone through the stained-glass win-

dows. Altarware gleamed softly. Lilies bloomed in tall vases. This is what she was looking for, a trustworthy melancholia, one that could be relied upon. Not the kind that came to her in her Victorian rooms, the London evening glooms, that seemed gaslit, undependable, wreathed in swirling fogs. She likes the catholic gloom of this cathedral with its counting of beads, the reciting of minor pieties.

What are the doctors doing to her coming to her with their steel devices with their iron instruments?

Names of benefactors are inscribed on benches and beneath the window and there is an atmosphere of everyday altruism, plain and undemanding, that would not allow augury.

She puts her hands on the mausoleum. *Uxor principas.* Outside the bodyguards are waiting for her beside the black Mercedes. She gets into the long black hearselike car. They drive her to the palace for lunch with the prince. The prince is remote. Every evening he attends the circus. As you grow older, he said, your capacity for melancholy increases. It is difficult to find ways to satisfy it. He likes to weep, to laugh until tears stream down his face. He liked the music of the circus, its evocation of lost ways of life, forgotten villages in Eastern Europe, its note of peasant gaiety with sinister undertones. There are themes of itinerant troupes of the Middle Ages, superstitions, fearful villagers making the sign against the evil eye. Clowns pad silently around the ring. Ornamented horses jingle their gorgeous harness. Costumed women parade. There is much here to be considered, the prince says. They notice how his persona has changed, having seemed himself to have taken on the characteristics of an itinerant pedlar of old, a vendor of gauds, a man leaning on a staff, quavering, a bearer of strange knowledge.

The black Mercedes, the mass car, brings them back to the Quai des Artistes where the dory for the Jonikal is waiting for them. The sun is rising in the sky. People catch sight of her in the car as it glides down the hill, tourists, sightseers, early morning workers. Others watch from moored yachts as she gets into the dory. The paparazzi are here now. She sits upright in the middle of the boat as it crosses the harbour to the waiting yacht and the people around the harbour take note. Here is something to be observed. The embarkation of princesses. The sight of her leads to speculation as to what gilded journey she might be undertaking, in whose playboy arms she might find herself, what spivish and unworthy sexual attention might be lavished upon her, what treatments, what laying of hands, what lavish gifts, allurements, betrayals.

Seven

Henri worked that night. He left the Ritz at 7.30 a.m. and stopped at the Bar Laurent. Monique put a Ricard and water on the bar.

'How was your night?' she said, lighting a Camel, inhaling and setting it on the edge of an ashtray on the bar, lipstick on the filter, the smoke curling from the tip, a composed, filmic gesture.

'Nothing much,' he said. 'Some trouble with night staff. Temporary staff. They steal. They pilfer. They get the shove. What do they expect? And your night?'

'You know,' she said, 'the girls.' She made a gesture with her hand to take in the whole bar, last night's smoke still hanging in the air, last night's promises, the girl voices pealing out rich and erotic and doomed. You could still almost hear them, Henri thought. The fluting sopranos. She said afterwards that she thought that Henri had been edgy all week. He would set his drink down on the bar suddenly and step away from it as if he didn't know what it was.

'Are you all right?' she asked. 'You look pale.'

'You think so?' he said. 'Maybe I need a tonic, a bromide, something like that. I have a feeling here.' He touched his stomach.

'Here,' Monique said. She put a glass of water on the bar and dropped an Alka-Seltzer into it.

'It's good for the liver,' she said. They would talk about their internal organs in these early mornings. The heart, the kidneys, the bowels. They affected gloomy prognosis, faked symptoms to each other, palpitated their livers, peered into the veined linings of each other's eyelids looking for the telltale sign. It made them feel like

50

veterans of some kind. They discussed constipation, addressed glandular issues. Monique dropped her voice to recount grim tales of the female system. Ovarian cysts, dark malignancies of the reproductive tract. A repertoire of doubtful headshakes, sharp intakes of breath, non-verbal exhalations accompanied each session. Henri felt admitted to the feminine sphere when they talked like this. He imagined that they were women, girlfriends, their heads bent over coffee, exchanging glum truisms. Henri had no problem in admitting that he had a feminine side. He was a fan of popular psychology, of Desmond Morris. He told Monique that they were all apes walking upright.

'Some of the hairy bitches in here,' she said. 'You could believe it. You drink too much of that Diet Coke shit.'

Henri admitted he drank four or five cans a day, each time remembering the warning that Nutrasweet caused cancer in laboratory rats.

Monique was thin, dark-skinned with a sharp nose and black curly hair. She wore halter tops with no bra so that you could see her small dark-brown nipples through the material. One day she lifted her T-shirt to show him a tattoo on her shoulder. A locker-room gesture. Henri noticed that she didn't seem to take other girls home, but that she had favourites among them. She liked the sullen fat girls who came in from the suburbs wearing leathers, black eye shadow and nose studs. They were slovenly and ungracious, exuding an air of half-hearted sadomasochistic practices. They permitted Monique to court them in a despairing way.

'You ever go with a man?' Monique asked Henri.

'Me?' Henri said. 'Of course. I've been had in all positions by men in every walk of life.'

'Be serious, Henri.'

'I spend too much of my life being serious. You know these hotel hookers nowadays? The way they wait until the client goes out in the morning then they start to order room service, full breakfast with champagne mimosa, they want a body wrap, a pedicure?'

'How do you get them out?'

'You ring the room, tell them the client's wife is coming.'

Henri finished his drink and left the bar, the bead curtain parting for a moment to admit the morning light, then closing behind him. That was the thing about sex, Monique thought, picking up his glass. You ask a question, you never get a straight answer. Sex was a thing of skulked-through doorways, of hand-on-heart perjuries with infidelities lurking in every corner. She polished the glass and put it on the shelf over the bar. Early morning customers started to drift in, drug-hazed couples, dazed emissaries.

Henri went home and slept for four hours. He rarely slept for more than four hours at a time. He woke and sat straight up in the bed, got out of bed feeling stale and groggy, went to the fridge for a Diet Coke. He lay on the bed with the curtains closed. He shut his eyes and thought about Belinda. The way she said she liked his stupid jokes, his man jokes, his sex jokes. The night he met her in the bar in Pigalle. Henri was drinking pastis, keeping an eye on a client, a Belgian businessman who was liable to get himself knifed. It was after 2 a.m., the shady time, the vice time, the crew gathering in the Bois for business, in Pigalle. The hookers, the rent boys, the dykes, the twinks, the trannies, the smack whores, the crack whores, the crystal-meth whores, the lost and the diabolic. She was sitting at the bar, smoking menthol Camels, glancing at her watch and watching the door with a stood-up look to her. The Belgian was sullen now, hunched over the bar having taken tawdry as far as it could go without spilling over into full-on sordid. Henri went over to her. Brunette hair to her waist. Strapless sandals. The dress looked Gucci. She picked up her cigarettes and her lighter and put them in her bag. He introduced himself as deputy director of security, Ritz Hotels. She said her name was Belinda. That she came from Marseilles. That she had grown up on the docks, close to the abattoir. He told her about his upbringing in Brittany, close to the sea. These were things they had in common. Spindly kids racing through the streets on bicycles. He thought that there was something shadowed about her, as if the cell structure held a memory of deprivation, of undernourishment. There was a home-made tattoo on the inside of her wrist, an inked-in hieroglyph that she showed to him and laughed about. A jail mark, Henri thought. She had a wharf-rat allure. She told him that she had been waiting on a bigshot, the owner of a Renault franchise, a man with gold jewellery and a pasty wife. She was a little clumsy, dropping her cigarettes and her lighter. He told her the one about the lorry driver and the prostitute. He told her the one about the nun. He ordered a pastis and then another. The Belgian was pulling at his arm. He took her number. When he looked back she was still sitting at the bar, smoking.

Henri showered and got dressed. He wore slacks, open-neck polo shirts. He liked clothing with the little crocodile on it. He wore Lacoste V-necks, deck shoes. He had an appointment at 4 p.m. at the DGSE. Just before he left the apartment the telephone rang. It was Masson from the DGSE. He said that he wanted to change the meeting place.

'A bar or a restaurant,' he said. Henri suggested a bar in Montmartre. He drove the Mini over, parked it on the pavement. It was 39 degrees. The street was empty. Henri with the Lacoste draped over his shoulders. The bar was old-fashioned. There was a zinc counter. There was a jukebox in the corner, a one-armed bandit and a pinball machine. Henri got change from the barman and went to the pinball machine. Running his fingers over the buttons. He used to play in a cafe like this when he was a teenager, winter nights with the dark coming in early, sea spray blowing off the harbour wall. You hit the pinball buttons, a Camel unfiltered in the corner of your mouth, America in all its bounty right there, the words US Patent No 653329707 on a metal plate on the corner of the machine like something encrypted. He hit the button and sent the steel ball rifling through the chutes, the bells and lights, the numbers racking, the racket, the manic contraption.

When he let the ball slip through the flippers and stepped back from the machine, Masson was standing at the bar. He had a long dark face with big cheekbones. He had big hands. Features that made Henri think of primitive agricultural implements. A rudimentary spade, an adze. Despite the heat he was wearing a heavy wool suit and an overcoat. He was from the south somewhere, a sun-blasted littoral near the Italian border, and he carried an air of vendetta with him, of accrued menaces. There were stories of trade

53

unionists falling down the stairs of suburban gendarmeries. There had been postings to Algeria, to sub-Saharan Africa. Henri thought of him as being adept in the politics of the souk, the polity of the stiletto.

Henri sat down beside him. Masson did not shake hands.

'There are British operatives paying attention to the Ritz Hotel,' Masson said.

'What are they looking for?'

'You tell me.'

'I don't know,' Henri said, 'there is nobody of importance staying at the hotel.'

'Anyone due?'

'Spencer is supposed to be coming. Diana Spencer.'

'When?'

'I'm not certain.'

'What do you mean? I prefer certainty.'

'It's Dodi. He never tells anybody what he is going to do. He is always changing his mind. You can't keep up with him.' Henri feeling querulous starting to seep into his tone.

'What is wrong with you?' Masson turned to look at him for the first time. Henri didn't like it when Masson looked at him. Henri spent time with cops. He knew their unscrupulous view of the world. He knew the flat-eyed nihilist look, but Masson's stare was different. There seemed to be a different level of consciousness there, something vast and dimensionless.

'A woman?'

'Yes,' Henri said, 'a woman.'

'Why do you let this happen to you?'

'It's frustrating. She won't let me near her.'

'Take what you want from her, Henri. In the meantime, the business at hand.'

'I suppose,' Henri said, 'that the British would have someone in place if Spencer is coming to town.'

'Yes,' Masson said, 'but normally that is handled by their mission in Paris. These are freelance people with intelligence backgrounds. A man called Bennett who does not have a good reputation. A man called Harper. A woman called Campbell.'

'You think they intend some harm to her?'

'What makes you say that, Henri? Why does that thought cross your mind?'

'I don't know.'

'Is that what such people contemplate? Harm to others?'

'I wouldn't know,' Henri said.

'It would fit,' Masson said. 'If one was to think of such an operation then one would contract it out.'

'To who?'

'There is a world of such people. Ex-military, ex-intelligence. The British called them Detached. Or the Increment. We will sit down now.'

They moved from the bar to a small table beside the jukebox. Masson took photographs from an envelope.

'This is Harper,' he said, tapping the first one with his fingernail. Early fifties, Henri thought, stocky, grey hair cut short. Slouching against a sunlit wall in the Place Vendôme, a cigarette cupped in his hand as though to shield it against some northern European drizzle, squinting as if he looked out on a barren and wintry centre of urban decay.

'Looks like a cop,' Henri said.

'He was one. Special Branch. Anti-subversive operations in the 1980s in Belfast. Dismissed from the service. Seems to have been problems with drinking. There was also an incident involving a witness falling off a ferry. I'm trying to get more information on that. Harper disappears for ten years then turns up in the employ of Michael Bennett.'

Masson turned up the photograph of Bennett. The location wasn't clear, but Henri thought it was an airport departure lounge. The plastic chair that he sat on looked injection moulded. Henri could almost smell the flame-retardant textiles in the carpet and seating areas. The lonely verities of mass transit seemed to hang in the air around Bennett. He was the same age as Harper, Henri thought, thinner, wearing a black suit and white shirt. He was pale with bad teeth. Henri imagined a sickly childhood, an anxious mother hovering.

'Bennett worked for MI5 until 1992 then apparently left to set up his own company offering, it seems, risk assessment to corporate clients.'

'It seems?'

'Difficult to know what Bennett is doing. He travels extensively in conflict zones. Has associations with Harper going back to Belfast.'

'And MI5? Why did he leave?'

'Who knows why he left, or if he left at all. He has an office in London. The woman, Grace Campbell, started to work as a typist with George Kennedy Young, former DG of MI6. Then worked in Communications at GCHQ Cheltenham and at Menwith Hill.'

He handed Henri a head and shoulders shot of Grace. She was looking straight at the camera. Mid-forties, he thought. Thin face. Good eyes. The hair long and dark, parted in the middle in a style she was too old for. A look conceived in the mid-seventies, he thought, at a three-day outdoor festival. It had the feel of muddy campsites about it, of trampled fields, of accumulated drug lore. The eyebrows were plucked and badly drawn-in. Henri told Monique that you could read a woman's eyes, and the markers of this woman's adult life, the defining indices, were there to be seen in the crow's feet, the puffiness, the veins that had acquired a permanent look to them. A drinker, Henri thought, a smoker of marijuana. This was an adept of the minor depravities, of the abasements they brought in their wake. There was a wan imperiousness to her look.

'Why did she leave the service?'

'Disciplinary issues are cited,' Masson said. 'She was Harper's girlfriend in Belfast for a while. She met Bennett there as well.'

'None of these people look like much of a problem.'

'No, you may be right. I suspect they may be representing an interest which wishes to keep an eye on Spencer and Al-Fayed without intervening. However, I want you to be alert and to stay in touch with the DGSE.'

'Of course.'

'And report approaches from any other agency.'

'Yes.' Henri got to his feet. 'Anything unusual. Anything at all.'

'Good.'

Masson watched Henri cross the street to the Mini. There was no one about in the mid-afternoon heat. He noted the way the man walked. There was a jauntiness there that he hadn't noticed before. Masson's hand rested on his attaché case. It contained bank statements from each of the sixteen bank accounts that Henri thought no one knew about, each containing FF200,000. Masson would find out where the money came from. And when he did he would own Henri.

Eight

Hôtel Quimper
29th August, 11 a.m.

Grace had fallen asleep on top of the bed without closing the curtains. When she woke the morning sun had been shining on her for
several hours. She was dehydrated and her head was pounding. She
went into the bathroom. She looked in the mirror. She was swollen-
eyed, her eye shadow was smudged, her hair fell limply about her
shoulders. She looked less like someone with a hangover than someone who had spent days ravaged by a terrible grief, an
all-consuming loss. She looked as if she could open her mouth only
to utter primitive expressions of mourning, guttural sounds.

She stood under the shower. In the bedroom the telephone rang.
She could see the outline of her body through the condensation on
the sink mirror, a pale and elegant thing that seemed to have col-
lected to itself the commonplace graces that had long since been
stripped from her real body.

She wondered if princesses did this. The Graces and Carolines.
The sorrow-burdened Stephanies. Standing in their bathrooms,
nude and ordinary, buffeted by complex woes.

She put on her dressing gown and went back into the bedroom.
She sat down at the dressing table and started to remove the rem-
nants of last night's foundation and mascara before applying fresh
make-up. Going for the pastel shades, the low-gloss, applied in
scant quantities. Working the hair into a severe bun. She picked out
a knee-length skirt and flat shoes. This was the way she would see
herself today, purse-lipped, spinsterish.

As she finished dressing there was a knock on the door. Before she answered it she knew it was Bennett. There was something furtive about his knock. As if he sought entry at the spy-holed door of a backstreet vice den. She swung the door open. Bennett walked in, closing the door carefully behind him, then scanned the room slowly, taking in the bed with its rumpled slept-on cover, her old clothes piled in a corner, the bottle of Gordon's on the dressing table. Grace sat down at the dressing table again. She started to wish that she hadn't let him in. The room had started to acquire a lurked-in feeling.

'Are you fit to do anything today?' he said, sitting down on the bed. 'You look like shit.'

'Thank you for that,' she said, 'what is it that you want me to do?'

'Keep an eye on Henri Paul. Try to get a bit of gen on him.'

'What is Harper doing?'

'Harper is doing his job. Trying to find out more about Mr James Andanson. He's a fishy fucker by all accounts.'

'So where do I start this top-secret surveillance of the evil genius Henri Paul?'

Bennett got off the bed and stood behind her. He was too close. She could smell his aftershave. A heavy, cloying scent that strove for undertones of brutish masculinity. Denim, Old Spice, one of those. A cheap reek that caught in the back of her throat.

'Where did you get the rig-out?' Bennett said. 'Did some dowager die and leave her frocks to Oxfam?'

'You don't scare me, Bennett,' she said. But the truth was that he did scare her sometimes. She could see him in the mirror, standing so close to her that she could see where the buttonholes of his black suit were a little frayed, the seams a little stretched, the cloth looking prone to mildew, fungal rots. His hands resting on the back of her chair were pallid and the nails long and yellow. Bennett was like something exhumed by lamplight. Sometimes he seemed to share the sickly and death-addled preoccupations of the Victorians. He put his hand on her shoulder. She got up from the chair quickly.

'You're a fucking low-life Bennett, you know that?' Bennett moved a few steps to the side of the chair. She stood in front of him, fists balled. What she knew of men contained in her stance. The ones her mother had brought home when she was a teenager, the shambling, kaftaned veterans of a hundred casual sexual encounters. They drank home brew, and tried to get into her bed when her mother wasn't looking. By the time she was nineteen she knew all she needed to know about men. Their folk-music LPs, their smiling bearded faces, their Rizla papers, dated slang, promises broken, misogynies harboured.

'Easy, love,' Bennett said. He was smiling. 'No need to lose the head. We both got jobs to do. Let's get out there.'

She picked up her handbag. Her body needed fluids, rest. She did not know what she would achieve following Henri around. What Bennett referred to as covert activity. One of these days she thought real spy work would be out there, a dark and thrilling espionage. There would be seething treacheries. Moral dilemmas would arise. Defectors would be exchanged at heavily guarded border crossings, microfilms switched. Betrayal would lurk at every turn. Men would stand on street corners with their collars turned up, smoking.

She felt giddy, the alcohol still in her system.

'Henri Paul lives in Rue Cambon,' Bennett said. 'He doesn't usually leave his apartment until about eleven o'clock. There is a gay bar underneath his apartment, and a lesbian bar across the street. It's a right den of fucking queers.'

'Why do you want me to do it?'

'Because Harper's trying to see if he can get a line on Andanson.'

'What did Henri do yesterday.'

'Henri goes home from work, has a drink in the lesbian bar. He goes into the apartment for four hours. Then he spends an hour in a bar in Montparnasse with a bloke I think is Colonel Masson of the DGSE.'

'Doing what?'

'Talking. But we don't know what he's talking about. We think there is a woman but she hasn't appeared yet. She might be a contact.'

'Why does he need a contact?'

'According to the principal he had money scattered in bank accounts all over the city. He's up to something.'

'The money. The money he has scattered around Paris in various bank accounts. He's up to something.'

'The security people in a big hotel are assets to any intelligence organisation. I'd say our Henri is taking money off anybody who comes through the door. Question is, what is he taking it for?'

'What kind of thing could he be doing?'

'Putting listening devices in rooms. Video cameras. When a subject checks in. When he checks out. Who he sees. Who he phones. Who he screws. Could be a right busy little bee, our Henri.'

They went down in the tiny lift. Grace aware of Bennett close to her, and of the smell of last night's drink on her breath, the sweetish acetone scent like some lab residue, an organic compound. On the street she could feel the heat.

'No fucking wonder the frogs get out of Paris in August,' Bennett said. 'Get a cup of tea for Christ's sakes. Stay off the booze. Henri's shift starts at five so I'll see you then.'

```
Place de la Concorde
          11.30 a.m.
```

Harper went to the Hertz agency in the Place de la Concorde and hired a Renault Clio. He parked it on the street opposite the Sygma agency. He was watching for Andanson's white Fiat Uno. Mid-morning. The temperature at 32 and rising. He opened the file on his knee. He put the photograph of Andanson on the passenger seat. Bennett had added notes in longhand, a weak and halting scrawl which Harper had difficulty making out. In the margin Bennett had written the letters UKN several times and underlined them. Harper had heard of UKN. Part-timers who worked for MI6. Media people, owners of yachts, remote properties. Anything that Six could use. Who thought they were insiders. Harper knew they were wrong. You weren't an insider until the civil service paid you. Until you took your place in the hierarchy.

Above Andanson's address Bennett had written *Flies Union Jack Outside House!* Beside this he had drawn a flag. Across the bottom

61

of the document he had written *Order of the Solar Temple*. Beside this he had drawn a sun with rays emanating from it. The name *Bérégovoy* was written in pen beside the names typed under the Known Associates heading. Sentences were defaced with slashes. Multiple question marks were appended to the end of sentences. Arrows linked words for no discernible reason.

Harper closed the file. It seemed like a fragment from a vanished civilisation, an incomplete scroll preserved through millennia. Something to be pored over in a temperature-controlled environment. He took out the top page and looked at the sun that Bennett had drawn. It had an esoteric look to it. Loaded with symbolism and portent. The Order of the Solar Temple. Harper had never heard of it. He looked at the photograph of Andanson again. It was a fat man's face, hearty, brutal, hypertensive. There was nothing to associate that face with something called the Order of the Solar Temple. You couldn't see him as an acolyte, pale and robed.

Bennett was a different matter. Harper had seen that type of handwriting before, the freakish marginalia. He had visited colleagues in mental institutions so often that it had come to seem an integral part of Special Branch work. Red-brick buildings in remote locations. Men broken through drink or gambling, lost in complex sorrows of their own devising. Men wearing pyjamas who had learned to shuffle in long corridors as though the shuffle and the averted gaze were the melancholy attainments of their state, as though they were required to excel in a delusionary craft. These were the men who pressed pages torn from cheap jotters into your hand, their faces arranged in expressions of conspiratorial guile. There were diagrams on these pages, sentences written and crossed out. Single words underlined. Their enemies were out there. World Jewry. Papists. Sinister forces were arrayed.

Harper started to wonder if Bennett had joined their ranks. The file in his hand seemed to point that way. Towards a man hemmed-in. Alerted to a catastrophic narrowing of possibilities. Panic-stricken in a drawn-out kind of way. He started to wonder how he had allowed Bennett to talk him into coming to Paris. He should have stayed in Belfast. He should have stayed with providing site security. He should have put the phone down on Bennett.

He should have resisted the undertone of lurid potential in Bennett's voice. Harper had a tendency to respond to the lure of real cruelty, even it meant being out of his depth. He knew that there was something big about all of this. That there was more to it than the street-level chicanery common to men like Bennett and Harper at this stage of their lives. Washed-up, burnt-out, limp with moral fatigue. Something meticulously planned and executed was on its way. An operation planned by men in their fifties with well-toned bodies and chilly eyes. A mischief of drastic proportions was looming on the skyline and at the minute he couldn't summon the means to get out of the way.

He saw the white Fiat coming down the street, fast. There was a brusqueness to the way Andanson drove that made Harper think that he had professional training. The Fiat was old. It was missing two hubcaps. You could tell by looking at it that it was never washed. Andanson got out of the car. He was a big man, bearded, sweating, wearing a T-shirt and shorts. Harper thought he looked like a character actor, one who had browbeaten his way through a dozen minor parts, but capable of surprising charm off-camera. A man who would possess a fierce and depraved inner life. He went into the agency. Harper got out of his car and went over to the Fiat. The inside of the car was a hymn to neglect. There were food wrappers, water bottles, toll receipts, a packet of Bisodol on the dashboard, the back seat covered in dog hairs, the seat belts chewed.

Andanson's Fiat resembled a Q car, the kind of unmarked surveillance vehicle that Harper had seen used by covert military forces in Ireland. There were careful parameters for Q cars. They had to be common models. They had to look uncared for, unwashed exteriors concealing a tuned engine. They had to be capable of hiding high-powered transceivers, have hidden compartments for the concealment of modified weapons. It was part of the lore that the interior of the car should be filthy, a kind of maleness in the interior, a pungency like something spoored at the base of a tree, redolent of long stakeouts. In the eighties Harper had developed an instinct for spotting Q cars. He thought they stood out. They seemed to create an aura of grubby dramatics around themselves. An amateurish and lethal sense of purpose. The amateurish part was important. It implied back-room boys, professorish types, boffins in white coats with a genius for eccentric inventions.

Harper went back to the Renault and waited. After thirty minutes Andanson came out of the agency and turned left down the street. Harper got out of the Renault and followed him. Andanson went to a bakery where he bought a box of ornate cakes. Harper followed him for an hour. Andanson bought dog biscuits in a Prima. He drank English tea in a cafe. He paid for everything in cash, producing a bundle of 100-franc notes every time. He browsed through a range of specialist photographic shops. Long-distance lenses. Low exposure films. Miniature cameras. He seemed to drift through the afternoon with an elaborate lack of purpose which made Harper suspicious.

At 4.30 Andanson bought a copy of the Daily Mail at a kiosk selling international papers. He went into a bar off the Rue des Petits Carreaux. Walking past Harper saw that he was standing at the bar. He had ordered a demi. There seemed to be three or four other men sitting at tables in the bar. There was no cover close to the bar so Harper waited under the shade of a plane tree further down the street. He felt that the afternoon had been tending towards this moment. He waited for fifteen minutes then walked back up the street on the other side, slowing down as he approached the entrance. Two men were standing either side of Andanson. Andanson was gesticulating, his hands moving as if he was trying to shape an intricate and dolorous thing in the air. The two men were very still. As if judgement awaited the edifice of blame and consequence taking shape between Andanson's hands. Harper walked to the other end of the street and stood by a lamp post. He waited for ten minutes.

Andanson came out and turned left. His shoulder struck a lamp post and he staggered slightly and kept going. Harper considered following him but it was almost time to meet Bennett. He thought about going into the bar and ordering a drink but the men in the bar would know him for what he was. He was wary of these men. Their stillness. There was a corruption at the heart of it. Harper had been around enough shadowy brotherhoods to recognise the men as party to one. Andanson rounded the corner at the end of the street and disappeared from view. As he did so a white Mercedes C220 with Paris plates turned into the street behind him. It stopped outside the bar and the two men came out. Both of them were wearing open-neck shirts, cotton trousers. One of them was blond. The other was dark-haired. The blond man had sunglasses on the top of his head. He opened the door for the other man and they both got in. As the car door closed the Mercedes started to move again. There was a slickness about it. Ex-military, Harper thought. The car turned left at the end of the street and disappeared. The street seemed very empty when the car was gone. Harper walked past the bar again. The owner was brushing the floor. Harper moved quickly to the top of the street. He could not see Andanson.

Place de l'Etoile
12.30 p.m.

Grace had a café au lait at a pavement cafe. Her mother had been to France once and had told her how they charged more to sit at a table than to stand at the bar. Sitting in Wimpys in Margate or Ramsey. Somewhere windswept, off-season. Her mother whispering it. Double the price to park yourself at a table. The waiters looking down their long noses at you. Men in waistcoats and pencil moustaches. Her nerves were gone at the end of it. She never enjoyed a drop of the coffee. The theme of her stories was always the same. The world was full of put-downs, cutting remarks, people whose purpose was to make you feel small. You had to move warily. This was the instruction a daughter required of a mother. To be shown where the anxieties lay, the primal unease.

After the coffee she went to a garage off the Place d'Etoile and picked up the hire Citroën that Bennett had arranged. She had always driven big old cars, prone to breaking down. Fifteen-year-old Volvos, ageing Saabs. They had noisy exhausts and leaked oil. They broke down on motorway hard shoulders en route to sustainable-living festivals. Long trips often took days. It seemed important that an epic note be struck on every journey.

There was a street map in the glove compartment and she used it to plan a route from the Place d'Etoile to Rue Cambon. The car had been parked in the sun and the seats and steering wheel were hot. There was a mildly toxic smell of hot plastic. She drove with the map beside her, catching the rhythm of the traffic, the semi-hysterical career of cars through massive intersections. She liked the headlong feel of it. When she turned into the streets around the Place Vendôme she felt the silence, the canyoned stillness, heat radiating off the walls.

She turned into Rue Cambon and found a space just down the street from Henri's apartment. She took this as a sign. Her mother had taught her to have faith in such things. To read her horoscope every day. To be alert to signs, portents, synchronicities, things of moment taking place in other spheres. Her mother read the tarot at the kitchen table. A crystal hung over the front door. She consulted a palmist when difficult decisions loomed concerning Grace. She had her child's fortune told in gloomy caravans. Growing up, Grace felt surrounded by women in hoop earrings and dirty fingernails. Her adolescence was swept along in a storm of foretelling.

Henri came out of the apartment. He was carrying a model aeroplane, its wings removed and placed parallel to the body. Henri opened the car door and placed the model carefully on the back seat. He returned to the apartment and came back with a remote control. Bennett had not mentioned model planes as an interest, although it fitted in with the fact that Henri was a pilot. It fitted with the things that men did. The way they were hobbyists in matters of the heart. Henri examined the remote control before he put it in the car, frowning, owlish. Her mother's boyfriends had dismantled motorcycle engines in the living room. Had carried out repairs to rusting camper vans in driveways. Some of then purported to earn a living by making things, affected a veneer of artisanal values. They were makers of pots, of teepees, of wattle fencing.

She drove behind him to the Bois, the traffic light now. She thought about trying to conceal the fact that she was following him but decided against it. It was the kind of thing that Harper was good at, she thought, one of the dark crafts he brought with him out of Belfast, dragging guile behind him out of the shadows. Henri

66

pulled into a small car park and parked in the far corner under a line of spruce trees. She parked several cars away from him. She got out of the car and could not see him for a moment then realised he had reached into the back seat for the plane. When he stood up she thought that he was going to speak to her for a moment, but he was looking beyond her at the sky, his eyes narrowed, as if to assess what might await him there, as though hazard lurked in the cloudless sky in the form of downdraughts, sudden thermals, treacherous squalls.

She watched him assemble the plane, fastening the wings on, then testing the rudder, moving it from side to side, taxiing it across the grass. The plane looked clumsy on the ground but when it got into the air the engine revved to a two-stroke whine with a waspish edge which left her uneasy. She had never liked insects, the stingers and biters, creatures of ill-intent.

At 12.30 Henri looked at his watch. He guided the plane to the ground, and quickly removed the wings. He looked at his watch again and began to walk quickly towards the car. He started to look furtive, to glance around. Grace stepped back into the trees. They had moved into a different context. She scanned the park for cover. Suddenly the park seemed like a strange and empty place. There was a feeling of depopulation about it now. She looked around but couldn't see anyone. Where had all the people gone? she thought. The children playing, the young couples, the pensioners, the women walking miniature dogs, the commonplaces of park life. She seemed to be in a different park now, a place skulked through and noirish.

Henri walked quickly through the gates of the car park. Grace was a hundred yards behind him. She could see that there was someone standing beside Henri's Mini. A woman. As Grace closed on them she started to register details about the woman's appearance. The long dark hair held back from her face with a wide band. The Chanel bag on a gold chain over her shoulder. The calf-length camel skirt with leather boots. The cigarette in her hand. The red blouse with long collars. The look was Jackie O, Grace thought. She had the air of having stepped into the car park from some other narrative. She looked like a 1970s divorcee, greeting Henri with a weary lift of the hand which held the cigarette. A gesture she could not have made if she had been dressed in any other way. That was why she wore the clothes, Grace thought. She was a jaded sophisticate, a deliverer of wry soliloquies in empty cocktail bars.

When Henri reached her she kissed him on both cheeks, then leaned in close to him, keeping a hand on his upper arm and talking fast and urgently. Henri stepped back from her. Grace tried to move closer but she realised now that Henri had chosen the isolated corner of the car park because it was difficult to approach unseen. Grace saw the woman open her bag and take out a map which she opened out on the bonnet of the car. Henri stood back as she talked animatedly, pointing to areas of the map. Grace moved a little closer, keeping in under the pine trees. She knew that a proper surveillance would involve the use of a directional microphone at this stage. At GCHQ she had transcribed conversations recorded that way. The tapes hissed with background atmospherics. Tech drama leaching into the conversations. As though they were trying to speak through a storm of buzz and clutter.

Henri studied the map frowning. He opened the driver's door and reached into the glove compartment, coming out with what looked like a city guide. He opened it beside the other map and seemed to be comparing features. The woman took a small gold pen from the Chanel bag and traced a route on the map. She folded it then and handed it to Henri. He said something and she laughed, the laugh carrying through the air, a woman's rich baritone laugh. She went around to the passenger side of the car and got in. Henri got in beside her. Grace waited for the engine to start. When it didn't she moved closer. She saw that the car was moving, rocking slightly from side to side. She could not get close enough to the car to see Henri and the woman without exposing herself to being seen, but she knew enough to recognise what was going on. In Margate she had spent enough time in parked cars with acne-scarred local youths, expressions of terrible yearning on their ravaged faces as they reached for her. It was the first time in her life she had the opportunity to be a channel of unaffected tenderness, a bringer of solace. She knew the textures involved in these car encounters, the synthetic pine fragrances, the feel of auto acrylics, the way there was never enough room.

She had liked the boys. They knew what life held for them. They knew that rudimentary sex acts in parked cars brought as much solace as they could hope to find in rainswept seaside towns, and were determined to make the most of these interludes.

Henri lay back against the headrest, his eyes closed. Grace could see the top of her head moving over his lap. Understanding the need to be painstaking, to search for the rhythm. Grace could not open her heart to the idea that some depravity was involved here. There was enough of the backseat voluptuary in her to see that an equilibrium had been arrived at, that the woman had settled into what was required, and that Henri had the good grace to accept the episode as sincere and without strings. Grace started to like him for that. She got into the Citroën and waited for them to finish. When she next looked the woman was walking across the car park. The woman had the effortless ability to give an on-location look to the space she occupied. In this case Grace thought she looked like the lead from a dated mini-series with a sweeping orchestral intro, and themes of infidelity.

Nine

Bar du Cercle
5 p.m.

Harper met Bennett in the Café de Flore. Bennett was drinking a Ricard. Harper sat down and Bennett called the waiter. He seemed to have taken on the air of an impoverished intellectual, an exiled dissident, a man who battled ill-health and wrote long into the night. The waiter seemed to defer to him on these grounds.

'Andanson had a meet with these two boys,' Harper said, 'ex-army by the look of them.'

'Nationality?' Bennett said.

'Never got near enough to tell.'

'Could they be English?'

'Could be English, could be French. This car picks them up, a white Merc. The way it worked, it wasn't the first time they done a pick-up like that.'

'What about Andanson?'

'Whatever they says to him, he was in a right state about it. Looked like he had to do some fast talking.'

'Where did he go?'

'Back to the agency, far as I could see. I had to come back here.'

'He's in with some shady gents then by the look of it.'

'By the look of it.'

'Did you see anything else?'

'They had a map with them. Spread out on the bar.'

'What kind of a map? You never mentioned a map.'

'I'm mentioning it now. It was a street map of Paris. Andanson had it in his car.'

'What happened to it?'

'Andanson took it with him.'

'Why the fuck did they have a map?'

'How would I know? What do you use a map for? Planning a route. Finding a street or a place,' Harper said. He watched Bennett. He knew what he was thinking. That a map in the hands of men like those acquired other properties. They saw kill zones, firing points, points of ambuscade and extraction. Their maps referenced safe houses, friendly foreign embassies, the map taking on other properties outlined in spare military jargon.

'Hello,' Bennett said, 'here comes our little spy-mistress now.' Grace was walking through the front door, looking around for them.

'So she sucked him off in the front seat of the car,' Bennett said.

'I wouldn't put it that way,' Grace said. Like so much of Bennett's vocabulary the phrase sounded archaic. It had the patina of schoolboy obscenity, of genitalia drawn in biro on the back of toilet doors.

'You seen him do it?' Harper said.

'I wasn't exactly there,' Grace said, 'but it was fairly obvious.' She had managed to strike a note of prim disapproval, which went with the tweed skirt and flat shoes.

'What else was there?' Bennett said.

'He went to the airport. He met the woman in the car park. They looked at a map.'

'More maps,' Harper said.

'What map?' Bennett said.

'I couldn't get close enough to see.'

'Was it a country map? A map of France maybe?'

'Or a city map, you know, a guide map,' Harper said.

'I couldn't see,' Grace said.

'Did you cop anything else about the woman?'

'Long dark hair tied back with a hairband, wore sunglasses. About thirty, I would say. Well dressed.' She decided the Jackie O reference would be lost on the two men. The complex matter of lost glamour. She could not imagine them grasping the aura of ghostly chic the woman had aspired to.

'I don't get this map thing. Andanson was looking at a map with them two characters,' Harper said.

'She looked as if she was explaining something to him,' Grace said. 'She was tracing lines on the map with her finger.'

'Them two boys did the same with Andanson.'

'What's the link between the two?'

'Between Henri and Andanson? Search me. Far as I know the two of them never met.'

'We're going on fucking crumbs here.'

'They've both got connections with the intelligence community,' Grace said.

'What connections has Andanson got?' Harper asked.

'People's inclined to die around Andanson. Like Bérégovoy.'

'Who the fuck is he? I seen his name on the file you gave me.'

'Pierre Bérégovoy,' Grace said, 'former French prime minister. Found dead in a canal in Nevers in 1992. Single gunshot to the head. Ruled suicide but various factors including the lack of powder burns around the entry point indicate otherwise.'

'I'm impressed,' Harper said, 'but what's this got to do with Andanson?'

'Andanson was friendly with Bérégovoy. Andanson was in Nevers the day Bérégovoy was killed and never made it known.'

'See? You fucking see, Harper? I'm beaming with pride here at what this girl can do. She's a walking encyclopaedia.'

'It doesn't tell me anything,' Harper said.

'It tells us that here are two shifty customers,' Bennett said.

'Does anybody want a drink?' Grace said. She knew that both men would disapprove so she slipped the question in while their attention was on each other. She had become good at feints, at stratagems, at exploiting social interstices in order to get a drink in her hand unnoticed. She ordered a vodka and tonic. 'Where did that come from?' Bennett said. 'Fuck. You couldn't watch her.'

'It's been a long day,' Harper said, 'let her enjoy it.' He knew that the only option in the face of her inevitable slide was to be gracious within limits, that world-weary candour was the only response capable of embracing all likely outcomes. He had been a heavy drinker himself once. He knew that Grace had commenced work on the patient edifice of self-delusion that would carry her evening through to its end. Bennett got up from the table.

'I got to go back to the gaff, see if anything more has come through.'

Harper ordered a Johnny Walker with a Stella chaser. Grace understood. Her latent havoc was being acknowledged in its own currency. He drank it quickly and ordered another for both of them.

'I don't feel good about this,' she said.

'Which bit?'

'Any of it. You. Me. Bennett. What we're doing here. I'd feel better if Bennett told us more.'

'I don't think he knows any more.'

'I mean why us? We're not exactly the KGB. There's plenty of people better at this kind of stuff. We're the dregs.'

'What if that was the reason? If whoever the principal is doesn't trust any of the other guns for hire in the business.'

'And why would he not trust them?'

'Because they are the people we're watching out for.'

'Just us?'

'Maybe there are others. Maybe the Ritz isn't the only place that is being watched.'

'In other words they know something is going to happen but they don't know when or where.'

It felt like the times at GCHQ when they knew that something was going on, signal traffic building in the east, nothing defined, but you could feel the anxiety out there in the networks, the deep unease. Operators bent over their screens. Transmissions coming in in dense clusters. If you touched one of the cables you could almost feel it, the coaxial hum. A feeling that events were moving on the ground. Everyone getting connected. Trying to access the information clusters. Knowing that they had to get beyond the commonplace, that powers akin to divination were required, that you had to use the ancient parts of the cortex, access the primordial neural pathways. They were trying to filter out the clutter and find their way to the pure message.

She saw Bennett coming across the bar. He had a flimsy sheet in his hand, a fax paper, ink-smeared.

73

'I got a fax, forwarded from the principal, an order for four gendarmerie vehicles and six motorcycle outriders to Le Bourget tomorrow. A contact sent it on to the principal, got a requisition for twelve SPHP personnel, armed, to proceed to the same location. They're to provide an escort to the Windsor villa and then to the Ritz Hotel.'

He spoke urgently. Grace felt that everything was heightened. She felt as if she was floating above the bar. There had been much discussion of the out-of-body experience when she was growing up in the house in Margate. The near-death experience.

'It has to be for Spencer,' Grace said.

'Why?' Harper said. She could feel Bennett watching her.

'Mohamed Al Fayed bought the lease to the Windsor villa in 1986.' She was talking rapidly. 'But he put the contents up for sale. They're due to go for auction on September 11th. The papers are speculating that the reason for the sale is that the couple are going to live there. Makes sense that they'd go to see it.'

'Al Fayed owns the Ritz,' Bennett said.

'Al Fayed has an apartment ten minutes from the Ritz.'

'Where are they now?' Bennett said.

'In Sardinia. On board the Al Fayed yacht, the Jonikal.'

'The French will have to give her a proper escort,' Harper said.

Grace could see that Harper wasn't getting it. He was thinking about it in technical terms. She could see that he was thinking close protection details, route variation. Men with cropped hair and aviator sunglasses. Motorcades sweeping through sanitised downtown locations. Grace knew that it wouldn't be like that. That the visit would be improvised. There would be paparazzi, knots of onlookers. People getting too close to Spencer, reaching out to her. All those stories Grace had read. The picture sets in Hello!, in OK! That was what people were drawn to Grace realised. Calamity stalking Spencer through the dense colour-saturated pages. The shadow never far away. They wanted to know how you behaved in the face of it. Your comportment in the vicinity of last things.

'Do you have a flight time?' Harper said.

'No,' Bennett said, 'but the security is ordered for three o'clock, so it'll be in or around then.'

'She won't take it,' Grace said.

'What?'

'She won't take the security.'

'Why?'

'She never does. She thinks they spy on her, report back.'

'So who will she go with?'

'The two bodyguards. Maybe somebody from the hotel.'

'Somebody from the hotel,' Bennett said, lying back in his chair. 'Fuck me. That would be Mr Henri Paul, wouldn't it? Well, fuck me pink.'

'Al Fayed probably has a regular driver as well,' Harper said.

'You're probably right, Harper. But if our Henri is part of their security, and Henri has been got at, then there's a problem.'

'In the meantime, what do we do?' Grace said.

'We do what we're told to do, which is watch and report. Harper, you go to Le Bourget tomorrow, follow them in, see what activity there is, if there is anyone else following them, that kind of thing.'

'What do I do?' Grace said. The night was hot but she felt cold. Circulation her mother had said. There had been poultices, hot compresses. Homely suburban mystics in worn cardigans had focused meditative energy on her extremities. She felt scared. She wished they were there now. That they would chant for her. That they would speak mantras to drive away the fear.

'You watch the Ritz,' Bennett said.

'Where are you going?' Harper said.

'I have to talk to somebody,' Bennett said, getting up. 'Keep her off the sauce.'

They watched him leave, the folder under his arm, as though he bore dispatches.

'You want another?' Harper said.

'You heard the boss,' she said, 'he doesn't approve.'

'Fuck him,' Harper said.

They went back to the Hôtel Quimper. Harper followed her up the stairs without touching her. She opened the door of the room and he walked past her and waited until she had locked the door, then turned to her with an air of grim expectation.

Nothing had changed since the first night they had spent together. She indulged in sexual behaviour inappropriate to a middle-aged woman. She simpered. She spoke to him in lisping baby talk. There were themes of abasement. She stripped in the middle of the floor, a demeaning burlesque she had first performed for him in a hotel room in Belfast years ago. She wanted to know if over the years he had indulged in forbidden practices, what foul services had been provided for him. She couldn't stop herself. There was a melancholia hovering in the room and Harper seemed to understand that she was trying to hold it at bay. He spoke to her brutally. He issued curt commands. His vocabulary was precise and explicit. She responded by being girlish, making coy suggestions, pretending to be shocked. She knew there was a parallel narrative out there somewhere, one in which they had been married for years, a narrative where he would clamber on top of her in a lumbering, husbandly way, would afterwards roll off and fall asleep. Not the uncouth act being visited upon her.

Afterwards she took a packet of green Rizlas and a small brown lump of hash from her handbag. She rolled a joint using one of his cigarettes.

'What do you think they want the maps for?'

'Fuck knows. Not sure if I give a damn either.'

'I can understand Andanson having one. He's a paparazzo. If she is coming in tomorrow, then he'll want to know the route.'

'But who are his dodgy friends? Why was he showing the map to them?'

'And why would Henri and his woman friend have a map as well?'

'If I were you I'd go home,' Harper said, 'you shouldn't be here.'

'Why?'

'It has the feel of something that could turn dangerous. Andanson and Henri Paul. Them's two fly boys. And where there's two fly boys there's always more.'

'Do you include you and Bennett in that?'

'I do. I include myself in it in particular.'

She lit the joint and offered it to him. He waved it away.

'Keeps the sadness away,' she said.

'You're in a post-coital situation. You're allowed sadness.'

'No,' she said. 'You're not allowed sadness. Not fucking ever.' She turned on to her side so that her back was to him. She felt that it was the time to assert her right to be moody and difficult. Time to let a note of complaint seep into her voice, a note of dissatisfaction. It was time to drag up old wrongs from the past, barely remembered incidents. Hauteur had to come into it somewhere. They both understood this. She let the smoke wreathe from her mouth. The smoke felt hot in her lungs. She imagined a fragment lodged in the tissue of her lung. Terror of cancer had been a recurring theme in her upbringing. Whispered tales of growths, of malignancy. Big as your fist. Cancer working its way into the family lore. Spreading into the nodes, the ducts, the secret pathways. Women sitting at the kitchen table, smoking, authoritative, speaking with lowered voices about the bowel and the pancreas. Knowing themselves to be custodians of cancer worries and the other heartfelt anxieties, knowing they had to nurture qualities of endurance when the time came.

In the middle of the night Harper got up and left. Grace lay awake listening to the traffic noises outside, a man's voice and then a woman's, arguing in a harsh tongue, a Middle Eastern language she thought, hawk-like and unforgiving. The woman's voice taking over, settling into a chant as though she were reciting a text, a lament, a recitation of historic wrongs.

Hôtel George V
1.05 a.m.

Max stood at the window looking down on the Champs-Elysées. He knew that something was afoot. Mischief stirred in the night. He had spent the day on the phone to sources and now reports were coming in. A K team from Mossad was rumoured to be in transit from Geneva. Men getting off flights from Durban, from London, from Prague. Messages going out on the coded channels. Missives marked Urgent. Missives marked Eyes Only. The talk was of crack squads. Of elite units. He knew that most of the talk was no more than speculation and hearsay but it still suited his purposes.

77

He knew that Andanson was in Paris. Andanson had not phoned but it didn't matter. Events were moving forward. He was confident that Andanson would play his part. The American contact had also phoned. He had told him that according to the transcripts Spencer was about to declare support for the Palestinians. He had no idea if this was true or not. It did not matter. It was enough that the concept of the Middle East had been raised. It meant that everything had opened out into another dimension. The involvement of the Al Fayeds had pointed in that direction, but it hadn't been enough. The narrative needed the addition of political conflagration, the spectre of street protests, men firing Kalashnikovs into the air. People needed to start thinking about the oil, the energy needs, the crude tonnage coming out of the Gulf. Another whole strata of players would become involved if Spencer's support for the Palestinian cause became public. The risk assessors and oil analysts working even now on the data, figures and volumes swirling around them. The Palestinians brought a whole rich texture to the events. Max considered their contribution to world affairs. Hijacked aircraft parked on isolated runways. Corpses of martyrs being borne through the streets.

And then there were the landmines. Spencer in Kevlar and goggles moving across a minefield. Watched by street children in ragged clothes as though such children held a right to arbitration at such events.

The American contact had informed him that the transcripts were being transmitted through Zurich within the next twenty-four hours. He liked the idea that they were coming through one of the old cities. Zurich. Vienna. Berlin. America did not have these monochromatic cities. Their jackboot-trampled Strasses. Their dark amassed textures. The old cities were the places where he liked to do his business. They understood the brokerage that he was engaged in. In their silent freight yards and cattlepens. In their airy mid-century stations and tramsheds. In their grimy autobahn interchanges. Cities that had done vile commerce and would do so again. A patronage of shadows bestowed on the transactions carried out by men such as Max.

He turned away from the window. He knew that he should sleep but he could not. He refrained from prediction. He could not say for certain what the next twenty-four hours would bring, only that it could only bring advantage to him. He wondered if other men stood awake as he did. Three or four across Europe perhaps, he thought. Not more than that. Men who slept little. Men alone in well-appointed spaces. Who understood the night-time stirrings of a fearful citizenry. An unsleeping oligarchy who watched and did not rest.

Ten

Henri came into the Bar Laurent wearing tennis whites. He played every Saturday morning. Monique had a photograph of Billie Jean King on the wall. She told Henri she didn't like modern tennis. Too much sweating and grunting. She liked the era of players like Miss King. Their brisk and mannish style of play.

'Billie Jean was gay?' Henri said.

'Of course,' Monique said. You imagined locker-room trysts. You imagined robust underwear, items that were elasticated. An atmosphere of the forbidden. Tennis stars of the sixties and seventies exchanging steady glances. That was what Monique liked about them. They were ardent. They would not flinch away from the exercise of illicit passion. Monique had been kissed several times at school by an older girl after exercise class. She had been kissed in the gym, in the locker rooms, at the entrance to the shower room. These stark high-ceilinged rooms with their smell of rubber gym shoes and perspiration had been for ever associated with the girl's cool dry-lipped kiss, and Monique recognised these places in memory as the light-flooded anterooms of transgression and desire.

Henri told Monique that he liked Saturdays in Paris. He asked her if she ever left the bar, she seemed to be there all the time.

'No,' she said. 'I do other things. I walk. I jog. I go to the Seine to look at the girls. Their summer dresses.'

'Really?' Henri said.

'Yes,' she said, 'I look at them and dream romantic things.'

'Romance? You're no romantic.'

80

'No, really.' She knew he would not understand. On Saturday mornings she was sick of the girls, of love being a thing of hierarchies. There was a tyranny there. Of aids and plugs and straps. Of lubricants and gels. The vocabulary you had to learn, the literature you had to delve into. Of tops and bottoms. Topless and crotchless. She wanted to be an old lady in a mantilla. She wanted to hobble, feed stray cats, eye the world with rheumy and de-sexed authority.

'And you?' she said, 'how is the romance?' Since Henri had separated from Laurence Pujol she had refrained from asking him about his love life. She had the impression that he didn't want to talk about it. There was something about Henri that she couldn't quite put her finger on. An absence about him in matters of the heart. She knew that he read books on psychiatry, on anthropology. As though he could deduce love from first principles. As though there were rules, species barriers, exact scientific principles and regulations which could be applied to the heart.

One of the regulars had told her that she had seen Henri in a bar with a tall black-haired woman. The regular was a pasty-faced waitress from the north, some flat industrial zone on the Belgian border. Underworld argots sprang to mind when you talked to her. She was a snitch, a tout, habits of sly ingratiation seemed to be inbuilt.

'I seen him,' she said, 'the Ritz man. Henri. He was in the Swan with this woman, taller than him with black hair. All over each other the two of them.'

'What age of a woman?' Monique asked.

'Thirties,' the girl said, 'tall and skinny. The type I like myself. I only seen her from the back. I never seen her face, but they were getting stuck into each other rightly.'

Monique could see the glamour of a secret assignation, a mystery woman. But her informant could only grant the encounter the seedy attributes of a sex crime.

Afterwards Monique would say that she thought that he was remote that morning. It would have been easy to have ascribed wraith-like qualities to him, to say that doom pooled in the corner of the bar where Henri drank his Diet Coke. But Monique was a hard-headed woman. Not given to overstatement. All she said was that he seemed preoccupied. None of the generalities pertaining to sudden death seemed to occur to her. She did not seem compelled to reach for the commonplaces, the banalities with which death ornamented itself.

Lignières
10 a.m.

Andanson rang the Palais de Justice. He rang the Elysée. No one was taking his calls. He rang the DGSE demanding to talk to Colonel Masson. They denied that there was such a person as Colonel Masson. It had been going this way since the death of Bérégovoy but he couldn't believe the way that access had become narrower and narrower. People had begged to be photographed by James Andanson. Had gone down on their knees. He had photographed Hussein of Jordan. He had photographed Agnelli. Small dark men, dapper, taut with the instincts of power, with the rigours of it. Now it was publicists, small-time celebrities. Once there had been a grandeur to what he did. Powerful men called for him.

He took the map into the darkroom and turned on the infra red. He spread the map out on the table. He liked to be in the darkroom. He liked the feeling it gave him of underground control rooms, map rooms. He had been in NATO strategic command headquarters once during an exercise. Maps on the wall showed the disposition of divisions, of vast army groups. There were live satellite feeds. Men bent over screens on which vectors were arrayed. They were talking nuclear into mouthpieces. They were talking high-altitude bursts, dispersal rates. That was living, James thought. He liked the tech argot. The cut-off words. Abrupt and brutish. STRATCOM.

It wasn't working for him now though. He hadn't put all the elements of what was happening together yet, but he knew that it was bad news and the map confirmed it. The red darkroom light seemed to emerge out of the gothic imaginings of post-war film studios. It was the lighting scheme of early technicolour, overblown, metaphorical. You expected Rank film studios credits to roll on it, Karloff or Christopher Lee, actors with long faces and sunken cheeks and an ability to project tenebrous malice.

He clipped down the corners of the map. The blond man had been very precise. Andanson thought that his accent sounded South African. There was an element of the dusty veldt. Old-fashioned though. As of countries vanished into history. Rhodesia. You thought about men in high collars. You thought about men with elephant-hide whips hanging from their belts. The other man hadn't spoken for a while. Andanson wondered about that. The way that people in the service developed the ability to remain silent. He wondered if it was something that was taught. The way they stayed quiet so that a subject started to project everything into the silence. You wanted to blurt out matters of consequence merely to fill the void.

'You are to take this route. Here,' the blond man had said. His finger followed the route. Rue Cambon. Rue de Rivoli. Whoever had drawn the route on the map had taken time over it. It had been done in pencil with little shaded-in arrows to show the direction. Dotted lines ran through intersections. These touches led Andanson to believe that a woman was involved. The fastidious way it was done. The arrowheads given a little decorative flourish at the corners. Rue Cambon. Rue de Rivoli. Cours la Reine. It was like an eighteenth-century plotter's map. There seemed to be subplots, false trails. He realised he was in that space now. An awareness of political assassination hanging in the air.

'I'm not sure about this,' Andanson said. 'I got blood pressure. Maybe you're looking at the wrong man for this.'

'I'm looking at the right man, James. You are a good driver. That is a reason for you to be there. You are a photographer. That is a reason for you to be there.'

'My heart. My blood pressure.'

'Fuck your blood pressure. And your heart.'

Fuck you too and the horse you rode in on, Andanson thought. He could feel his right fist go into spasm as it always did when he was nervous. He realised that he was holding on to the counter. His family had always been prone to vertigo, to disturbances of the inner ear. There were delicate mechanisms that could be disturbed. He compared it to the mechanism of a camera. The shutter leaves that could be jammed by a particle of dust. That is what you are messing with in my head, he wanted to say. There are delicate mechanisms at work, fine tolerances. Think of the whorls and tympanum. He could describe the architecture of the inner ear in detail. The membraneous labyrinth.

'What happens when it is over?' Andanson said.

'You get the fuck out of the way. Get out of Paris.'

'I'll be seen. There will be bystanders. The other photographers.'

'They will see a fat man in a dirty old car. They will think, so what.' It was the first time the other man had spoken. The voice was clipped and precise and heartless. Andanson thought that there was a Germanic flavour to it. It was the voice of a minor and debased Middle European aristocracy, inbred, jaded, an aficionado of exquisite cruelties.

'Don't worry James,' the man said, 'you're only a tiny part of a bigger picture.'

'Fuck me,' the blond man said, 'he's sweating like a pig.'

'Sweat is good,' the other man said, 'I like a man who can show his fear. That way we all understand each other. It is us who must strike fear into others. It is people like James here who must respond. The sweats, the twitches. We are always looking for the small involuntary signs.'

'He has too many involuntary signs. His body is one big involuntary sign.'

'Don't worry about James. People have died on him before and he didn't crack up.'

Andanson said nothing. There were too many dead. Bérégovoy and the others. He could see the dead faces sometimes, floating up out of the emulsion, in the unresolved image in the developing fluid, their ghostly personas. The fear was with him all the time now. His finger followed the route drawn on the map. Rue Cambon. Rue de Rivoli. Cours la Reine. He had wanted to tell the two men that he was a photographer. He took the picture and then he developed it. His friendships with politicians and celebrities were by-products of his work. That his job was to bring them to gleaming and exalted life. He worked in the medium of silver bromides, mercuries, Ilford photographic papers. He had relationships with several security agencies, that was true, but that was only so that he could come and go as he pleased. A man who had his access was valuable to them. He was on first-name terms with cabinet ministers, with stars of the movies and of the world of fashion. He was on close terms with actors who you saw on your cinema screens. Famous actresses arched their swan-like necks when he approached. It didn't mean anything. It didn't mean that he had to be part of this. He wondered if he got down on his actual knees and pleaded with them. What did they know about his medical history? His parents were broken down before their time with circulatory ailments. There were aneurysms. There were arterial blockages. He wasn't a fucking commando, a man scaling down a building with a knife in his actual teeth.

'You see, James,' the dark man said, 'I think you have a grasp of the issues here. You understand what is involved. Unknown forces are at work. Powerful men operating in the shadows. The issues involved are complex and have many dimensions. Are you capable of foreseeing all possible outcomes?'

'There is only one possible outcome if he doesn't do as he is told,' the South African said. Andanson thought that the man had an aura of violent death about him. He would be an expert on rarefied and hard to detect forms of assassination. He would know the pressure points, the vital airways.

'We are not entitled to the overview,' the dark-haired man said. 'Our function is to follow orders. I want you to go home, spend some time with your wife. Attend to domestic chores. We'll be in touch. Don't worry about that. We won't abandon you.'

'We'll be there,' the South African said with a grin.

'Think about it, James,' the dark man said.

They had said that their names were Oates and Furst. Andanson presumed that the names were false. There would be false passports, elaborate identity fraud with their names appearing on passenger manifests. There were whole departments devoted to such things, Andanson knew. Skills that were thought of as artisanal. Frauds involving inks and adhesives and paper densities. Crafts that should properly be handed down from father to son.

85

They got up to leave. Andanson found himself noticing small things. The South African's boots which laced halfway up his calf. They were an item that you bought in a specialist shop. They would be lightweight, built for endurance. The South African would know the importance of good equipment, of things not letting you down. He wore multi-pocketed khaki combat trousers and knew the purpose of each pocket.

'After all,' the dark man said, as he turned away, 'you are known to be an admirer of the monarchy, is that not right? You fly a Union Jack in front of your house, don't you?'

Andanson nodded. It was true that he had always been an admirer of the British royal family. Of the queen in particular. He admired the bulldog spirit, the Dunkirk spirit. He admired cheerfulness in the face of adversity. There was the island spirit, the Blitz spirit. The island he thought overflowed with variations on a theme of cheery self-reliance, of forbearance from spiritual hunger. He liked Princess Margaret in particular. He thought she projected a bleak and soulless sensuality. He liked the way the royals talked, the way they barely opened their mouths, as if to do so would permit a howl of the damned to spew forth. He thought that the men in front of him might be loyal to some abstraction of monarchy. They were knights of atrophy. They were apostles of ruin.

Andanson folded the map and put it back into his pocket. He imagined he could see the photographs that would appear in the Sunday papers and he derived no comfort from them. Mortality had no real place in Andanson's portfolio. He stood up. He imagined his face in the blood light of the darkroom. He imagined himself a count or a lord from the films, scion of a decayed line. He would sit alone in a darkened chamber, consumed with horror and malice. Wisps of mist would rise in lonely graveyards. Virgins would toss sleeplessly in canopied beds. The fear would follow him out of this room on to the street. Rue Cambon. Rue Royale. Cours la Reine. Cours Albert Premier. Place de l'Alma. It would follow him.

Harper thought that in different circumstances it would have been a pleasant thing to watch men playing tennis on a Saturday morning. He sat on a green wooden bench fifty feet away from the courts. He had played tennis in the park at Warrenpoint, a dry salty wind coming in off the lough, seagulls on the air currents above the court, and looking back Harper could see that a geometry accrued to the scene. Of men in white flannels seeking the angle of service, the long parabolic glide adopted by the gulls, a draughtsman's precision to the way they found the arc.

Henri and his partner were in tennis whites, Henri wearing shorts which came down below his knees which looked a little old-fashioned. Harper though of amateur sportsmen of the twenties and thirties. Men of forthright demeanour bringing a hard-won diligence to their game. A range of manly virtues on display, that by their honest endeavouring there were aspects of the world that could be put to rights.

Henri wasn't tall but he served well, following the serve up to the net. He chased unwinnable points and disputed several line calls. He was belligerent and controlled. He talked to himself as he walked to the back of the court to serve, working towards the introspection he required, bending over and staring at the ground just before he served as though instruction for service were written there. The court was made of red clay. Harper was used to grass or tar. The red clay brought a sense of dusty arena to the court. It made Harper think of bullrings and other places where acts of greater jeopardy took place.

They played three sets. Henri winning the first and the last. When he had taken the final score he turned and walked slowly towards the pavilion, letting the top of the racket bounce lightly off the toes of his tennis shoes. The game had distracted him, Harper thought, but now it was over he had to face the day and what it would bring.

Harper waited for him at the entrance to the park. Henri drove back to the Ritz, Harper following. Henri parked in the Ritz garage. Harper called Bennett.

'They're coming in this afternoon,' Bennett said.

'Who is?'

'Spencer and Al Fayed. Their plane has a take-off slot at Olbia in Sardinia at 1.04. They get to Le Bourget around 3.00.'

'You're very precise in your information. The right times and all.'

'Stuff gets around. It's not that hard. You reckon when that plane touches down there won't be a dozen photographers that got tipped off, that got the old nod?' Somebody is talking to somebody, Harper thought, but Bennett isn't talking to reporters. It has to be the principal feeding him information.

'What do you want me to do?'

'I told you. Go out to Le Bourget, follow them in. Grace is going to watch the Ritz.'

'You reckon she'll sit there all afternoon?'

'It's got a bar in it, don't it? She'll watch it like a hawk.'

Harper put the phone back in its rest and went back to the car. He saw a black Mercedes 600 with tinted windows outside the building opposite the Ritz. He read the sign. Etoile Limousines. It had French number plates. Behind it was a black Range Rover with GB plates. An Algerian man was waxing the bonnet of the Mercedes, working the wax into the lacquer. Harper looked into the low gleam in the paint on the flank of the Mercedes and it seemed for a moment that in the paint itself was represented some kind of clandestine regalia or livery, misshapen and strange, and then he realised that it was the distorted reflection of the street and of its inhabitants. He saw Grace crossing the street in front of him. She was wearing a long skirt with a floral pattern and a loose cotton top with a drawstring. She was wearing dark sunglasses. He was glad that he couldn't see her ravaged stare. There was something remorseless and unblinking about how she looked early in the morning. As though she was covenanted to her own abasement.

A truck drove between Harper and Grace and when he looked again she was gone. He saw Henri come out of the front door of the Ritz. He crossed the street and went into Etoile Limousines. Several minutes later he came out with another man. The two men stood beside the Range Rover talking. They looked as if they were planning a route. Things are picking up now, Harper thought. The operation was acquiring a momentum. You had to be aware of the unforeseen. He knew that VIPs were most vulnerable in transit. The way they hit Kennedy. The way they hit John Paul. He looked more closely at the vehicles. Neither of them was armoured, he was certain of that. There was no projectile resistant glass. You could tell from the window frames, the fact that the cars did not ride low on their chassis. He looked at his watch. If Bennett were correct the Al Fayed Gulfstream would be touching down in an hour and a half. Henri got into the driver's seat of the Range Rover. The other man got into the Mercedes. Harper turned the key. He could feel the familiar sickness in his stomach, the metallic taste in his mouth telling him that this was real. That some carnage lurked at the end of this matter.

He stayed behind them as far as Le Bourget. At the airport turn-off he saw a group of motorcyclists at the side of the road. As he drew near he realised that they were photographers, paparazzi. Some of them sat on the motorcycles smoking. Others were checking camera gear, peering through shutters, polishing lenses. Harper looked for Andanson's face among them, but he could not see him. They seemed sombre, barely glancing up as the Range Rover and the Mercedes passed them. They had the air of men carrying out wayside rituals, commending themselves to the minor deities.

Harper wasn't aware of any other pursuit but a motorcycle cop on a panniered Honda 750 was waiting on the hard shoulder as the Range Rover and the Mercedes took the airport turn-off. He allowed the cars to pass him then accelerated away from the hard shoulder until he was in front of the Mercedes. There was no point in staying with them, Harper thought. They would sweep through locked gates, enter VIP areas, access secure zones, be issued with laminates. Harper dropped behind and tried to pick up the signs for the short-term car park. There was a smell of jet fuel in the air, a kerosene tang that Harper liked.

He drove into a multi-storey close to the terminal building. He found a space on the third floor. He was alone as he locked the car. It was very quiet and the locking mechanism made a loud noise. Sound travelled strangely in these buildings. Small noises were subject to unusual amplifications. A barrenness of the soul stalked the echoing prefabricated spaces. You felt as if you were in a cathedral of modernist faith. You had the feeling that acolytes of non-belief were scurrying unseen in the pillared gloom.

Harper was glad to cross to the terminal. The departure lounge teemed with people. He felt the mood of anxiety as soon as he entered. People were dry-mouthed, tight-lipped. They clung to their children. Their unease was being channelled in ways that they did not understand. They passed through customs, passport control, security and emerged into duty-free areas. Men and women wandered from shop to shop, seeming lost in troubled interior monologue. Their identity was being questioned in an environment of luxury consumer goods.

Harper went upstairs to departures in the hope that he could see out on to the apron. Airports used to have viewing balconies, he remembered. Lounges from which you could observe the actual commerce of the airport, the taking off and landing of planes, of passengers being disembarked by smiling stewardesses. Passengers and crew aware that a certain type of behaviour was required. They had been buffeted in the icy jetstream and had still observed certain civilised values. Cocktails had been consumed at forty thousand feet. They had travelled Club Class, Clipper Class. They had travelled in aircraft bearing names such as Constellation, TriStar. The language of the heavens had been bestowed upon their voyaging.

Now travellers sensed that this transcontinental glamour had been snatched away from them. The glamour of vast distances crossed. They were herded into echoing concourses, deftly patronised by airline staff. Passengers sat with their backs to windows, feeling earthbound, resentful. Harper found a window where he could see at least some of the apron. He knew that the plane would be directed to a remote part of the airport assigned to the disembarkation of VIPs, some lonely perimeter area. There were conventions in regard to this. A windswept corner had to be found.

He looked at his watch. 2.35 p.m. The Gulfstream was due at 3.00 p.m. He bought a coffee and returned to his seat. As he did so he glanced to his left. A tall man was standing at the glass wearing a heavy overcoat. Masson. That was what Bennett had called him.

The man he had seen with Henri in the cafe. The DGSE man. Harper was getting that feeling again, the awareness that something was going on. He positioned himself so that he could watch the man. He had the feeling that Masson knew he was being watched and knew exactly who was doing the watching. He had been in the same line of work as Masson. They had each extinguished certain values in themselves, had watched them flicker and go out in the dimly lit stairwells and corridors of provincial police stations. They had seen the men in shirt sleeves at work. They knew the routines. The concocted witness statements and the false confessions. Without knowing Masson's history Harper knew that they were of a kind. That he had worked through civil strife. He would be familiar with the raids, with men being batoned into cells and the way they called out into the night for succour and you knew, you knew that you had set this in motion, the crying out, the moans, the sounds of a dread machinery brought clanking into life.

Harper followed the man's gaze. Masson was looking at the Range Rover and the Mercedes. They were just visible in the distance. Out beyond the corroded fuel storage tanks, the freight handlers, the industrial units, almost lost in the heat and dust and jet fumes. It was a setting for a drug deal or a hostage exchange, Harper thought. It was ideal for an illicit trade and it seemed right that the two cars should have found their way to a hazy and filmic locale.

Harper watched Masson closely. There was an exotic quality to him. The glossy dark hair and the strange bone structure. North African, Harper thought. Berber, Tuareg. An ethnic group with a nomadic lifestyle and a reputation for ferocity in warfare. Harper looked at his watch again. 2.40 p.m. The Harrods Gulfstream was due in twenty minutes. Harper looked up into the sky although he knew that the plane was still many miles away. Masson stood without moving, his eyes fixed on the vehicles in the distance. As though an unknowable obligation detained him there. A tie of blood or kinship. You couldn't work out anything from his demeanour, Harper thought. Whether he was simply observing the arrival of a VIP. Or watching a pre-planned operation unfolding. Or ensuring that Henri observed the terms of whatever accord he had arrived at.

Harper could see a figure leaning against the bonnet of the Range Rover, slight and almost unresolved in the distance. Henri. He could tell that he was gazing up into the sky. There were patterns there that Henri could read. He would know the language of holding patterns, of descent rates, airspeeds and wind sheer. He would know the direction from which to expect the private aircraft, the jetstreams it would follow to get to Le Bourget, borne up out of Africa by temperate zephyrs. He would be able to pick up the contrail unique to the Gulfstream. Harper looked at his watch. 3.08 p.m. The Gulfstream was late. He thought about an air crash. The Gulfstream disappearing off air traffic screens. Personal effects scattered over vast areas. Smoking wreckage located in remote and hostile terrain. It would be appropriate to a public figure. Death in an air crash attracted a certain glamour. There was a seemliness to public figures dying in fireball aircrashes. There was public satisfaction at the immolation.

Probably just a delay, he thought. There would be no announcement. People like Spencer and Al Fayed were not required to account for their comings and goings. He saw Masson turn and look towards the main runway. 3.17 p.m. It was difficult to make out the planes as they approached the airport. The late summer air was soiled, grimy with city dust, atmospheric pollutants. The sun reduced to a dull glare. It seemed as if some grim scientific prediction had come true. Then Harper saw the Gulfstream, descending towards the runway nose up as though dropping down into a poisoned biosphere. It touched down lightly and taxied fast towards the waiting cars. Harper got up and went over to the public phone on the wall. He called Bennett.

'The plane's here,' he said, 'twenty minutes late touching down.'

'Any sign of her Royal Highness and the Arab?'

'The plane's heading towards the cars now. Masson is here.'

'Who?'

'Colonel Masson. You mind he met Henri Paul.'

'What is he doing?'

'He's watching the Gulfstream coming in. It's not a coincidence, if that's what you're getting at.'

'Not on your fucking life.'

'The likes of Masson never do anything without a reason. You better get talking to your principal.'

'That a fact?'

'Sure as I'm fucking standing in this airport, there's something bogey going on here. This thing reeks Bennett. And getting nicked in la belle fucking France was not part of the pension plan.'

'Keep your shirt on.'

'Listen, Masson's got me made. He knows what I am. Probably got the sheet sitting on his desk courtesy of some speccy bastard in the MOD.'

'You got to be kidding. The MOD wouldn't give these jokers the skin of their shite.'

'I'm worried here, Bennett. You never said nothing about French secret service taking an interest in me.'

'Where is he now?'

'He's about twenty feet away.'

'What's he doing?'

'Looking out of the window.'

'Maybe the man's a plane spotter. Maybe he's took a recreational trip to the airport for the purposes of observing aircraft movements.'

'Wise up, Bennett.'

'All you got to do is follow them into Paris. That's all. Stay well back. Anybody takes a sideways look at you, pull out, let me know what's happening.' Bennett hung up. When Harper turned around Masson was gone. Don't start pulling this shit now, he thought. Don't be fucking at it. He couldn't see where Masson had gone. He went over to the window. The Gulfstream had come to a halt beside the cars and the aircraft door seemed to have opened. He turned towards the exit. He didn't need to be grasped by uncertainty, a pall of the esoteric descending over the day.

Eleven

Olbia Airport, Sardinia
1.30 p.m.

The Gulfstream had missed its take-off slot at 1.04 p.m. and had been delayed by thirty minutes. It was waiting for the party from the Jonikal. They had disembarked the Jonikal at 11.30. The Jonikal's launch had docked at the Cala di Volpe Hotel where they were met by two Mercedes. Spencer and Al Fayed were accompanied by Al Fayed's butler, housekeeper and masseuse. The two bodyguards accompanied the couple in the first Mercedes with the staff following behind. The drive to Olbia Airport took thirty minutes. *The flowre ne more doth flourish after first decay.*

Spencer is wearing tan Jaeger slacks with a matching jacket. She is wearing a dark Dior top and Ray-Ban sunglasses pushed back on her head. They sit down in the leather aircraft seats. They put on their seat belts. There are magazines on board for them to read. There is Hollywood Reporter for Al Fayed. There is French Vogue for Spencer. She opened Vogue on her knee as they waited for clearance to take off. Scents rise from the page. The complex inks and colourants, the rustling processes. The inserts impregnated with various perfumery. The whispered excess. Vanderbilt. Estée Lauder. Yves St Laurent. There are new therapies. Electrostimulants. Depilations. Hydrotherapies. Spencer phones her friends from the aircraft. *Go to my love where she is careless layd.* In GCHQ, in Menwith Hill, the intercepts are made. The townhouses ring to their laughter. The suites. The parquet-floored apartments. Revelations are hinted at. Meetings are planned for the following week in London. Their talk is subtle, coded, allusive. The Gulfstream taxis on to the runway.

In GCHQ and in Menwith Hill the intercepts are transcribed. They are relayed up to case officers. The difficulties inherent in the transcribed conversations are acknowledged. There are references to second homes, weekends at country retreats, yachts, holidays in temperate climes. Weeks spent in listless repose in Caribbean arcadia are taken for granted. *Uxor Principas*. The conversations are scanned.

The Gulfstream lifts into the afternoon sky. Climbing over the sea. Thirty thousand feet, forty thousand feet, up into the ionosphere, following the curve of the earth into the blue-black zone. Taking Spencer right up there, it seems, into the satellite belt. In among the sleek Intelsats, the drifting space junk of the 1950s, the long-silent Telstars.

Twelve

Place Vendôme
2.30 p.m.

Grace saw the woman come out of the Ritz and turn left. Bennett had said to follow her if she saw her again. The Jackie O look was gone. She was wearing a simple two-piece suit, dark glasses and a silk headscarf which she had tied under her chin. It was Audrey Hepburn, Grace realised, although she thought that the women lacked the requisite gamine look. She didn't have the features for Hepburn. The face on the verge of some bright and superficial insight. Do Jane Russell, she wanted to say. Do Monroe. Out on some blowsy edge.

Grace found herself walking after the woman. She was taller than Grace had thought, with a narrow-hipped walk which Grace found herself copying. Grace had always fallen down in matters of deportment. At school she had been accused of slouching, of walking with her toes turned out. She had responded to this by developing an aesthetic of graceless and slovenly habits. She bit her fingernails, developed unsightly cold sores, cut her fringe herself with nail scissors, stood accused of crossing her legs in a mannish way. Grace thought that she could smell the woman's perfume in the warm air, a classic and understated fragrance. She noticed that every gesture that the woman made was correct. She developed a picture in her head of the woman's upbringing. There would be an elegant suburban maman. Piano or violin lessons. Gloves and hats worn on Sunday. There would be rules, strictures, proverbs on the subject of personal grooming handed down from long-dead grandmothers. Never leave a room empty-handed. There would be a madness lurking in the perfection. There always was. Intricate punishments would be imposed for small transgressions.

The woman took a Line 8 train going south. Grace realised that she didn't have a guide on her and she couldn't understand the map opposite. The woman changed trains twice. Each time she got up and stood at the door so that Grace had time to follow her. Grace had no idea where she was. She had to fight claustrophobia. Travelling on an underground train always left her on the edge of panic. The Metro was worse than the London underground, she thought. Although it was layered in ancient grime it had longevity on its side. It had sheltered the cities' population through hostile bombardment. Victorian engineers with a background in public sanitation had designed its tiled corridors and brick tunnels. Stalwart mentalities had been brought to bear. The Metro was different. The materials were new, lightweight. She worried about what held the ceilings up, what untried technology. She imagined the tunnels and trains designed by bespectacled utopians, men with high foreheads and radical political views. She kept losing sight of the woman in circular tunnels composed of futuristic materials, then almost running into her on platforms.

After half an hour the train emerged into the daylight, the tracks running between apartment blocks. The woman got off at the first open-air station. Grace got off too. The train pulled off until they were the only two people on the platform. Grace avoided looking at her, but she could hear her heels walking towards the exit. Grace waited until the footsteps were no longer audible then she followed.

The station opened out on to a concrete plaza between two apartment blocks. There was no one else around. Heat haze rose from the concrete. It looked solid, black. It looked like a primal matter, hard and unyielding, obsidian or another stone with supernatural properties assigned to it. It wasn't the kind of place that Grace had thought she would find her in. There was a burnt-out car at one end of the plaza. A window was boarded with plywood. There were alien cooking smells in the air. The woman could no longer be seen.

After lunch Max waited for Bennett in the bar of the George V. When Bennett came in the bar manager started to walk towards him, but stopped when Bennett turned to look at him. Max recognised the man's reaction. There was seedy carnage in that stare of Bennett's.

'Mr Bennett.' Max stood up, extended his hand.

'All right, Max.'

'Please, sit. How are we getting on?'

'I got the team in place. Nothing to worry about on that score. You're in safe hands.'

'I am pleased to hear that. You received my fax about the security detail ordered for the airport?'

'I got it. Thing is, Grace says that the bloody woman won't take the security. Says that they spy on her.'

'Does she indeed? She may be correct. But it does leave Spencer and Al Fayed a little underdefended.'

'We're still there. Michael Bennett and Co.'

'I don't want you to intervene. Remember. Watch and report. What is the current state of play?'

'They should have landed at Le Bourget. Harper's staying with them.'

'They are en route to the villa?'

'You tell me.'

'That is what they intend, yes. It is rumoured that they intend to move into it.'

'That wouldn't go down well with the old in-laws, would it? Moving into the gaff belonging to the Windsors. Be a bit of a poke in the eye for the palace.'

'It was an interesting time. The duke had fascist sympathies you know.'

'A lot of people did in them days. Listen, Max. I don't want to be caught up in no illegality of any nature whatsoever.'

'If an illegal event was to occur,' Max said, 'do you not think that you are caught up in it already?'

'I fucking hope you're joking, Max.'

'Relax, my friend,' Max said. 'I have no knowledge of any illegality. It is a fantasy.'

Max liked the way he had said 'relax, my friend' to Bennett. It made him feel roguish, amiable, an archetype of plausible villainy. Bennett didn't seem to notice. He was eating cashew nuts from the bowl on the table, cracking them between his teeth.

'How are your team finding things?'

'All right. Grace is boozing a bit, but that's to be expected. She's a marvel, that girl. Harper's a pro, does what he's told. He don't like the heat.'

'Only another day or two.'

'You never did tell me what interest you have in HRH. You know, when you said you were protecting an interest.'

'Your's not to wonder why, isn't that so?' Max could quote from Tennyson, Keats. He had read the greats of English literature. He was eloquent on the subject of chivalry and courtly tradition, a theme which he thought might be wasted on Bennett. He thought about telling Bennett about the transcripts. Bennett was uncouth but he wasn't stupid. He would appreciate the intricate mechanisms at the heart of Max's plans. The schemata. The broad sweep.

'I'm wondering all right. I'm wondering when I'll get the rest of the money.'

'You will get your money,' Max said, trying to project disappointment, a gentle chiding in his tone, trying to make Bennett feel like an errant son. Trying to make him see that there were bigger issues at stake.

'What now?' Bennett said.

'I want you to keep maintaining a watching brief,' Max said, liking the phrase. Even after all these years of speaking English, he was always pleased when he found the correct words. For many years he had kept a notebook where he wrote down sentences that he had heard. Slang words. Business parlance. He knew how unreliable language could be. He thought that by repeated use of these phrases he could finally rid himself of his Austrian accent, the hacking, guttural consonants.

'The two men that Harper saw with Andanson. I don't like them being around the gaff.'

'I have made enquiries. Two men fitting the description flew in from Pretoria yesterday. Their names are Furst and Oates.' There was a stillness in the room. Max poured more tea for himself. He liked English tea. Earl Grey. He thought that you got a connection to more civilised times. There was a colonial feel to it. The temperate hill stations.

Bennett was staring out of the window as though something in the zinc-coloured sky had caught his attention. He looked as if he had suddenly become aware of the need to ration out words.

'Nothing is known about Oates. Simply that he accompanied Furst,' Max said.

'Who's the other bloke then. Furst?'

'Former member of the South African Defence Forces with connections to Boss and to Armscor.'

'How do you acquire your information, Max?'

Max noticed a harsh formality in Bennett's tone now. As though they were strangers met far from habitation. As though they were two men standing alone in the windswept barrens and a wayfarer's formality was required.

'There are ways, channels. You should know that. The men's arrival in Paris was noted at immigration at Charles de Gaulle. They flew from Pretoria on Wednesday. These are small things. Their presence was simply notified to me. Now, if you'll excuse me, I have some phone calls to make.'

Before Bennett could stop him Max got up from the table, waved a hand at Bennett and started to make his way across the bar. He smiled at customers, stopped to talk to the restaurant manager, winked at a waitress. His passage across the room was ornamented with bons mots, cheery greetings, mild sexual innuendo. He seemed to know everyone in the bar intimately. Spirits were uplifted. Tips were dispensed. When the attention of the room turned back to the table where he had been sitting, to his companion, Bennett looked like a figure from an old tale, a ragged and unwelcome traveller.

It wasn't like any surveillance that Harper had mounted before. He was accustomed to dour pursuits, dogged and relentless. This was different. From the start it seemed to have elements of carnival to it, ritualised events with their roots in penitential processions. Leaving the airport the motorcycles fell in behind the Range Rover and the Mercedes. A gendarme motorcycle rode in front of the Mercedes. Harper noticed cars as well. A black Peugeot 205 seemed to make up part of the procession, getting between Harper and the paparazzi.

When they reached the A1 the gendarme peeled off. Spencer and Al Fayed were completely open now, Harper thought. He was thinking culvert bombs and infrared switches. He was thinking shaped charges, Semtex boosters, Czech-made PTUs. He couldn't help himself. There should be outriders. Pennants should flutter on the front wings. The Mercedes crossed traffic into the fast lane. The Range Rover driven by Henri followed. Harper looked at the speedometer. 140 kph. The motorway signs flashing up. *A gauche.* The pace of the weekend was being set. It would be pellmell, subject to an unstoppable impetus. The paparazzi bikes were enduros, motocross-spec machines with long-distance tanks in primary colours and ridged highwall tyres. They kept close together in a pack behind the Range Rover. Every so often one of them would move into the inside lane and overtake the Range Rover and draw alongside the Mercedes. Harper could see the rider lean towards the Mercedes with a camera held in one hand, the strap dangling, the flash rebounding from the paintwork of the black car. Harper looked around for Andanson's white Fiat, but he couldn't see it. Andanson would be wily. Andanson would have a vantage point. The motorcyclists were fast and skilful. There was a Latin feel to the way they rode. Taking things to the edge, keeping one hand on the handlebars, standing on the footpegs to get a shot over the top of the Range Rover. The older ones wore biker jackets and bandanas. They had watched the motorcycle films as adolescents, the James Dean films, the Peter Fonda films. They knew their Hell's Angel lore. They had delved into the subgenres.

Harper could see the camaraderie between them, the way they called to each other. That was a good thing. They would know a stranger. They would recognise an assassin in their midst.

He had to remind himself that he was not there as a bodyguard. He had to adjust his sights downwards. His function was to observe and to report. Don't get fucking involved Harper. That was Bennett's instruction. Count the bodies. Watch for operatives in the crowd. Look for the lean-faced ones. The men that hunger for secrets. Look for the patterns, seek for the further layer down there where the deep anxieties gather, the 4 a.m. fears. Watch for the outlines of a malign itinerary emerging, these dusty end days of August counted off in some almanac of the dire.

As the A1 joined the Périphérique the cars slowed to 120 kph, the traffic heavier now, the driver of the Mercedes finding gaps, punching holes in the traffic, Henri following smoothly, the paparazzi spread through all four lanes now, scattering and merging, trying to anticipate where the Mercedes would be four or five hundred yards ahead, hunched over the handlebars, getting in front of the Mercedes sometimes now, discharging the flash directly into the driver's eyes. The Nikons flashing. The Rolleiflexes. It was tempting to apply the terminology of stalking, of hunting packs moving with silent purpose, but Harper knew that this was different. It was disordered, chaotic. He wondered who made the plans. Al Fayed he thought. There was a feeling of a rich man's whim about the idea of the couple being in Paris.

Harper was finding it hard to keep pace with the cars now. Vehicles were moving aside to let them through, pulling on to the hard shoulder, then closing up again. Looking in their wing mirror and seeing a black Mercedes bearing down on them at speed. The chromium trim. The raked grille. Burnished, speeding, expertly handled. They knew what was happening. Stepping on to the subliminal level. Catching a glimpse. The blonde head in the rear window. *The flowre ne more.* They stared after the car as if a long-held faith had been confirmed, as though a prophecy had come to pass. Henri coming behind in the Range Rover with the bodyguard beside him, crossing two lanes at 120 kph, talking to Kez Wingfield the bodyguard, everything under control. He had done the Mercedes advanced driving course for five years running from 1988. He had learned the defensive driving techniques, the high-speed pursuit techniques. He knew how to keep momentum with the front tyres shot out.

They were approaching the Porte Maillot exit. The exit for the Windsor villa. The Mercedes showed no sign of slowing down. Then as it drew level with the exit it suddenly turned right on to the ramp, losing most of the paparazzi. Henri stayed on the Périphérique. Harper followed the Mercedes. He couldn't believe the lack of security. He was the only car staying with the black Mercedes. He looked through the windscreen to see if there was a police helicopter. A Bell packed with sophisticated surveillance equipment, live feeds going back to a base station somewhere, stony-faced operatives scanning the footage, knowing the signs.

The Mercedes turned left on to a narrow avenue leading towards the Bois de Boulogne. Harper's Renault was the only other car on the street. The kind of street usually referred to as being quiet, residential. It looked expensive. Many of the buildings had high gates. Cameras were angled at the approaches to some houses. Harper was uneasy. It had the quiet of the embassy district of a troubled city. Mobs roaming in the centre. Unrest reported in outlying areas.

There was no surveillance. There was no cover. There had been nothing since the Gulfstream had touched down at Le Bourget. Two things, Harper thought. They made her vulnerable when her cover was withdrawn. And they didn't want anyone to be there to see how events unfolded. There were plane trees at intervals along the street. The Mercedes reached the end of the street and turned right. Harper went down the gears to catch up with it.

The next street went along the edge of the Bois. The Mercedes had slowed down now. Further ahead Harper could see the paparazzi bikes pulled up along the side of the street opposite a set of ornate wrought-iron gates. The photographers had gathered at the gates on foot. Harper couldn't see any gendarmerie at the gates. He scanned the cars parked at the side of the road for plain-clothes police but he couldn't see any. The gates stayed closed. Harper wondered why that type of gate was always done in stylised flower patterns. Something to do with the properties of iron. Some way the metal addressed itself to stamen and pistil. The Mercedes was stopped now, ten feet short of the gate, the driver easing it through the paparazzi who were pressing their cameras against the car windows now, banging against the paintwork, swearing hoarsely in several European languages. The gate should be opened as the car was approaching, Harper thought. Some of the photographers still wore their motorcycle helmets pushed back on their heads so that the car looked as if it was being mobbed by aliens, examples of higher intelligence from early science fiction with high, domed skulls.

Open the gates. Open the fucking gates, Harper thought. He was almost level when the gates began to swing open. He could see the house beyond. Stuccoed, gilded, turreted. It didn't look as if it belonged in this park. It looked like it belonged in another city, a place full of winter palaces and mock-gothic opera houses. It looked like a place where gay balls were held while a half-starved peasantry looked on sullenly. The Mercedes got to the gate. The paparazzi fell back, some of them holding their cameras to the rear windscreen as the car moved on to the gravel drive. The gates started to swing shut. The photographers began reaching for phones.

Harper pulled in and called Bennett.

'Jesus, Bennett, she has no cover at all. Nothing. No gendarmes, no plainclothes, no coverts that I can see. The area around the target is completely sanitised.'

'Where are you now?'

'At the Windsor villa. They just went in. The place is coming down with paparazzi.'

'Any sign of Andanson?'

'No.'

'What about Henri Paul?'

'He stayed on the Périphérique. He's driving the Range Rover. He's got the staff on board. He's either headed for the Ritz or Al Fayed's apartment.'

'The apartment. Stay there and pick them up when they come out again.'

Harper put the phone back in his pocket. He looked up. There was a motorcycle at the end of the street. This one wasn't an enduro like the ones driven by the photographers. This was a big touring bike with a full fairing in gunmetal grey. Harper could see the cylinderheads. A BMW. An R100, something like that. The rider was wearing a white half-face helmet and goggles and one-piece black leathers. He sat without moving. Harper felt sweat trickle down into his eyes. He knew that one of the services was represented here. DGSE, or SIS or Det or some other agency of despondency. The man was an operative, one of havoc's outriders.

Thirteen

Grace had gone back to her hotel to change. She put on a black sequined top she had bought in a vintage shop. She wore it with black strapless sandals with a high heel. She knew she would have difficulty walking in the heels later on. She didn't consider herself a delusional drunk. She insisted on clarity. But she thought she could pull off a certain tainted glamour with the sequins and heels. Like Minnelli or Taylor, ravaged by alcohol, by failed romance, by addiction to prescription drugs. All she needed was a handsome alcoholic husband.

The Ritz doorman held the door for her. She stepped carefully in. The air conditioning making her shiver. She stopped at the door and looked around as if she was trying to spot a friend. She could see other guests, men in business suits, women sitting at tables in the lobby, not doing anything. There was a general impression of marble and gilt. The lighting reminded her of department stores when she was young. John Lewis. Chandeliers hanging from the ceiling and table lamps of nymphs entwined. She looked at the guests, the way they inhabited the space. They lounged, they smoked cigarettes vacantly, they walked with purpose across marble flooring. The men were stern-faced. There were responsibilities which came with luxurious surroundings.

She walked towards the bar. She knew she was out of place. She could feel women's glances passing over her. The vintage blouse was wrong. There were sequins missing on the hem. The women in the Ritz were wearing Valentino. They were tanned and blonde. They took their place in hierarchies that Grace could only imagine, the pan-European elites. She felt a tremor in her hands. She wished she was in a lounge bar, a place with a Formica counter and a smoke-yellowed ceiling, a place for daytime drinkers seized of the need for temporary and shifting alliances. Mid-afternoon. A place where you could harbour small treacheries, make generalised commitments at no real cost to yourself, make promises to yourself that you had no intention of keeping.

She took a table close to the door of the bar where she could watch the foyer. When the waiter came over she ordered a gin and tonic, paying for it in cash, feeling that she was being watched as she fumbled the papery franc notes. The waiter kept looking towards the door. The barman kept glancing up. They knew that Spencer was due. In the foyer she saw two men in suits and ear-pieces moving to the front door. People in the foyer started to feel something in the air, rearranging their space. Anticipation began to flood the lavish hallways, the period interiors. Doormen in top hats and frock coats took up position either side of the front door. She saw someone standing next to the porters' desk. He fitted Harper's description of Masson, the DGSE man. He was watching the door. Grace lifted her drink. She was starting to feel more comfortable. Masson's presence was reassuring. He had the air of a veteran about him. She could tell that he was grounded in post-war spycraft, of the fifties and sixties, its grainy and monochromatic terrain of defectors and mail drops. His presence made her feel that she was a legitimate party to any intrigue that might be in the offing. She looked at her watch. 4.15 p.m. Spencer must be due soon. Hotel management were gathering at the door as well.

She wondered how she would have described Paris to her mother. How she would say she had been in the company of a princess, had been party to the intrigue that surrounded her. Grace knew that she would imply that she had got closer to Spencer than she actually had. Her mother would not believe any of it. She knew that this was part of her birthright. To be devastated when her accomplishments were belittled, to be the recipient of the crushing remark. A certain wan bravado in the teeth of a mother's sharp remarks was her birthright as a daughter.

The rooms of the villa are empty. All of the furniture is in storage and is due to be auctioned on 11 September. Al Fayed stays behind talking and she walks through the rooms on her own. There are marks on the wallpaper where paintings have been removed. The floorboards are stained in places. She stands in the drawing room and phones several numbers in London. She has a way of standing when she phones. The phone held to her ear with the right hand, the left hand supporting her elbow with the shoulders slightly hunched. The left foot in front of the right, tracing shapes on the ground, her attention seemingly on the moving foot. There are bluebottles in the windows, cobwebs, dust, motifs of decay.

Afterwards they said that she was planning marriage and that Al Fayed intended to propose to her. That he had bought a ring *Tell Me Yes* which he intended to collect that evening. She speaks to columnist Richard Kay.

confirm confirm

She leans against the fireplace, one hand in her jeans pocket. The room she was in seemed almost designed to induce sadness of a certain kind. You were expected to mourn the deaths of melancholy and sickly princes. The little dead tsarinas. Evocations of pre-war ruling classes seem to hover in the dust-laden air. Lives of empty privilege. Heavy-handed symbolism seems to lurk in every corner of the room but Spencer doesn't feel it. She is a veteran of all types of big-house melancholia, the empty country seats reached by dripping lime avenues, the crumbling plasterwork, primogeniture gone awry. She was familiar with the vices of the inbred, the ward-of-court heirs drooling in asylums.

adjust upwards 20megahertz repeat up20megz confirm previous please

Spencer must be aware that her phone is subject to intercept. That they are drawing her narrative up into the ether. The men in headsets. The men in shirt sleeves. The indiscretions murmured into the handset.

She walks through the villa with Al Fayed. The guide recites the names of those who had stayed in the Villa. The entertainments that were provided. The lavish banqueting. The driveway lined with Daimlers and Lagondas and Bugattis. The misfit couple greeting guests in the entrance hall. The weakling duke and the divorcee wife.

planning an accident for me a car accident he is

Novotel
4.30 p.m.

The package had been delivered to the front desk at 4.15. Furst brought it up to his room and put it on the bed. There was a decal on it indicating that it had transited through Geneva. He checked his watch. Spencer and Al Fayed were due at the Ritz now. He opened the package. It contained a cardboard box without markings. He opened the cardboard box and removed its contents from the packaging. The device was sprayed battlefield green. The housing was robust with rubberised switching to keep rain out. The lens, which was as big as a small plate, was rubber mounted as well to protect it from shocks. He moved it from side to side, letting the fine ground glass catch the light. He could see the wire element clearly, and the housing of the element, the unflawed silvering. It was good, the fact of up-to-date technology concealed in a utilitarian housing.

He knew about glass. Binoculars and telescopic sights, the objects that had to be finely calibrated. It had a grain you had to work against. It could suffer from blooms which spread like viral matter. The finer the glass the less resistance it had to being spoiled. It reminded him of the eyes you saw at night in the bush, reflected in car headlights. The things that stood in the brush, impala and antelope. Prey turning their eyes towards the light.

He took the battery pack out. The LEDs told him that it was fully charged. He pulled the curtains and checked the door. He clipped the battery pack to his belt and attached the HT lead to the pack and to the device. It had a grip like a gun with a trigger. The measure of luminous intensity is a candela. The battery pack wasn't

109

light. The heavy elements coming into play, the alloys. Cadmium, lead, nickel. The weight of the pack suggesting the power available, the pent-up processes.

He passed his hand through the stroboscopic beam. There was a memory there. Off-duty soldiers at discotheques. 1976 in Johannesburg. Off-duty in Mombasa. The Kinshasa Hilton. Outdoors in Freetown in 1978. Ramshackle capitals in death zones. Walking round the dancefloor in khakis and camouflage T-shirt. Everybody knowing who they were. Reading it from the mercenary strut. There was always a strobe. The Africans liked it. What it did to the dancers, turning the whole thing into some kaffir voodoo rite. The strobe flickering, people dancing, skeletal, jerky, in the grasp of some rigor, knowing what was out there beyond the light, amid the minefields and the corpses, night's militias stalking the bush.

He switched off the strobe and turned it over. There were faint markings on the underside where the plate bearing serial numbers and tech data had been removed. He checked the charge again then replaced the device in its packing and put it under the bed. He took out the Falkplan and opened it at P16. He traced the route with his finger, feeling that there was a city now uncovered beneath the Paris he had seen, a city of elegiac concrete vistas and moody underpasses. He had driven the route that morning, noting the traffic cameras. He had been told that they would be off which he thought was a pity. The film would add an extra layer of mystery to the events of the night, the grainy and indistinct close-circuit theatrics.

He stripped to the waist and started an exercise routine. One-handed press-ups. Twenty on each side. One hundred sit-ups. He felt the need for a gym. To exercise in a machine. Watching yourself in a mirror. Seeing the muscles under the skin, the flex and torsion. The smells of deodorants and antiperspirants but underneath the human rankness of it. He knew that Spencer went to the gym. It gave him a connection with her. He thought he knew her. One of the leotarded woman. He knew the blonde hair, the brittle stare. Padding over the non-slip matting. Haunting the asexual spaces.

The BMW had been left in a multi-storey car park on the

Périphérique. It had false Marseilles plates. The engine number had been filed off. Furst started the bike and eased it out of the shadows. When he was a teenager he had raced bikes across the veldt at night. Stripped-down Nortons and Triumphs. Two-stroke cafe racers with clip-on handlebars, lying flat over the tank to get more speed. He read English motorcycle magazines which were six months out of date when they reached him. Motorcycle Mechanics. Superbike. He dreamed about flat-out racing along rain-slick A-roads in the English Midlands, in the industrial zones. The Great North Road. About motorway cafes, jukeboxes. Riding all night on his own and dreaming of mods and rockers and white-knuckle amphetamine camaraderies. The man in the sports jacket looked like those were the places he came from. The flyovers and underpasses. The wind-scoured urban spaces.

He had taken the motorcycle to an Elf station in the suburbs. He had filled it with petrol and checked the tyre pressures. Then he drove it to the Windsor villa to watch Spencer and Al Fayed arrive. He wanted to get a feel for the target. Spencer and the Arab. Driving through Paris with an Arab and band of paparazzi, a ragged troupe in bright-coloured motley her only escort and following. Chaos at the gates of the Villa Windsor. Two bodyguards the only protection that he could see until he spotted the Renault Clio. Recognising the man in it as an operative. Could be Eastern European he thought. Something dated about him. His creased sports jacket. Representative of some down-at-heel intelligence service. Furst turned the bike and drove slowly into the Bois. He stopped under a stand of pine trees and called Belinda.

'The bike is ready,' he said.

'What about the targets?'

'They're at the Villa Windsor.'

'They'll be leaving for the Ritz shortly.'

'Where's the Breton?'

'Don't worry. He'll be at the hotel when we want him there.'

'There's no guarantee they'll go through the tunnel.'

'The Breton will take them through the tunnel.'

'There are men watching. Professionals.'

'They don't know anything about us. They've been told to watch the targets and report their movements and that's what they're doing.'

'I was told there wouldn't be anybody watching.'

'Don't worry about them. Go back to the hotel until you are ready to move.'

Furst went over things in his head. The plan was fluid, improvised but he had a sense of it coming together. Of confluences, forces moving, the cryptograms of conspiracy, false trails, feints and ruses. Men and women moving in the darkness unknown to each other but all bent to one purpose. He had felt it in Angola. He had felt it in Oman. He finished his exercise routine and went into the bathroom where he stripped off for a shower. He gazed at himself for a long time in the mirror. The flat abdominals. The flat pectorals. A perfection he knew to have everything to do with death. His profession required self-absorption, a honing down of the self. You kept your contact with women at a professional level. He had known women like Spencer and he despised the weakness, the eating disorders, the public settling of scores, the Arab boyfriend. He looked at his watch. They would be leaving the Villa Windsor now to drive to the Ritz Hotel. He stared at himself in the sterile, semi-darkness of the Novotel bathroom, posing his nude body this way and that, thinking of himself an athlete, a thrower of the discus or javelin from ancient games, though there was no audience to the dark Olympiad allotted to him, nor medal nor acclaim.

```
                              Ritz Hotel
                              4.34 p.m.
```

Grace could tell the car had arrived. Everyone in the foyer had turned their faces towards the door. The manager straightened his tie. The doorman held the door open and people flooded from the street into the foyer, the hotel staff closing around Spencer and Al Fayed. Grace found herself craning so that she could see them, catching sight of the blonde hair. There seemed to be people closing on them from everywhere, Henri Paul there, keeping them moving towards the lifts. She could see the paparazzi outside the glass now, the doorman holding the door closed. They were holding their cameras up against the glass so that the flash penetrated the foyer. The place bathed in an eerie morguish light. The crowd parted so that Grace could see Spencer for a moment, standing with her back to the bar. She was thin, Grace thought, with a slightly round-shouldered stance. Devoid of any kind of radiance. Grace doing a womanish inventory of tan Jaeger slacks, white blouse. Matching tan jacket slung over her shoulder.

It took her a moment to realise that the man standing beside her was Al Fayed. She had thought that the photographs showed an ordinary looking man but she had not expected him to be so anonymous. She hadn't expected him to possess the usual playboy attributes, but she thought that there should have been a wan charm. She had expected some kind of weakling allure. The type of man that women took on for complex reasons to do with authoritarian fathers. He had the tan, the Gucci loafers.

They were going upstairs to the Imperial suite, Grace thought. She had read about it in Hello! the first time they had stayed there. Former residents include was the way they put it. Former residents include Goering, Churchill, Nixon. Grace wondered if they left something of themselves in the room. Her mother would have held a seance. The ideal setting. The dim lighting and heavy velvet curtains to the floor. Is there someone there called Winston? Is there someone there called Hermann? There would be a sudden reek of cigar smoke in the room. One of the participants would start to speak in a man's voice, heavily accented.

The entourage moved out of her sight line, in the direction of the lifts. She could almost position Spencer by the eyelines of the people remaining in the foyer, a moving triangulation fixed on the Jaeger suit. People already running through how they would relate their encounter, taking in the details of the foyer, looking for the fixed points in the narrative. Spencer and Al Fayed waiting for the lift doors to open. Stepping into the mirrored interior. People willing the doors shut. Wanting it to be over so that they can order it in their minds. Grace could tell when the lift doors closed. People in the foyer started to look introspective, wondering about their audience, on who first to bestow the bounty of this sighting.

Grace didn't see Bennett until he was standing in front of her. The doors were still barred against the paparazzi and she wondered how he had got in. He sat down on the edge of the chair opposite her and lit a Gold Bond.

'What do you know about the Order of the Solar Temple?' he said. 'Sounds right up your fucking street.'

'Order of the Solar Temple?' she said slowly. 'Founded 1984, I think . . . Luc Jouret and Joseph Di Mambro . . . why do you want to know this?'

'Keep talking.'

'Headquarters at Cheiry and Grange-sur-Salvan . . . it was a cult. They thought they were going to find a better life on one of the moons of Sirius.'

'Bunch of fucking retards.'

'They all died. A suicide pact, supposed to be anyway. 1994 at Cheiry and Grange-sur-Salvan. The buildings were burned. The bodies were found to have been arranged in a star pattern. The following year there were deaths in Quebec. Bodies arranged in a star pattern as well.'

'The cops found something different though, didn't they? The Plod found that there wasn't too much suicide going on. Load of them were shot in the head before being burned.'

'Suffocated. Some of them were suffocated.'

'That's right. It's coming to me now.'

'There's one other thing,' she said.

'What's that?'

'The theory was that the shot people took sedatives and then one of the others shot them and turned the gun on themselves.'

'And?'

'They never found the gun.'

'There would have had to have been a gun, that right?'

'Yes. But there was no gun in the wreckage of the building.'

'Somebody else killed them and done a runner.'

'Nobody ever proved it.'

'Nobody ever bloody does in cases like that.'

Bennett fell silent. She could see him taking it in. It was all there. He knew what he would find if he looked into it further.

'Why are you asking?'

'Andanson. Seems he's mobbed up with them some way. Don't sound like the type to me.'

'They were supposed to have something to do with Grace Kelly's death.'

'Fuck me. Here we go.'

'The land her car crashed on was owned by them.'

She waited for him to pour scorn on her but he looked haunted. Aware of what all this meant. Of the global narratives unfolding. The edifices of conspiracy. He had been in the covert world too long not to believe. The way these stories connected deep in the cortex, in the ancient pathways. Mutable and troubling events. Charlatan preachers in white robes. The practitioners of mass suicide. Of souls decamped to distant moons, to the outworlds.

'What has Andanson got to do with them?' she asked.

'I don't bloody know. Principal thinks that they got some kind of hold over him. That he's afraid of them.'

'Where is Andanson?'

'Not sure. I followed him out to the Périphérique this morning. He was driving south. He lives in a place called Lignières with his missus. He's spooked about something. He's got a right case of the twitches.'

'What do you want me to do now?'

'Stay here and keep an eye. And for Christ's sakes don't drink any more.'

'I want to go home.'

'Go bloody home tomorrow. The job's over then.'

'Something's going to happen.'

'Let's have a bit less of the Gypsy fucking fortune-teller about it. You mind your business and do your job and I'll have a big wad of cash for you tomorrow. You see them about to move you call me. Harper's outside keeping an eye. They got a dinner reservation at some place at the George Pompidou Centre at half nine.'

'Chez Benoit. It's where they go when they're in Paris.'

'That's a girl.' Bennett got to his feet.

'Where are you going?'

'I want to talk to the principal, see if I can find out any more about this bloody cult thing.'

She watched him leave the bar and walk towards the lobby doors. He looked shabby and misbegotten but the doorman moved to open the door for him and inclined his head as if he knew that there was a hierarchy in which men like Bennett toiled, an authority which was due recognition. Grace lifted her drink and finished it. When she looked up again the lobby was almost empty and then she saw that Masson was still standing in the same place, beside the porter's desk, his eyes fixed on the front door as though he expected nemesis to burst forth there.

Place Vendôme
6.25 p.m.

Harper had parked the Renault in Rue Cambon several streets away. By the time he got back to the front of the Ritz Spencer and Al Fayed had already entered. The paparazzi had their bikes on sidestands at the edge of the pavement. They were talking on mobile phones. They were checking cameras. They were eating high-energy bars taken from multi-zippered pockets. Harper thought of scenes from a stage of the Tour de France. The paparazzi bikes streaming out in an amoral peloton, primary coloured.

Harper couldn't see Andanson. It felt wrong. He thought that Andanson wouldn't like to associate with the bike paparazzi, that Andanson would work on direct access. He would use connections to try to get inside the Ritz. He would work out itineraries and be lying in wait. But he should still have come across him, Harper thought. Andanson should be in sight.

He cupped his hands to light a cigarette. He hadn't eaten since morning. His skin felt grimy and he needed a shave.

A gendarme van drove slowly through the square and he found himself backing behind a pillar.

He knew he looked as if he shouldn't be there, that he looked as if he belonged in a run-down arrondissement, a place of narrow streets with a history of petty crime. The van slowed and he knew that he was being watched from behind the dark glass, a cop making him for a small-time practitioner, an archetype of stubbled villainy.

The van did another slow circuit of the Place Vendôme. Harper saw Bennett coming out of the Ritz. Bennett crossed the Place and joined him just as the police van drew level. As Bennett joined him the van sped up and drove out of the Place.

'Cops taking an interest, were they?' Bennett said.

'I need to clean up.'

'You got crook written all over you right enough. But there isn't time. Grace is watching inside. They've gone up to a suite.'

'What now?'

'Stay here. Let me know when they come out.'

'Where are you going?'

'Back to the principal. See if he knows anything more about Andanson. Wouldn't be surprised if he's up to something.'

'I been watching for him. Could your principal not tell you where he is?'

'Is that sarcasm there, Harper? Are you trying to come over all barky on me?'

'Far as I can see he knows everything.'

'He's got widespread contacts in the intelligence community.'

'So it's a community now?'

'He only knows what they tell him.'

'And you only know what he tells you. Or doesn't tell.'

'He says Andanson's in with some cult.'

'That's all I fucking need.'

'The Order of the Solar Temple.'

'For Christ's sakes, Bennett. Did you tell Grace this shit? Send her right off the deep end. You did, didn't you?'

'I'm going to try to find out more.'

'You know what, this buck is pulling your leg. I'm in with a cult too. The cult of getting paid for what I do. Make sure you get the cash off him. Get it tonight. Andanson can get beamed up to the mother ship or wherever it is he's going, and I can get back home.'

'He hasn't put us wrong yet.'

'Doesn't mean he isn't going to. I mean this cult thing is away with it.'

'Sounds a bit quaint all right.'

'Quaint. Jesus. Fairies is quaint. This here is more than quaint. Is Henri Paul still in the hotel?'

'Far as I know. Stay here.'

Harper watched Bennett walk away. He considered following him, tailing him to the principal. But he had a sense of complex events unfolding and he knew that the Place Vendôme was at the centre of it. As if to confirm it he saw the DGSE man Masson coming through the front door of the Ritz. A Renault with a plainclothes at the wheel slowed down at the kerb and Masson got in. The Renault drove off at speed, the driver placing a blue light on the roof and turning on the siren, an old two-note siren, a notification to citizenry that alarm was abroad in the city, off-key and mournful.

Fourteen

Andanson left the house at Lignières when he got the call. She told him to drive to the Sygma office and to wait there for a further call. He drove fast but carefully. In situations like this he liked to drive. He had fixed the CV joint. He had new brake linings and the steering bearings had been replaced. Outside the car was dented and soiled, but it was fast and handled well now. He took pride in his driving. He used to go to the circuits. Le Mans. Monaco. Brands Hatch. The smell of high-spec auto fuel hanging in the air. He went to see Graham Hill. He went to see Jochen Rindt. These drivers were actual heroes. Men in goggles you could look up to. Being lifted from the open cockpit begrimed, limp with fatigue. These were men for whom the word fireball was not an exaggeration. There was sudden death at every corner. Andanson could identify with them. He knew that a truthful analysis would put him in the group of known risk-takers. When he shut his eyes at night he could see the great drivers of the era. Standing with their arms folded before the race, jaunty and reckless. He was haunted by the deaths of racing drivers, flung from cockpits like rag dolls against dramatic 1950s skies or slumped broken-necked in the wreckage.

The ear-splitting V12 thunder made your heart race. He challenged anyone not to feel it. He defied them.

Andanson was man enough to know when he was in deep. He had been there before. It was the price of access. There were secret worlds out there, hidden networks. The world was not what people thought it was. He had stood in rooms with powerful men. He

knew the feel of a secret handshake. The intricate finger movements. People said paranoid but Andanson said what paranoia?
That was the world. They would crush him if they wanted to.

With this Belinda said that all was paid. In addition there would
be a future of instant access to top-level summits and major sport-
ing events without let or hindrance.

He had expected the autoroute to be busy with people returning to
the city, but it was quiet. He passed a few lorries carrying dusty produce. Oil tankers labouring towards the city. He turned off before
the first toll plaza and took the A road instead. She had told him to
avoid the toll sections. There were tickets which could be verified by
date and time. There were cameras which recorded. Do things right,
she said or there would be serious consequences. They used phrases
such as higher consciousness. Andanson understood that it wasn't
personal. It was right to feel fear. Fear was the correct instinct when
faced by people with eyes that burned. It was right to feel dread
coming into the city, slowing at the interchange, the exhaust fumes
and heat making a kind of burning dusk although it was only four
o'clock.

He kept the Nokia on the passenger seat beside him but it did not
ring. He thought that was strange. Usually his phone rang all day.
Airport employees. Hotel porters. Security guards. All touting
information on arrivals and departures, cosmetic surgeries, adulter-
ies. Confident that Andanson could broker these hushed exchanges
into glossy cold-set images. They relayed news of raised voices in
penthouse suites. News of rendezvous, of starlets incognito in wrap-
around sunglasses. They wanted money but they were also
concerned that happenings within their sphere would take their
proper place in the world. That Andanson could give shape and
meaning to the pallor of their days.

But the phone was silent. Andanson wondered if his calls could
be filtered. The subterranean burble of his informants. He glanced
at the phone. Its everyday outlines had been transformed by its
silence. It seemed to have taken on the dimensions of a formal
object.

He had always kept up to date with technology. Telexes, faxes.

His office was full of tech clutter. Psions. Garage openers. Anything that operated with a remote. He opened them up just to look at the interiors. The transistors and chips. He did not have names for all the things he saw inside even your common or garden radio. You had to be in awe of the dense circuitry, the delicate loops of copper, the solder beads at precise points.

He had owned one of the first mobile phones. It was an object you could heft in the hand. It had the weight and sombre purpose of early electronica. He felt let down by the lightweight Nokia on the seat beside him. He didn't know what it was capable of. He wondered if the people in cars around him could tell of the fear eating at him. The silent phone looked as if it had been turned to some other purpose. He had heard stories about mind control. About sleepers who were ordinary members of the citizenry until they received a signal and then left what they were doing to obey the order they were given. Stopped at lights he lifted the phone and put it to his ear. He was afraid to press the button. The Nokia looked as if it might emit a stream of alien phonics. A series of interplanetary bleeps and pings. He took a Kleenex from the box on the passenger seat and wiped his forehead and palms. The Michelin No 10 was open beside it but he didn't need to look. Rue Cambon. Rue de Rivoli. Cours la Reine.

He pulled up outside the agency at six. The building was closed. Aluminium shutters pulled down over the front windows. The street was empty. Heat still radiating from the walls and pavements. Andanson sweating in the heat. He put the phone on the dashboard in front of him. When it started to ring he thought about letting it go for five or six rings. But he knew they were not interested in his bravado. When he picked up the phone he heard Belinda's voice. The tone was kind, sympathetic to his predicament. Andanson hadn't expected a representative of the Temple to sound like that. He had expected an inhuman voice, pitched at some icy register, toneless and precise.

She told him to drive to the Alma Bridge and find a parking place. She asked if he had eaten since he left Lignières. She told him that he had time to eat. She explained that nothing was going to happen until after dark. Her voice was warm, cadenced. There seemed to be layers of comfort, a warm stratum of understanding.

She told him to drive to the Alma Bridge. To find a parking place. To leave the Nokia on the seat beside him.

Andanson parked just off the Rue de la Reine. He put the Nokia in his pocket and walked to a phone box. He wanted to keep the mobile clear for the call. He called Max.

'Max.'

'Hello, James. How are you?' Max cautious. Knowing that DGSE could be picking up the call. Routing it through the exchanges.

'Never mind that. I'm an actual dead man walking if I don't do this thing. You know that, Max? We're talking very serious people here. I know what you're thinking. You're thinking he's lost it. James Andanson has finally cracked under the pressure.'

'I'm thinking nothing of the sort, James. I have every confidence. What thing are you going to do? Confide in me, James.'

'They done it before. Those people in Switzerland. They never committed suicide. The Order of the Solar Temple.'

'You are babbling now, James. Who are they?'

'People hear cult they think Hare Krishna. But this lot aren't any Hare Krishna.'

'If you told me what was about to happen . . .'

'What? Give you info, Max, so you can trade it? That's the way to get myself killed all right.'

'I could talk to the police.'

'Forget about it, Max.'

Hôtel George V
6.45 p.m.

Max thought a lot about belief. It was natural at this time of his life. The twilight years was how they referred to it which made these days seem shaded, evening-textured. That was not how Max perceived it. He had seen the elderly who went to live in Florida. The palsied refugees from the outlands of the dying. Max could see the fear in their eyes, trembling, liver-spotted, lost in the terrors of the aged.

In foreign capitals Max had taken to attending churches of different denominations. He would sit at the back if a service was in progress. He used to have a weakness for priests with beards chanting but now he found himself drawn to Lutheran churches, the bare liturgies, the unadorned rites. Men who framed the narrative of last things in wintry tones. The kingdom of God was hedged about with difficulties and rigorous tasks and was attainable only by the righteous few. Max liked the bluntness of their vision and their cold zeal.

He thought that Andanson was probably in Paris. Max's information was that Andanson believed that he was involved in an operation controlled by people associated with the Order of the Solar Temple, a defunct cult formerly based in Switzerland and Canada. Andanson had received calls from public phone boxes in France and untraceable contract mobile phones in Switzerland over the previous five days. Sometimes a man rang him and sometimes a woman. They directed him towards Paris. Non-specific threats were made if he did not comply. Max thought that it was more likely that the calls came from covert operatives of some kind, but if Andanson believed himself to be pursued by a cult then Max would not interfere. If he believed in cults and their sprawling liturgy of messianic leaders and mass suicides then Max would not intervene.

There was a soft knock at the door. Expecting a chambermaid Max opened the door. He recognised the two men as plainclothes. They did not try to show him a warrant card or any other form of identification. Everybody knew the moves. From now on the evening would be conducted in a ballet of world-weary gestures. Max picked up his jacket from the bed. In the foyer the men walked close behind him. There were no handcuffs but there didn't have to be. Max could see the concierge's eyes flicker towards him. The way the porter held the door open. These men knew the dynamics of custody.

Once the unmarked car had pulled away from the kerb the driver put on the blue light but didn't use the siren. They drove north, towards the suburbs, the driver using streets Max didn't recognise. The streets opened out into broad boulevards between apartment buildings. There were green spaces between the blocks. They pulled up outside a newly built suburban gendarmerie. Max was disappointed by the well-lit civic spaces, the use of glass and concrete. He had expected to be brought to one of the city centre stations. Weathered old buildings with begrimed stonework. Quai des Orfèvres. He expected to be led along distempered hallways under yellow lights. To sit on steel-framed chairs. To be held incommunicado in rooms where men conducted conversations on the subject of guilt and consequence, interspersing those conversations with acts of violence. He wanted a building that was equal to his troubled soul, that gave a debased context to it.

The tall man in the foyer introduced himself as Colonel Masson. They did not shake hands. Masson led him into a side room where there were computers and filing cabinets and other objects in moulded plastic. Masson sat down at a table. Max sat down opposite. Masson put a plain blue folder on the table and removed three photographs from it. Max approved of the folder, its edges scuffed and foxed. The way it bulged. The way edges of A4 sheets protruded. Documents pored over as the connections were sought. It was the way this whole business should be handled. The folder bulking out as the days went on, mystery accruing to the text.

Masson put the photographs on the table. They were old file photographs in monochrome.

'Bennett, Harper and Campbell,' Masson said, 'they are working for you. They are carrying out a surveillance on an employee of the Ritz Hotel, Henri Paul, also of two prominent guests of that hotel. Also of the photographer James Andanson.'

'They are in my employ. I hired Bennett and he hired the other two.'

'I requested all three files from my colleagues in the British security services. To what purpose have you employed them?'

'As protection to the prominent guest of your republic.'

'Who would wish to harm Spencer?'

'She is in a dangerous position. She is an embarrassment to her former family. She is the mother to the heir to the throne and proposes to marry a playboy Muslim. Her campaign against landmines caused much anger in certain quarters.'

'How do you know she plans marriage?'

'I have seen transcripts of her telephone conversations over the past three years. I know also that she plans to espouse the Palestinian cause.'

'What interest do you have in this matter?'

'The transcripts belong to me. I propose to do business with them.'

'To sell them?'

'There are interested parties on all sides.'

'You wish to protect Spencer then.'

'At least until the transcripts are sold. They contain many interesting details. Some people are too trusting of their telephones.'

'These are classified documents?'

'In the United States they would be considered so.'

'What is your relationship with James Andanson?'

'We trade information.'

'Since you arrived in Paris you have received three calls from Andanson.'

'We keep in touch.'

'He seems to be afraid.'

'He imagines that he has got himself involved with a cult. That they will do something to him if he doesn't do what they tell him. I believe that the balance of his mind is disturbed.'

'Do you think he represents a threat to Spencer or anyone else?'

'I don't know.'

Masson got up from the table and walked to the window. Max knew that the whole thing was troubling him, his instincts telling him that there was something wrong, there were undercurrents out there, that in the warm evening a malefaction was abroad. He knew the kinds of people who got swept up in the wake of people like Spencer. The cultists, the stalkers and loners and pale compulsives, out there on the margins, a citizenry of lost. Masson knew that he could not be blamed for all the members of Spencer's fame-haunted entourage, someone stepping forward out of a crowd with a revolver in their hand and phrases of borderline insanity on their lips. But he felt there was something else out there.

'There are always conspiracy theories,' Max said.

'There are,' Masson said, 'but the fact that there are conspiracy theories does not mean that conspiratorial politics do not also exist.'

He knew what he was dealing with in Max. He had read his file. His name came up in connection with the OSS. His name came up in connection with the Red Brigades, Grey Wolves and other underground movements heavily infiltrated by the security services.

A teenage prostitute had overdosed in his room at a Los Angeles hotel. A street girl. He had sent word through to justice to see if extradition proceedings were in train, but it was the weekend, the last days of the holidays. Offices were deserted.

'You should get Spencer off the streets,' Max said, 'get her off the streets and draft in extra personnel.' Masson was silent. Max took his silence to mean that Masson had already requested help from his superiors and been turned down.

'I'm sure it is nothing,' Max said, 'there are always rumours.'

But Masson thought there might be a real operation out there, labyrinthine in its execution. False trails would have been laid. Forged documentation employed. Rumours had reached him about sleeper cells being awakened, hitmen from former Eastern European secret services crossing the border on false passports. Masson could feel it, the deep and transgressive undertow.

'Harper. The Belfast man. He says he saw a motorcycle.'

'One of the photographers.'

'No. It was a BMW, a touring machine. They don't ride those. One man on it. He said he looked like a professional.'

'Where?'

'At the Windsor villa.'

'It's not enough. It is reasonable to assume that someone would have her under surveillance.'

'Harper was sure there was something wrong about it.'

Masson turned away from the window and walked to the door. 'I think it's better if you stay here for a while.'

126

She returns from the hotel hairdresser to find the suite empty. Al Fayed has gone to the Repossi jewellers on the other side of the Place Vendôme and has not yet returned. She phones a correspondent and discusses the hostile comment on her relationship with Al Fayed. She pretends to be unable to understand why the press do not like him. She asks if it is because he is a millionaire. Afterwards she starts to dress for dinner. She selects black Phillippe shoes, white Gucci trousers and blouse, a black Oscar de la Renta blazer. She hasn't eaten since breakfast. The suite is empty and she stands in front of the gilt-framed mirror in the bedroom.

comprehensive blood chemistry panels are important in detecting possible occult metabolic complications

She inspects herself. Bringing forensic scrutiny to bear. The line of the blazer improving the profile of the sloping shoulders. She puts her hand on her abdomen. At night she goes downstairs to the kitchen. A midnight processional barefoot through the royal apartments, the draughty palaces. Balmoral. Kensington Gardens. Old buildings awash with narratives of ghost sightings, unquiet spirits in the corridors, drifting in the shrubbery. She walks in pyjamas past psychic hotspots, scenes of paranormal events. She works out the routes to the kitchen beforehand. There are arts of concealment, treacheries to be practised on the self. She looked at herself in gilded mirrors as she passed and knowing that she was working her way beyond the rational. That the image projected back to her is not to be trusted. She opens the fridge door, chilled air wreathing out of the fridge like ectoplasm. The room filling with freon hum.

History has never interested her. But the names of the suffragettes stick in her head. Mrs Emmeline Pankhurst. Mrs Davidson. Mrs Burns. She read how they were force-fed in Holloway. *They forced my mouth open with an iron instrument.* Their faces in Unwin's History of Britain. She knows the meaning of the shadows under the cheekbones.

She stands in front of the mirror in the Ritz Hotel. This body has had its brushes with the infinite. It was known in its entirety. Its capacity for betrayal.

The long feet, almost masculine in their dimensions, that she thought clownish when she was a teenager, a circus memory of Pierrots walking, a sinister padding in the ring sawdust. Lately she had taken to emphasising the eyes, the eyeliner drawn on heavily, the mascara also, until she came to resemble the girls that she and her friends had laughed at. The girls out of Plaistow and Manningtree. The girls who came into the West End on a Saturday night with the hoop earrings and boyfriends in Ben Sherman polo shirts. Eyelashes if they had access to harem girl erotics. More knowing now than she thought. Aware that second-hand mystery is better than no mystery.

She goes to the window, standing to the side of it and holding the curtain back in a parody of backstreet nosy parkers, doing it so that the paparazzi can't get a shot of her. On the other side of the Place Vendôme she can see the Mercedes outside the Repossi jewellers. Al Fayed in the shop buying the Tell Me Yes ring. In the distance the noise of Saturday night traffic from the Champs-Elysées, the engine noise blending together, a lone, wolfish harmonic rising above the city.

Fifteen

The Mercedes 600 crossed the Place Vendôme. Harper kept pace with it on foot. He could see Al Fayed in the back. The bodyguard Wingfield was in the front seat. Spencer was still in the Ritz. He couldn't see any of the paparazzi around which meant that they were waiting somewhere else, that they had been tipped off about the couple's movements. He thought that the Mercedes would stop at the front entrance of the hotel but it drove past, Harper crossing the Place Vendôme at a diagonal, half-running. The Mercedes rounded the corner of the hotel, going towards the rear entrance. Harper followed it, crouched over, feeling like a fictional detective, a gone-to-seed aphorist in a cheap suit. As he rounded the corner he saw Al Fayed go into the hotel followed by Wingfield. The Range Rover that had driven from the airport pulled in behind the Mercedes 600. He could see exhaust fumes, both cars kept their engines running. Harper walked back across the Place Vendôme. He got into his Renault. The radio was tuned to an Arab station. Filling the car with souk clamour, and over it a man's high voice chanting, semi-falsetto, invoking the names of God. Harper looked left as he passed the entrance to Rue Cambon. He saw the BMW again, the same silver-grey machine he had seen at the Villa Windsor.

He turned the corner and parked several car lengths back from the Range Rover behind the Ritz. He called Bennett.

'I seen it again. The BMW. The motorcycle. In the Place Vendôme. Did you get anything from your principal?'

'He's not there.'

'What does that mean?'

'The cops took him in. The concierge at his hotel seen them going out with him. Done very discreet.'

'Discreet is not getting arrested in the first place. What the fuck was he lifted for?'

'I don't know. He's too smart to give them the excuse.'

'He better be. He's got bills to pay.'

'One thing's for sure.'

'What's that?'

'There'll be no bills paid if you don't do your job. Keep with them for now and watch out for that BMW. And Andanson, whatever the fuck he's up to.'

Bennett hung up. Terse exchanges seemed to be in order. It was important that dialogue was clipped, utilitarian. Harper lit a Gold Bond. There were three left in the packet. He wondered if he would have to smoke French cigarettes when he ran out. A Gitanes or a Caporal. To join the sombre men in blue work jackets smoking them on park benches.

The Range Rover and the Mercedes 600 had their hazard lights on, flashing out of synch. Lighting up the buildings on either side, bringing an air of emergency vehicles to the narrow street, an atmosphere of roadside carnage.

Harper saw Henri Paul emerge from the rear entrance to the hotel. He walked over to the driver of the Mercedes 600 and spoke to him briefly then went back into the hotel. Harper could see the driver straightening his jacket. He switched on the engine of the Renault before he saw the door of the hotel open. Henri coming out first then the bodyguards. There was a momentary pause and then Spencer and Al Fayed came out. The couple were not allowed to stop, the bodyguards keeping them moving, giving their exit from the hotel the air of an embassy evacuation by helicopter, the couple hunched over, their faces averted as though against the rotor wash. As though in the empty street the clamour and press of bodies surrounded them. Henri kept looking at his watch. Harper wondered what calculation he was making. He looked like a man with somewhere to go. The door of the Mercedes closed. Harper looked at his own watch. 7.05 p.m. The Mercedes pulled away from the kerb followed by the Range Rover. Harper pulled in behind the Range Rover, tensing up, ready for the fast drive in traffic, his hand on the gear lever, trying to work his way into the headlong rhythm of the other two drivers, men driving big vehicles fast in traffic, the great Paris intersections coming up, the massed trajectories. You had to abandon yourself to the rhythm. The filter systems, box junctions, mergers, traffic spread out across eight thunderous lanes coming into the Place de l'Etoile.

He could not rid himself of a persistent feeling of getaway about the way that the couple travelled, of dissidents in flight. As if some regime bore down on them, or nameless state organs sought them out.

He knew from Belfast how easy it was to find yourself out in the dangerous hinterlands.

Five minutes took them to the Rue Arsène-Houssaye. The paparazzi were waiting. A changed atmosphere to the drive in from Le Bourget where they had seemed to be pursuing the same route, where they seemed to be fellow voyagers, steeped in philosophies of wayfaring. Where there was a sense of a shared destination. The Rue Arsène-Houssaye was different. The paparazzi were hemmed-in, clamouring. They surrounded the Mercedes. Camera housing banged against the bodywork of the car. The source again, Harper thought. What was Al Fayed doing in the Repossi jewellers shop in the Place Vendôme? If he had bought an engagement ring then that accounted for the mood of the paparazzi. They wanted the shot of the engaged couple. They wanted the shot of the ring. The source feeding them the information. It had to be somebody close to the entourage.

Al Fayed's decisions were too random to be anticipated long in advance. A rich boy improvising. There had to be an insider, a disaffected courier feeding their movements to the paparazzi.

Either that or they were subject to close monitoring. Being tracked through the base stations. The installations where Grace had worked. It would have to be priority work, highly resourced in terms of personnel. Moving across the frequencies. Instant interception and transcription. Somebody working the phones, feeding their movements to one of the paparazzi. That was another thing he had learned in Belfast. When you lifted a phone you never knew who was listening. In the seventies you could sometimes tell. There were buzzes, clicks, telltale feedback on the line. Army engineers with earphones and regional accents trying to work the manual exchanges, using crocodile clips to connect recording devices. Harper used to lift the phone and wait for the switch noise and then the whirr of the reel to reel. Now he thought there was something comforting in the idea of outmoded electronics, a nostalgia lurking, a longing directed at the analogue hiss, the gimcrack contraptions.

Ahead of him the Range Rover had overtaken the Mercedes 600 and pulled up on the pavement, the bodyguards getting out, trying to hold the photographers back, the flashes going in one continuous burst, casting a ghastly light on the faces of the couple in the Mercedes 600. Uniformed security guards were coming out of the building. A wordless noise rising from the photographers. Passersby stopped on the pavements. Their focus no longer just on the Mercedes 600 but also on the paparazzi themselves, men surrendering to primal urges, screaming at the security guards, spewing invective, making lurid threats.

This would be the place for the lone gunman. A Mark Chapman. A ill-gotten post-adolescent in jeans and a heavy metal T-shirt looking for an event in which to invest disappointments which he regarded as epic. Harper scanned the edge of the crowd that pressed around the cars and the entrance to Al Fayed's apartment building.

Two uniformed security men from the apartment building moved on to the pavement, trying to push the photographers back. One of the bodyguards opened the door of the Mercedes, pushing it back against the photographers. Rees-Jones and Wingfield stood over the couple as they left the car. Photographers pushing the bodyguards. Holding their cameras at arm's length above their heads, straps dangling. Spencer being jostled. The whole maul moving sideways then, carrying Spencer with it, eight or nine men locked together around her, off-balance, the momentum carrying them five yards down the street, crabwise, the whole thing like a scene from silent film, gestures being exaggerated, fists shaken. The characters attempting to get beyond the melancholic drollery of early comedy. Harper saw one of the bodyguards guiding Spencer by the arm into the entrance of the building, Al Fayed following, gesticulating at the paparazzi.

Spencer was gone and the photographers took out mobile phones, flasks, bottles of water. They leaned back against the railings or sat on the kerb. Two of them were on the boot of a parked car, their feet on the bumper, smoking a Marlboro. Another straddled his motorcycle facing backwards. It was important that they inhabited urban space in a variety of ways in order to stress the outcast dimension to their work.

Harper rang Bennett.

'Where are you?'

'At the Al Fayed apartment.'

'Are they inside?'

'They're inside. The photographers is all over them. They got no protection.'

'Any sign of Andanson or that motorcycle of yours?'

'In the Place Vendôme. Outside the Ritz.'

'Shit. We're working blind here without the principal. We should ring the cops. Tell them there's some fucking psycho on the loose, about to bump off HRH. Go home. Get the fuck out of here.'

'You taking the piss, Bennett? Nothing's going to happen.'

'I keep telling you about the conspicuous absence of police activity in the general vicinity of these two.'

'You're saying sanitised.'

'Dead right. Feels like that to me anyhow.'

Harper knew what sanitised was. Sanitised was the deliberate withdrawal of all security force personnel from the area surrounding a target in order to give a killing team a clean run. Sanitised was run between state agencies. Sanitised was eerie eighties suburbia, the prowled dark between car ports, the assassin's gloom, another era, not here.

'The woman's more likely to get run over by one of these boys on a motorcycle.'

'Just stay put, Harper. Keep on them. They'll be there for a while. Nose-powdering time. They got that dinner reservation at half nine. We know that much anyway.'

133

'Half of fucking Paris knows that by the way these photographers is setting in. What's Grace at?'

'Doing what she's told like she always does. Staying on Henri Paul as per instructions from the principal.'

'The amazing disappearing principal.'

'Shut up about the principal and sit tight. If there's something in the pipeline it's not going to happen yet. It'll be different after the restaurant.'

'Nothing's going to happen.'

'It'll be dark then is why. It'll happen after dark.'

Ritz Hotel
7.05 p.m.

Grace saw Henri Paul crossing the lobby. She knew straight away that he was on his way to an assignation. He had shaved somewhere in the hotel and changed his shirt. He looked light-hearted. Willing to carry goodwill into any carnal episode that might be on offer. She wished that men like him were drawn to her. Bearers of erotic bonhomie. Open to mild deviance, but only in the cause of mutuality. Not like her episodes with Harper, laced with trangsression of the worst kind, the rank physical commerce.

Henri shouted au revoir to the deskman. Going off shift on Saturday night, the evening city waiting outside. Henri doing the bachelor thing, patting his pockets for keys, wallet. Grace stood up. She could feel the three drinks. An out-of-body feeling. She felt a sudden urge to call her mother. To hear talk of tarot cards read, destinies foretold, unreliable prophecies falling from the old woman's lips. She wanted to be believed when she said that bad intentions were abroad in the warm night. She wanted the small consolations offered by her mother and her coterie of cardiganed soothsayers.

She wanted one last act of love. She saw herself in a tableau of mothers and daughters. Tear-stained, contrite.

She walked out through the front doors of the Ritz Hotel and set out to follow Henri through the evening city. The heat of the day starting to abate. He turned in the direction of the bars she had

134

passed on the way in. The Bourgogne. Harry's New York Bar. The Laurent. He had a rendezvous. An assignation. It would be happening on a higher plane, shining, cosmopolitan. She followed him along the street feeling that she drew a rank spiritual baggage behind her.

He stopped outside the doorway of the Bar Bourgogne and lit a thin cigar. She could see the place it took him to. The narrowing of the eyes against the smoke. It was the brand of the provincial cinema, the napped velvet seats. Henri seeing himself as a lone fatalist in spurs and a poncho.

He turned and went in. Grace walked past. She thought she could see Belinda sitting at the bar. She walked to the end of the street then turned and came back. Grace thought she understood Belinda now as a haunter of retro clothing shops and market stalls, a stalker through late twentieth-century milieus. She would understand the hoarders, the gatherers of trove. From childhood on Grace had been dressed from the nearly new shops of Margate. Her mother liked to dress her in big-house cast-offs, flapper hats, to tap into the twenties and thirties, feeling the epochal draw of these items.

The Bourgogne didn't seem to belong in the quartier. It had the feel of a Marseilles wharf bar. Young men smoking Marlboro were working the fruit machines along one wall. There was a pool table at the back. The older men sat at the zinc bar with a Ricard or an espresso in front of them. They wore T-shirts with cigarette packets in the sleeve, white shirts with the sleeves rolled tight to the shoulder. Fists were notched and battered. There were scars and tattoos. The emblems of disrepute predominated. The sports pages of Figaro were folded into a rack on the wall. Grace spotted Belinda straight away, sitting with her back to the room. She had known she was coming here. She was wearing jeans and a short leather jacket over a white T-shirt, her hair tucked under a cap. When she turned to put a hand on Henri's Grace saw a home-made tattoo on her wrist, a dagger she thought, pricked into the skin with a needle and gone over with blue ink. She resembled a depression-era stevedore, a union card buttoned into her shirt pocket. It was the right look for the Bar Bourgogne.

Belinda was drinking a Stella from the bottle. Grace couldn't see what Henri had ordered. There was a bar stool in the angle of the bar and the wall beside a payphone. Grace sat down and ordered a gin and tonic. The men standing at the bar ignored her. They exchanged terse remarks with each other in hoarse waterfront argots. Belinda and Henri got up and carried their drinks to the pool table. Belinda put the money in and racked the balls. Henri took off his jacket and chalked a cue. They played two games. Henri being competitive, Belinda working on getting the stance right, a boondock-era straddle of the table, putting the languor of early Americana into it, of men in jeans playing in downtown pool halls, redneck bars.

Henri went to the bar and paid. Grace waited until they had left the bar then followed them to the street. They were walking slowly, fingers laced, Belinda with her jacket slung over her shoulder. Playing into archetypes of summer lovers. Grace had to remind herself that this was a surveillance. These narrow streets with none of the dishes and aerials, the electronic mesh, to keep her reference points in the late twentieth century. Momentarily losing the watchers, pale and shirt-sleeved operatives at vigil over glowing screens. Data packets swirling through the night. Henri and Belinda taking on the look of 1940s lovers, a Parisian couple, striking classic poses as Henri unlocked the apartment door at Rue Cambon and stood back to let Belinda enter, then closed the door behind him, Grace finding herself suddenly alone in the street, erotic expectation seeming to hang in the shop windows and doorways, suddenly seeming a wan commodity.

Grace knew that they would not leave the apartment for a while. She could find a bar nearby where she could keep an eye on the street. There was a danger that she might lose Henri but she knew that this was not a proper surveillance, the target contained in a moving box, agents rotated, the patterns of covert logic rippling outwards from the lone individual. This was something different. The requirements in this operation were intuitive.

She had crossed half the distance between the doorway and the bar when she realised that the Laurent was a lesbian bar. Picking it up from the atmosphere before she saw that the couples along the wall and at the bar were all women. Part of it she could like. The smile she got from the girl behind the bar, one corner of her mouth turned up, a wryness in the matter of gender permeating the place.

Grace took a stool at the bar and ordered a gin and tonic. She felt as if part of her should be pierced or hennaed or tattooed. Rituals were being observed in the shadows and she didn't know what they were. Fetish glossaries were unfolding. She felt as if she was fourteen again. Trying to work out the meanings of the glances, the cool looks bestowed. Even then she had never been at ease with the feminine assay, the scrutiny that was brought to bear. She wished she was back in the Bourgogne. Among the wharf rats. Being looked up and down by a burly patron.

The bar stereo was playing Carly Simon. A TV screen set into the back wall was playing The Wizard of Oz on a loop. She slipped off her stool and went to the door, looking down the street to Henri's apartment. She thought that if she could see light behind the shutters. She thought she was in the right place for spying on lovers. When she turned back from the door it seemed that a dozen pairs of eyes followed her. Doomed operatives in the house of love. There was a payphone on the wall beside her. There were cards pinned to a cork noticeboard beside the phone promising various services. Photographs of dominatrices with long melancholy faces. Services rendered. A girl with long lashes and a bowler hat tilted over one eye. A card for a STD clinic. Masseuse intime. She kept finding innocence in unexpected places. She called Bennett's number.

'Henri has gone home. With the girl.'

'That's him for the night then.'

'I don't know. It's early.'

'You're right. Stay there and keep an eye on him. Get a mobile, Grace. If he goes walkabout, how are you going to stay in contact?'

'I don't like them. They give you cancer.' She could imagine a growth in her head. The brain tumour. The thing with its own dread vocabulary. Metastasis. Radiations being brought to bear. The thing that had the power to draw down future technologies.

'Cancer my arse. I can hear you piling coins into the phone. You ain't claiming expenses on it. I'm going over to Al Fayed's apartment. Let us know when he moves.'

Grace put the receiver back on the rest and turned back to the bar.

Rue Arsène-Houssaye
8.35 p.m.

Masson hadn't used the siren on the way back into the city centre. He told the driver to detour via the Rue Arsène-Houssaye.

'You know it?' he said.

'It is where Al Fayed keeps an apartment,' Max said. Masson didn't speak again until they reached the top of Rue Arsène-Houssaye. Max could see a small group of paparazzi waiting outside Al Fayed's apartment. They were smoking and talking among themselves.

'There is a blue car parked on the left-hand side of the street,' Masson said, 'can you identify the driver?'

'Harper,' he said. Masson took a fax from the file that lay on the seat beside him.

'Are you aware of his record?'

'I do not have your access, Inspector.'

'Collusion with intelligence services and paramilitaries . . . acted as agent provocateur for Special Branch . . . running of informers . . .'

'A patriot.'

'Perhaps. Left the service in 1988. Charged in connection with murder. Charges not proceeded with.'

'Murder?'

'A seventeen-year-old was drowned when he fell from the deck of the car ferry Ulster Princess. The boy was due to appear as a witness in Craigavon Magistrates' Court the following day.'

'Tragedies happen.'

'Harper and Bennett were the officers involved. They said the boy jumped into the sea before they could reach him. A witness said that Harper threw him from the ship. The witness later withdrew his testimony.'

138

'I did not ask for Boy Scouts to be in my employ.' Max liking the sound of Boy Scouts.

'That was not my point,' Masson said. 'These men are not reliable operatives. And if they commit an illegal act on French soil then you are also responsible.'

'I told you, Inspector. They are employed to watch and to report back to me. Which of course they are unable to do at the moment.'

'There are too many rogue elements involved.'

'Bennett tells me that the opposite is true.'

'What does that mean?'

'That there are not enough agents. That you would expect French intelligence to keep an eye on such an important person. Bennett says he can see none. He uses the word sanitised.'

'I think it is better if you stay in my custody for the time being.'

'Am I under arrest?'

'I will give you back your mobile phone. You will maintain contact with Bennett and relay all information to me.'

Max was convinced now that Masson was acting without contact with his superiors. Otherwise he would have asked for the phone traffic to be monitored. Otherwise he would have allowed Max to talk to Bennett on the phone and taken what he needed from the transcripts.

'Where are we going?'

'The Quai des Orfèvres.' Masson nodded to the driver. Max sat back in his seat. He had the feeling that events were moving beyond anyone's control. He wondered where Andanson was. He marvelled at the fact that in this burnished city princesses might be abroad, storybook evils might lurk.

Bennett opened the car door and emptied the ashtray into the gutter. He'd brought food with him. There were waxed sandwich wrappers and Coke cans in the footwell.

'Brings you back, don't it?' he said.

'Like fuck it does.' To Harper this surveillance had nothing to do with any other. It had nothing to do with rainy dusk at edge-of-town housing estates, a Walther PPK held barrel down in your right hand, atrocity and the rumour of atrocity being carried towards you on damp winds.

'A firearm would be handy,' Bennett said.

'Right enough. Off your turf and out of your depth. A gun would be just the thing. Frogs could really throw the book at us then.'

'This is a bit of history right here, Harper.'

'We part of the royal household now? Her Majesty's secret fucking service. Get a grip, Bennett.' Though Harper could see that Bennett could have emerged from some historical underhandedness, a thing of stilettos and conspiracy by night.

There were only a few of the paparazzi outside the apartment. Harper thought that they probably knew about the dinner reservation for 9.45, that they would start to gather again before then.

'Any word of the principal?' he said.

'Nothing,' Bennett said. 'Makes no odds anyway.'

'Makes odds if I don't get my money pal.'

'Told you, Harper. Cast-iron guaranteed. What if she's up the spout?'

'Who?'

'Spencer.'

'Talk to Grace about that.'

'Ain't joking, old son. Wouldn't like that at headquarters. Her Majesty would blow a gasket.'

'Why would that be?'

'Little brown lad a brother to the heir to the throne. Are you joking? And look who the old grandad would be. Having Grandad Mohamed round to tea. You can just see the look on her face.'

'And then there's the landmines.'

'Too fucking right, old son. They'd bump her off for the fucking landmine campaign.'

'Jesus. Wise up, Bennett, you fucking retard. She's supposed to be marrying an Al Fayed. Who is married to Adnan Khashoggi's sister. Who is one of the biggest arms dealers in the fucking world. Landmines and all.'

'So our girl is not the brightest then. She hasn't quite thought things through.'

'I've seen brighter operators.'

'So there's nothing to it? No op aimed at Spencer? Maybe I'm just

being paranoid is what you're saying. Maybe the French aren't taking an interest because they just aren't interested.'

'That's about it.'

'What about the BMW?'

'Who knows. Could be the French service after all, checking her
out.'

'And Andanson?'

'Mad, far as I can see. Candidate for the floating hotel. Stick him
in the padded cell, pump him full of the happy stuff. Henri Paul is
supposed to be involved some way. But according to Grace, Henri
has gone home for the night. If there ever was an op then it's gone
off the boil.'

'Hello. Looks like the happy couple is about to vacate the prem-
ises.'

The paparazzi were on their feet. Strapping on open-face helmets,
zipping up jackets. Several of them had started their engines. The
four-stroke noise, blipping the throttle, valve clatter echoing in the
eventide street. Harper started the engine of the Renault.

'Face it, Harper. It still beats the shit out of doing security work
in Belfast. There's a bit of the old glitz about this.'

Harper thought that if this was glitz he didn't want it. Late at
night he hankered after the grim allure of early Belfast, rainy nights
after curfew, the short wave crackling with tidings of civil unrest,
everybody craving a hangdog glamour.

The Range Rover and the Mercedes 600 turned into the street.
Driving slowly in formation, two paparazzi bikes side by side
behind them. Everybody working at achieving the perfect formation. Acknowledging the tumult to come. The paparazzi at the kerb
moved back to allow the cars to park, perfectly distanced at the
kerb. Preliminary formalities were being observed. Two private
security men in uniform opened the door of the apartment building.
Photographers got into position, checking light meters, kneeling,
leaning across car roofs. Checking shutter speeds, exposure settings.
Wingfield and Rees-Jones getting out of the Range Rover. Then as
the apartment doors swung open, even before anyone emerged, the
photographers were shooting off film, the high-pitched motor drive
and shutter chatter merging into a high-pitched edge-of-reason

whirr. The couple emerging, the photographers shouting to them in a broad range of Western European accents, imploring them to look, to bestow the bounty of a glance. Asking to see her hand, her left hand, for her to hold it up to them. Wingfield and Rees-Jones holding their arms out and facing the photographers to shield the couple as they walked swiftly, head down, from the apartment building to the car. The photographers still trying to get a shot of the left hand and asking to see it as though there was a troth that might thereby be pledged.

Harper put the Renault in reverse. The Range Rover and Mercedes 600 moved away from the kerb. Harper swung the car into the middle of the street and reversed hard away from the two other vehicles as they bore down on them.

'Fuck's sakes, Harper, they got us made now,' Bennett said. Harper swung the car rear first into an entryway so that it was facing the road. The Range Rover and Mercedes passed.

'We're not made,' Harper said, 'there's nobody here to make us. They're not looking, Bennett. About time you got that.'

He let the paparazzi go past, then pulled out after the last bike. The Mercedes turned right at the top of the street without stopping.

'Heading for the Champs-Elysées,' Bennett said.

                              Rue St Martin
                              9.41 p.m.

Furst parked the BMW on the pavement and walked around the corner into Rue St Martin. Both pavements in front of the restaurant Chez Benoit were lined with onlookers and with photographers. Ripples of expectation running up and down the street. Belinda had been right. Use publicity against the target. Make it difficult for her to move without crowds, without flashing cameras. Spencer's options kept narrowing. They could not have dinner at Chez Benoit now. There were too many people. The target was being directed towards the gilded suites, the still, interior spaces, a discipline of self.

Furst didn't trust the way these people behaved. How they reacted

142

to the woman. The way they gave themselves up to childlike awe. These were the people who camped out in order to get a good view of her wedding. They were the purchasers of commemorative figurines. They uncovered narratives in her which were denied to him.

The Range Rover and the Mercedes 600 pulled into the street. A sigh went up but it looked pitiable to him. A small harried procession. As the cars moved down the street Furst saw the blue Renault. This time there were two men inside. One of them was thin-faced, wearing a black suit. The other was wearing a grey sports jacket and open-neck shirt. These were the ones you relied on. The cops in ill-fitting suits. This one had been driving at the Villa Windsor. Furst had felt him watching. The steady corrupted stare. The car stopped at the top of the street. If they were Press they would get out, follow the cars on foot down the street. Furst knew they were Service. You knew it by their stillness. The way they sat in profile. Furst knew that without thinking they were scanning open windows, rooftops. Profiling the crowd. Looking for the person whose movements marked them out from the others. Alert to the furtive gesture. Furst didn't know if they had spotted him yet, but he presumed he had been seen outside the Villa Windsor.

He saw a man on the pavement talking into the mobile. Identified him as a Ritz employee from photographs supplied by Belinda. The cars started to pick up speed. The Ritz employee was ringing ahead. They were going back to the Ritz. Furst sensed the way things were going. Events falling into place. The moments that plotters everywhere sought. The moments that they craved. Things could still go wrong. The variables were still present. It might still have to be called off. Postponed to another time but only postponed. He could feel the momentum, something in history, a deep shift in the texture of things, the Range Rover and the Mercedes 600 passing him now and taking on the attributes of a cortège, the empty pomp, the dead being conveyed among the living, something ghastly in the texture of it, his helmet blocking out the sound so that it seemed as if the crowd gestured wordlessly after the car. He knew that was what drew them. He had seen it before, mobs on the streets, at demonstrations, at the township funerals, the crowd feeling that death itself was on the move, a ghastly boulevardier.

He wondered if the two men in the Renault felt it. Not as strongly as he did but he thought they would feel it tugging at them, in a corner of their consciousness they would feel the patterns beginning to establish themselves. The thin man most of all, Furst thought. He had the look of a man who had spent too long in the environs of the dead. He had a morgue attendant's pallor. The other one was different. More dangerous in a way. He would have made himself familiar with the matter-of-fact aspects of death. Prosaic understandings would have been arrived at in the matter of mortality.

The Renault passed him, both men looking straight ahead, not talking. Furst gave them a hundred yards before he pulled out onto the road. They were starting to pick up on it now, he thought. They were Service. They were death's familiars.

Sixteen

Andanson tried to remember the first time he met with Joseph Di Mambro. Di Mambro and that fraud doctor pal of his, Jouret. Most people fell for it, the Order of the Solar Temple stuff. Jouret was a real medical doctor. When he did lectures he made them sit up. The apocalypse is on us. The forests are burning. Species extinction. Women went for him big time. He remembered Jouret giving him his card. Luc Jouret, Physician. Love and biology. Setting out his stall all right. Di Mambro was more behind the scenes. The whole thing was his idea. The Order of the Solar Temple. Di Mambro had asked Andanson to do publicity stills. Andanson remembered that Di Mambro had paid in cash. One hundred dollar bills.

For half an hour he had watched bystanders gathering at the front of the Ritz. Belinda had said this would happen. People would know what route Spencer was taking. The woman said that people were attuned to her spiritual trajectory. Andanson thought they were attuned to Hello! magazine, to Paris-Soir, all the other media with her photograph on the front. In the last ten minutes they had been joined by paparazzi. The photographers were different. They were being fed info from maître d's, from chambermaids, from porters. Andanson wasn't stupid. He wasn't an actual idiot.

Di Mambro and Jouret built the place in Switzerland at Granges-sur-Salvan. Di Mambro kept in touch with Andanson. Brought him in to do publicity stills when things were going well. Jouret knew his clientele. His name spreading through the resort villages. In Chamonix. In Salvan. Andanson would go to Granges-sur-Salvan and stay with him. He could admire the way the thing was put together. The ski wives, the heiresses flocking to see Jouret. Smiling matrons with the chequebook out. But he couldn't believe the stuff that people would swallow, about going to live on the planet Sirius. At the height of the thing Di Mambro was faking apparitions in the basement. Creatures of higher intelligence from the outer fringes of the galaxy. Spindly humanoids in silver suits.

The DGSE turns around and asks Andanson to keep an eye on our hero Di Mambro. Turns out Di Mambro has convictions for fraud going right back. Andanson was happy to help keep an eye on the old trickster. He wasn't the only one. He recognised two French cops among the followers one day. Two men he knew from Paris. They walked past him without looking at him.

One day Di Mambro tells him dead confidential that Princess Grace is a member. Mind you he also says that they are the descendants of the Knights Templar and a lot of other old nonsense. Di Mambro starting to get a bit leery towards the end. Andanson had the feeling that the money wasn't going right. Then Jouret's son comes out and blows the lid on the whole thing. The son saying that the whole thing was a scam. The son turning against the father. The admissions to the cult starting to fall away.

Andanson got out of the car. He kept the mobile in his pocket. He went to a phone booth and telephoned the Hôtel George V. The phone rang in Max's room but no one answered it. He transferred back to the switchboard. They told him that Max had gone out. He got back into the Fiat. He saw the Range Rover and the Mercedes 600 enter the Place Vendôme. Andanson realising suddenly that darkness had fallen.

And with the fall of darkness the fear returning. And with the fall of darkness they come bearing instruction for the chosen and with the fall of darkness

Andanson couldn't believe how it all ended. Twenty-five poisoned and burned in the chalets at Granges-sur-Salvan. Twenty-three burned at Cheiry. All bar two shot in the head with

146

multiple entry wounds. Jouret and Di Mambro in the middle of it. The cops saying that it was suicide. Shoot yourself in the head then reload and shoot yourself again. That was what was supposed to have happened. Funny kind of suicide. Then four adults and a baby at Morin Heights, Quebec. Each time the bodies arranged in the shape of a star.

It is with unfathomable love pure joy and no regret that we leave this world. Men do not cry for our fate but cry for your own

Andanson drove up to Salvan six weeks afterwards. Both chalets roofless, charred. There were documents scattered in the snow, clothing and other personal effects. He found a photograph he had taken of Jouret, the frame broken and charred. Jouret taking the heiresses into the day room to test them for what he called psychic compatibility. Jouret on the podium, messianic, spittle-flecked. In the end even losing interest in the sex. Gathering intensity to himself, developing the piercing stare. He had started consulting horoscopes, searching for the signs, alert to the auspicious dates.

There were volumes of esoterica lying in the snow. Andanson picking through the ruined houses as the blue shadows came down the mountains, lengthening in the valleys. The smell of damp burned timber. He could picture the fire. The bodies laid out starwise. The hair going first, a halo of flame. Tendons gone bowstring taut. The body fats popping. He wanted to leave but he could not get away from the place. A man pottering in the ruins. Death by fire the thing that he feared more than anything and the woman on the phone knew it.

'Remember Lardanchet,' she said to him softly, 'remember Rostan?' Rostan and Lardanchet had been the two French policemen he had seen with Di Mambro at Salvan. Andanson presuming that they were plants not genuine followers. That they were under some kind of deep cover in the Order. If they were it did not save them. On 22 December 1995 they were found dead along with fourteen other members of the Order in the forest Vercors. The bodies burned. The autopsy picking up traces of phosphorous in the corpses.

The phone started to ring. The mobile phone lying on the passenger seat of the Fiat. He did not have to look to know that the number of the caller would not be on the screen. He put the phone to his ear.

'Spencer and the Arab are approaching the Ritz now, isn't that right, James?'

'Yes.'

'Two cars. The Range Rover and the Mercedes 600.'

'Yes.'

'Is there any other security?'

'Not that I can see.'

'That's good. You know the route.'

'Yes.' *Rue Cambon. Rue de Rivoli. Cours la Reine.*

'I want you in place at 11.30. They will dine at the Ritz and then they will drive by that route to the Arab's apartment at Rue Arsène-Houssaye.'

'What if they don't? What if they don't take that route?'

'An arrangement has been put in place, James. You do not need to worry about it. Are you clear in your mind what is required of you? We know you are a good driver. We would not ask you to perform something that was outside your capability. The bloodline will be grateful to you.'

'As long as you leave me alone.'

'Your obligation will have been fulfilled. Remember the route, James.'

Andanson put the phone back on the seat. Di Mambro had been the same. Rabbiting on about the bloodline. James thinking that it was part of the scam. He didn't have much time for our Middle Eastern chums either. Jouret too. He'd been part of some right wing nut thing. Jouret didn't know James had found out that particular dirty little secret. It wasn't hard. Industry and the aristocracy were rotten with Nazi lovers and Andanson spent a lot of his time snapping them. The aristos loving the idea of it. The secret networks. The safe houses. Andanson doing photosets for them. Doing captain of industry poses then taking him into a study. Place crammed with memorabilia. Death's head badges. Steel daggers. Signed photographs of Bormann, Hess. In love with the mystery of it. Lowering the voice confidentially. That was the thing with the whole Nazi deal. There were so many stories, so many tales to be told. Talking on into the night. The Vatican ratlines. Swiss vaults overflowing with looted Jewish gold. Then they'd start in on who else was a sympathiser. The whispered names. Figures in the media, in sport, in politics. Paranoid too. They saw treachery everywhere. Communist infiltrators, trade unionists.

Andanson opened the glove compartment and took out a packet of Bisodol. He tried to remember the last time he had eaten. His stomach in ruins. The bad taste he got in his mouth for days on end. The bile duct working overtime. Years of eating on the run had started the process. Stripped the stomach lining clean away. Disorders of the digestive tract. You name it he had it. Heartburn. Colonic spasm. He could barely put a spoonful of food near his mouth since June when he had received the photographs. The plain brown envelope with the Geneva postmark, the address printed in black pen. The ten autopsy photographs. Andanson knowing them to be the Granges-sur-Salvan victims. The leathery burned flesh. You couldn't tell if they were male or female. Laid out in rows on the mortuary floor. Shrunken and blackened, desexed in death. Jouret and Di Mambro in among them somewhere. The bodies contorted in different shapes as though each sought to find separate expression of the agonies that had consumed them. The faces mask-like. The expressions formalised. The police said that Jouret had rigged crude incendiary devices around the buildings. Plastic bags full of petrol hung from hooks.

Belinda had called him for the first time that night.

The Range Rover and the Mercedes 600 had come to a halt outside the Ritz. The paparazzi almost on top of the car. Shouting at the passengers. Which showed an actual lack of class. Andanson always used a person's proper title when he called out to them. You said Miss Taylor. You said Mr Onassis. A little respect went a long way. He couldn't believe that the Ritz staff hadn't cleared a path from the cars to the door. He caught sight of Spencer's blonde hair. Andanson knowing the way people projected on to people like Spencer. How they said to themselves she was kind, she would understand. Andanson wasn't stupid. He knew that she wouldn't understand what he was going to do. But the woman had said that there would be no bloodshed. She had said her name was Belinda, which he reckoned was some kind of code name that cult people gave themselves.

'What about the cameras?' he had asked. The route was lined with CCTV cameras. Andanson always aware of the lens being trained. Police sifting through the footage. The timeline running across the top of the screen. Andanson knowing the power of the images, the authority that accrued to them, the grainy authenticity, the smudged monochrome images, dirt on the tapeheads, the tape running too fast or too slow, the jerkily played out lo-fi dramas.

'The cameras will be dark,' she said, 'the tunnel lighting will be on. Get in front of the Arab's car. Slow it down. That is all I am asking of you. It is important that you get in front of the car before you reach the tunnel.'

Andanson thought then that there was a tension creeping into her tone. That she was answerable to a higher authority.

'You will exit Paris via the Périphérique. Open the glove compartment.'

'Why?'

'Open it.'

'You're scaring the shit out of me now.'

'It's nothing, James. Just do it.'

Andanson leaned forward and opened the glove compartment. He lifted out a plain white envelope. It contained an autoroute toll receipt dated 30 August 1997. It also contained the ticket and counterfoil of an Air France flight from Orly to Bonifacio in Corsica. The departure time was 9.30 a.m. on Sunday 31 August 1997. He tried to remember the last time he had looked in the glove compartment. He knew that there would be no point in examining the car for evidence of a break-in. The envelope could have been posted to him but it was important that he found it in his car. You were supposed to feel that your life had been taken out of your hands, that shadowy forces were at work. That certain predetermined and clandestine outcomes had been set in motion. Andanson wasn't stupid. Andanson knew that some covert agency was behind the whole thing. Using the Order of the Solar Temple as a front. Cult leaders could not produce a receipt for a journey that had yet to be made. They could not produce a forged airline ticket. Di Mambro and

150

Jouret would never have had the scope to their thinking that seemed to be behind this operation. Di Mambro in his last days, suffering from kidney problems, a yellow tinge to his skin, knowing that the thing had got out of control.

The receipt and counterfoil showed that the toll and flight had been paid for by Andanson's Mastercard.

'Use them if you are asked about your whereabouts on the night of the 30th,' the woman said before she broke the connection.

Andanson started the Fiat and moved it slowly forward. Spencer and Al Fayed were out of the car now, being jostled as they moved towards the door of the Ritz. Andanson starting to think beyond the fear, to concentrate on the job in hand. It was a quality he had. He could shut out everything. Feeling the head becoming cold and clear. After tonight it would be over. Men in positions of influence would start to take his calls again. By tomorrow evening he would be clear. And with the fall of darkness the bloodline would have gone back to the shadows they came from.

Bar Laurent

9.44 p.m.

'Looks like you got stood up, love.' Monique leaned on the counter beside Grace. Her English was heavily accented. She sounded almost German, Grace thought, the consonants flattened. Grace made a non-committal gesture with her hand. Monique knowing her to be English so that Grace started to see herself the way Monique saw her. Tweedy and maidenish. A habitual wearer of flat shoes. Monique was wearing a black silk blouse with a dragon pattern on the back.

'Are you on vacation?' Monique asked.

'Just for the weekend,' Grace said.

'What's your star sign?' Monique asked. Grace found the question touching. She knew that the woman wasn't making advances. The question was being asked in the way adolescents asked it. Someone wishing to be taken as resplendent with intuition. Nodding sagely. Centuries-old wisdom being called upon, the cos-

151

mos, the great wheel of the heavens.

'Capricorn.'

'Ah,' Monique said, 'a sensible woman.'

'Practical and prudent,' Grace said, 'but also miserly and grudging.'

'Which are you?'

'A mixture. Prudent and grudging.' Monique smiled.

'And you?'

'Scorpio.'

'Passionate,' Grace said.

'Jealous,' Monique said, 'possessive. I can see it in others. You were following Henri.' Grace stared at her.

'I saw you. From the flat upstairs. You stood for a long time looking after him.'

'Did I?' Grace realising that Monique was seeing this as a matter of the heart.

'Yes. You met him where . . . Sardinia, this July. He would like that, Henri. Meet a nice English lady on holiday. Somebody to laugh at his stupid jokes. He never mentioned that he met someone.'

Grace found herself nodding. Going along with the story. Hoping to elicit information about Henri but at the same time liking the way the narrative was emerging. An affair with a man on holiday, the melancholy mid-life atmospherics of it. Holding hands on a beach at dusk. Knowing that it can't last but grateful for last-minute encroachments on a spinsterish heart.

'This type he is with. Hard, you know. A bitch,' Monique said.

'You know her?'

'That is the first time I saw her, walking with him tonight, but I hear him talking about her. She is not good to him.'

'Have they been together long?'

'A few months. She always comes to him. I don't think he even knows where she lives.'

'You like him.'

'He is a friend. But not everybody likes him. You hear stories from the hotel. But he is faithful to her and a good person to talk to.' Monique looking surprised at having uncovered such stalwart properties in Henri.

'Sounds ideal.'

'Perhaps. I think your friend is here.' Grace looked up. Harper was crossing the floor.

'A cop,' Monique said.

'You never told me it was a lezzie bar,' Harper said, pulling up a stool beside Grace. Monique moved away.

'Doesn't like me,' Harper said, 'I can tell. Jesus, would you look at them two playing pool. Where'd you park the truck, girls?'

'Don't make fun of them,' Grace said. A pall of seediness seeming to descend over the bar. Harper seeing it as an extension of the sex industry, looking for the angle. Harper dragging an atmosphere of late-night venues, vendors of the carnal, into the room.

'What were you talking to your woman about. The boss?'

'I was getting information on Henri Paul and his new girlfriend. I thought it might be important.'

'Can't see how it would be important but good going on the Mata Hari front. Come on. Let's go.'

'Where are we going?'

'I booked dinner for us.'

'Where?'

'The Ritz. Bennett's going to meet us there.'

As she left Grace turned in the door and saw Monique looking at her. Monique smiled. The neon sign on the bar behind her flashing on and off.

Ritz Hotel
9.50 p.m.

The paparazzi had moved back to the centre of the Place Vendôme. Some of them were scanning the top half of the building in case Spencer appeared at the windows of the Imperial suite. Ritz security had erected two small barriers to keep the public back. There were about a hundred people waiting. Harper and Grace had to stay at the barrier while the concierge checked the booking. Harper was wearing a creased tie he had pulled from one of his pockets. The concierge looked as if he was about to query the booking, but when

153

Grace walked past him with an air of disheartened authority he had to let Harper follow. She had been quiet since she left the Bar Laurent. Star charts going through her head. How they had gone for the dark places. A zodiac of grudges and broken promises. They found Bennett sitting in the foyer. Grace looked around. Bennett had found a corner not covered by any security camera she could see. It was something he took pride in. Working along the margins, staying out of sight.

'Place is pretty quiet,' Harper said.

'August in Paris,' Grace said, 'it's not fashionable to be here.'

'I never had dinner in the Ritz before,' Harper said.

'And you're not going to now,' Bennett said, 'that was just a way of getting us in.'

'Where are they now?'

'In the dining room.'

'What are they wearing?' Grace said.

'What does it matter what they're wearing?' Bennett said. Harper closed his eyes and pictured the couple.

'He's wearing jeans, cowboy boots. A brown jacket. Suede maybe. She's got a black top I think. White trousers.'

'Sounds like they'll eat upstairs.'

'Why?'

'It's the Ritz dining room. He'll feel out of place. Underdressed.'

'She won't notice,' Harper said, 'but he will.'

'Hark at the cop turned society commentator. What's the queen going to be wearing at Goodwood this year, Mr Harper? If the Arab thinks he's underdressed then it sure as fuck leaves us a bit short on the class front. No class at all in fact.'

'Apart from Grace,' Harper said. He wasn't looking at her when he said it. She knew she didn't belong here. The look of shabby bohemianism freighted out of high street thrift shops. Lipstick stubs in the handbag, a pair of laddered tights. Things that were worn, bitten-off, frayed. She thought it was the nearest she had got to a compliment from him. Delivered as a gruff truism. She looked over his shoulder. She could see groups of bystanders outside the window. People anxious, clustered. Some of them looking dazed, shocked at their own behaviour. That they would cry out to a stranger. That they would beseech.

Sitting in the foyer of the hotel she realised the nature of the wolfish grace that Harper and Bennett still possessed. In a shabby and furtive way they were insiders. They knew the mechanisms. They assumed the worst and they were right.

'Hello, they're on the move,' Bennett said. The entourage coming out of the dining room. Managers, security, Wingfield moving ahead of them, scanning the lobby. Harper and Bennett turning their backs to the bodyguard. Knowing that he might recognise them. That something in their eyes would establish a bleak kinship with him. Grace watched for Spencer, but she had her head down, her face partly averted, the security men once again moving her towards the lift housing.

'What a fucking way to live,' she heard Bennett say. People clustered around her at the lift. Waiters in white jackets coming behind carrying silver dishes. The foyer seeming full of lonesome clamour. Everybody backing away from the lift as the door closed. Harper watching the numbers on the display.

'Where are they going?' he said.

'Imperial suite,' Grace said, 'eighth floor.'

'Safe enough there.'

'Safe enough anyhow,' Harper said, 'any word of that principal of yours?'

'Not yet.'

'You need to call him.'

'I'll call him.'

'We going to sit here all night?'

'You think they'll stay here?' Bennett said, turning to Grace.

'Probably not. All their stuff is back in the apartment. They'll need to get back if they're flying out tomorrow,' she said. Things that seem obvious to a woman. How you moved in the world, setting up wayposts, the formal arrangements of clothes and make-up. She knew that Spencer would have spent time unpacking, working off lists, putting order on the transited items, every piece of clothing or make-up with meaning because they stand for the deep places where you go to be replenished, the memory hoards.

'We stay with them to the apartment. Somebody waits there for the night. Go with them to the airport, then job done,' Bennett said, 'couldn't be easier.'

'You mind if I make a call?' Grace said.

'Go ahead,' Bennett said. Harper held out his mobile. She took it and walked to a corner of the foyer, stood facing into the wall, hunched. She would phone her mother to say she was coming home in the morning. She wanted to form the word home in her mouth. The way the word itself seemed to enfold something, the way the saying of it seemed to draw up sound from deep within the sternum. She wanted to hear her mother's voice, chiding and familiar. She wanted to have her shortcomings brought to the fore. Standing in the foyer of the Ritz Hotel Paris with two men who were steeped in moral squalor, pouring her unworthiness into the phone, her mother knowing that it would end like this, making sounds of grim confirmation. Grace could picture her face on the pillow. Often when Grace was a child her mother had stood her in the middle of the kitchen and examined what she called her aura. Grace had the idea that there was some kind of force field around her. What auras would these old ladies have now, Grace thought, a weakling emanation hanging in the air around their sleeping faces. Grace hung up and went back to the two men. The foyer starting to take on a late-night feel now. An airport lounge. A bus station. The two men looking like slumped transients.

Bar Laurent
9.55 p.m.

Monique was surprised to see Henri come in on his own.

'Can't stop,' he said, 'got to get back to work.' Monique knew what was going on. 'I thought you were off,' Monique said, 'I saw you going back to the apartment.'

'Place is a shambles,' Henri said, 'so they called me back in. The boss's son and the girlfriend are there.' Henri had shaved and changed his shirt but you could tell what kind of encounter he was coming from. There was a rank maleness, hard and amoral. You could tell it from the way he walked, the musculature subtly adjusted, the sinewy post-erotic shapes that he threw, walking on the balls of his feet, virile and alert. You could even hear it in his voice, Monique thought. The little resonances. She had an expertise in these areas. She could see the girls at the bar watching, coming to the same conclusion, exchanging glances and sotto-voce remarks, seeing themselves as a languid commentariat in matters of the flesh.

She held up the Ricard bottle. He shook his head.

'No time,' he said. He waved to the girls at the bar and went out. Monique followed him to the door. She saw him get into his Mini and drive off. She looked up at Henri's apartment. Belinda was standing at the window, her face half-hidden by the curtain. Monique didn't pay much attention at the time. She was used to women making use of the shadows, taking up moody and evocative stances in the hope that mystery might accrue to them. To Monique it was a case of a man leaving his girlfriend alone in an apartment. She would turn on the television, find a magazine, settle into the waiting hours with nail varnish or tweezers, working her way into the utilitarian female responses. As Monique watched the woman turned away from the window and disappeared from view. Henri's car turned right at the end of the street. He would be at the Ritz in a few minutes. Monique went back into the bar. The girls in the bar had heard that Spencer was in the Ritz. They were talking about her. Claiming her for themselves. They liked the fact that there was a certain physical ungainliness about her. They felt that if she walked into Monique's they could make way for her at the bar without compromising basic tenets.

Henri hoped that Spencer and Al Fayed would not stay at the Ritz all night. Belinda had said she would wait for him. Henri had poured a Martini each. When they had got back to the apartment he had closed the door then turned to her and kissed her, pushing her back against the door. She had taken him by the hand and led him into the living room. Taking control the way she had in the Bois de Boulogne.

'I am not a passive person,' he said, 'in bed. My turn.'

'No,' she said, 'your turn next. Later. You need to relax. Put yourself in my hands.'

He went along with it. The thing suffused with adolescent long-ing. A fully clothed groping on a sofa. The awkwardness with fastenings. A clumsy attendance on beauty. She steered him towards the teenage nights. Rainy nights with nowhere to go. Fumbling in cars. Up against schoolyard walls. The way teenagers found them-selves on the canal walks and derelict industrial sites and spooky old avenues and graveyards. Scaring each other with tales of lurid murder. Conjuring up wistfulness in bleak landscapes.

Afterwards he poured a drink. She wanted to hold hands and talk. She wanted to talk about when she was young. He realised how lit-tle he knew about her. That she came from Marseilles. That she worked for a news agency. He had considered the possibility that she worked for a security service. You heard stories about Mossad, the KGB. The honey trap. The way the Israelis had snatched Mordechai Vanunu, the female agent luring him to Rome. It excited him, the thought that sex could be used in that way. Wondering if he should have told Masson about her. About the thing she had asked him to do.

She asked him again about growing up in Lorient. She kept com-ing back to those years. He went to a drawer and found photographs. Henri at the lycée. Henri with long hair.

'Were there girls?' she asked. Coming back to the point several times so that he named them for her. A narrow stratum of longing. These dimly perceived entanglements. Girls called Marie. Girls called Florence. The faces smudged with longing. She seemed to be looking for the sadness.

'It will be tonight,' she said. 'I want you to do this thing for me tonight.'

'Impossible,' he said. 'They have already left the Ritz. Next time they are in Paris I will do it.'

'You'll do it for me tonight. I'll be waiting for you.'

Then at quarter to ten her mobile had rung. She reached across him to take it from her handbag so that he could smell her sham-poo. The unobserved moments that Henri looked for in a woman. She took out the phone and sat upright. She said okay several times into the mouthpiece then turned to him.

'The couple are on their way back to the Ritz to have dinner.'

'Shit.'

'You can do it tonight.'

'I'd rather be here.'

'I know that.'

'They'll go back to the apartment round about twelve,' Henri said. 'Mr Al Fayed always leaves from the apartment in the morning.'

'You'll be back here by one o'clock at the latest.'

'You'll be here?'

'Of course. Remember. Your turn next.'

When he left the apartment Henri had looked up. She was standing at the window. She smiled at him and waved. He looked again after he had been in the bar. She was holding her mobile to her ear, talking fast. He waved up to her. She gave him a vague smile and waved with her left hand. He got into the Mini. He liked the black bucket seats and the metallic trim. The big odometer and temperature dials. The interior of the car had the stripped-down feel of a prototype. It brought him back to the films he had watched when he was in the lycée. Men in rudimentary jet aircraft working to break the sound barrier. Laconic test pilots in fireproof overalls. Henri driving fast towards the Ritz, snicking through the gears, working the synchromesh. There was always that feel for the machine. That was the dream before he had been turned down by the air force. To be out there on the edge of the atmosphere, buffeted by the jetstream, looking down on the dreaming world.

Ritz Hotel
10.08 p.m.

The CCTV picked up Henri parking. Reversing backwards and forwards several times before parallel parking tight against the kerb. Henri getting out of the car and locking it then walking towards the Ritz. So much of the night captured on CCTV. The street lights' sodium glow like chemical flare-off. The framing that made you think of low-budget camera work, grainy and alienated. The smudged compositions, people walking in and out of frame. The out-of-kilter compositions. Henri crossed the Ritz foyer at five past ten according to the video timeline, the digitalised numerals scrolling in white across the bottom of the frame, counting off the seconds and the hundredths of seconds in a way that seemed to bring an unbidden urgency to the content.

Henri went to the concierge's desk. He examined the CCTV screens. He thought there were about one hundred people outside, maybe thirty more photographers with motorcycles further back in the Place Vendôme. Behind them a grey BMW R100 went past at walking pace, stopping just beyond the photographers. Henri's eye passed over it but he didn't attach any significance to it. He checked the foyer cameras and the bar camera. On the bar camera he saw Rees-Jones and Wingfield sitting at a table. He checked the interior and exterior cameras at the rear exit. On the exterior camera he could see the back of the doorman's head but no other activity. The interior camera showed that the corridor leading to the exit was empty. Other screens showed unpeopled corridors, flickering streetscapes, an unease settling in the transit areas.

Grace saw Henri first. She hadn't noticed him coming in but she saw him at the concierge's desk. He was talking on the phone. She felt the out-of-body feeling coming back again. The foyer seeming to be seething with portents. She started to notice detail that she hadn't seen before. The life-sized Nubian slaves in porcelain that stood on either side of the entrance to the main corridor. The garishness of the flower display in the centre of the room. The rococo ceiling.

'Look,' she said.

'Well, fuck me sideways,' Bennett said, 'it's old Henri himself.'

'Shit,' Harper said.

'This is going to be interesting,' Bennett said.

'You said that it would be different if Henri Paul was here,' Grace said.

'I know what I said.'

'Just in passing,' Bennett said, 'if anything happens tonight we're only on every fucking close-circuit camera in Paris following her ladyship around.'

'We should just get out of here now,' Harper said.

'Get out and go where?' Bennett said.

'The airport. The railway station.'

'That would look right and suspect, wouldn't it?' Bennett said. 'Fleeing the scene. They'd have us in a minute.'

'You know what I'm starting to think,' Harper said, 'I think this principal of yours has done a runner on us. I get the feeling I'm being set up.'

'No,' Bennett said, 'honest to God. He's straight up, kosher as they come.'

'You two are scaring me.'

'What's his name, Bennett?'

'I'm not at liberty.'

'I'm at liberty to pull you out of here, Bennett. I'm at liberty to come after you when this is over.'

'Stop it, you two,' Grace said.

'All right, all right, we're all pals I suppose. His name is Max LaFontaine.'

'What in the name of Christ sort of name is that?'

'It's the man's name.'

'And what does this Max LaFontaine do with himself?'

'I told you, he's part of the intelligence community. He calls himself a broker.'

'A dealer.'

'Something like that.'

'And what sort of deals would he be brokering?'

'He's got these transcripts coming in. Stuff from Spencer's phone calls. The CIA recorded them.'

'Help us here, Grace. Could these transcripts just be out there floating around?'

'Yes, of course. That sort of stuff goes missing all the time.' Information traded between agencies. Transcripts released on the foot of certain agendas. Data going astray. Disk drives plundered. Illicit downloads going unnoticed. Rogue operatives trading information. There were a thousand ways for information to escape.

161

'I'll sleep easier in the bed for knowing that,' Bennett said.

'And he wants to sell the information?' Harper said.

'Yes.'

'Be easier sold if she was dead.'

'Then it couldn't be verified.'

'I'm with you now. That's where we come in.'

'That was the idea. We keep the eyes peeled for threats. We report back to him. He decides what to do with it. He has contacts with European intelligence.'

'Except he isn't around any more, is he?' Grace said.

'That's right. Which means that we don't have any choice.'

'What exactly are we supposed to do,' Grace said, 'make a ring of steel around the hotel or something?'

'You try and stay sober, that'll be a start,' Bennett said.

'We stick to the plan we have,' Harper said, 'stay as close to them as we can.'

'We can't do anything,' Grace said.

'Nothing's going to happen for an hour or so. Maybe I should have a recce outside,' Harper said.

'Leave it for a bit,' Bennett said, 'they mightn't let you back in again.'

'I'm going for a look in the bar,' Grace said.

'Thought that might happen,' Bennett said.

'Let her be,' Harper said, 'go on, Grace. Keep an eye on them two bodyguards. If they get up we'll know the happy couple are on the move.'

They watched her leave.

'I should have known better than to have went along on one of your schemes,' Harper said.

'Let's keep the old head screwed on here,' Bennett said.

'If anything goes wrong here they'll have a field day with the likes of the two of us. And I can't see nobody sticking up for us either.'

Harper got up and walked to the window. It was air-conditioned cool in the hotel but outside the heat persisted. He was tired. Memories coming back of other hotels in other towns. The Europa. The York. Informants met and paid off. Drinking rum and Smirnoff. Men coming in from covert patrol. Faces taut with lethal chicanery. The black ops boys. The psy ops boys. Operations hatched. Touts and undercovers coming and going. Renegade nights. It was different here in Paris. There was no chain of command. There was no cover. Harper's eyes passed over the crowd behind the barrier outside. The instinctive sweep, right to left. He looked again. Without turning his head he beckoned to Bennett. Bennett got up and came over.

'What is it?'

'Look,' Harper said, 'there's faces in that crowd.'

'Faces?'

'I'm telling you. We're not on our own here any more.'

One man in the crowd that Harper recognised, older now, but he had seen him in one of those locations. Brize Norton. Thiepville barracks. The military compounds and off-limits areas of the ferry ports. You made them for MI5 or 6. Men wearing Aquascutum coats walking briskly in the restricted zones, some purpose of mayhem awaiting them in Belfast.

'I seen him before,' Bennett said. His voice was a whisper. 'And him,' he said, pointing to another man in a white shirt who stood in the second row of the crowd. The onlookers' attention was focused on the door of the hotel.

'There's a couple of others at the back. That blonde woman and the man. And there's a couple of heads sat in a silver Audi at the back of the square.'

'Could be they got wind of some tricky business. Could be they're on protection detail.'

'If they wanted to protect her they'd flood the place. Put personnel on the ground. Secure the fucking place and put the target out of harm's way. I don't see too much sign of that, do you?'

Harper was starting to wonder if anybody knew what was going on. If they were just responding to some shudder in the Intel fabric, an unease in the weft, picked up in the sunken command structures, the dust-free environments. An increase of signal traffic in the east. Sudden info flurries and flare-ups, going quiet almost as soon as they began. Intuition awakening in the infosphere. The Place Vendôme starting to fill with operatives, converging on this location. Harper looking out seeing the uplifted faces. As though called to witness.

Seventeen

Masson kept going out of the room and coming back again. Placing the calls, Max thought. Saturday nights, the building almost empty. Passing cleaners and janitors on the stairs, Masson forcing Max up five flights of chipped terrazzo steps.

'I have sent a request that all available cars look out for Andanson and his white Fiat,' he said, 'are you aware how many white Fiat Unos there are in this arrondissement alone?'

There had been clippings about the Bérégovoy affair on his desk when he got back. He learned nothing from them except for the fact that there were unexplained aspects to the alleged suicide of a former prime minister. There was no way of telling whether or not Andanson had anything to do with it. He did not strike Masson as the assassin type.

He had tried to telephone Henri Paul at the Ritz. They said he had gone home. He had not answered his mobile so Masson had sent a plainclothes to his apartment. A woman's voice had answered the intercom. She said that Henri was not there and she did not know what time he would be back.

'There is nothing you can do, Inspector,' Max said, 'if you put it out that there is to be an attempt on a famous life and that attempt does not take place, then it will be the end of your career. Washed up.' Max liked the phrase. It seemed the right setting for dropping in these fragments of dialogue, things he had picked up from the films. He always thought that the American precinct houses you saw in television had their origins in the kind of place he was in now. The distempered walls and desks piled high with paperwork. Battered filing cabinets. The decaying neighbourhoods. Something the Europeans had brought with them. A world-weariness in the matter of law enforcement. He could hear the voices of petty criminals and prostitutes being brought in, carrying up from the street four floors below. The reprobate badinage.

Masson put Max's phone on the desk. It was in a sealed evidence bag. Masson had gone through the calls. Calls made and received from Bennett in the previous forty-eight hours. Fifteen calls to numbers in the United States, recipient unknown. Four calls to a Swiss contract mobile. Two calls received from the same number. The Interpol directory gave the caller's name as Georg Kaufman, probably an alias. A call to Geneva confirmed the address given as that of a building used to provide registration addresses for shell companies. There was nothing more that Masson could find out on a Saturday night, his contacts out of town for the weekend, the channels closed.

'Call Mr Bennett,' Masson said, 'find out what you can. Ask him if he has seen Andanson.'

Max took the phone from the bag and dialled Bennett's number. He listened for a moment.

'The customer you require may be out of range or have their handset powered off,' Max said, putting the phone back on the table. Max thought it wasn't likely that Bennett would have his phone turned off. He would be worried about his money. Max wondered if Bennett was in an area where mobile phones had been blocked.

'It happens sometimes,' Masson said, 'the network goes down.'

Masson put the phone in his pocket then walked out of the room. Five minutes later two cops came into the room. They were wearing uniform trousers and shirts with the sleeves rolled up. Max was brought downstairs by a back corridor, brought through dingy basement areas. They passed a windowless canteen, a locker room. Max had been in custody before. He knew the penal gloom. He knew the way these old buildings lent themselves to a process of softening up. You were meant to see yourself as part of a numberless procession, padding unheard through badly lit corridors, trafficked in the shadows. There were urine smells, cooking smells. He knew he was being taken to the cells. He could hear the noise of them ahead. He could smell the disinfectant. At the desk they took his tie and shoelaces and valuables. Max had spent time in immigration custody and in low-security facilities. Other people might see it as degrading but Max regarded himself as a student of human nature. The policeman behind the desk met Max's eye when he instructed him to sign for his effects. The man appreciated that Max was not of the dregs. The money clip was made of gold with a US treasury logo in it. There were platinum Amex and Visa cards in the wallet.

The cell was windowless with a hard wooden bed. There was a wool blanket on the bed. The door was metal with heavy iron hinges and a spyhole at eye level. There were names carved into the wooden door surround and the frame of the bed. From the corridor outside he could hear the prostitutes and drunks. This was where he would see out the tumultuous night.

Masson waited in his office with the light turned down. He had transcribed Bennett's number. He tried it again. It was the same. He didn't like the fact that Bennett was unavailable. There was too much going on that was out of his control. The last days of the summer vacation. Key people on holidays with their families, preparing for the next day's journey home. Lost in rented properties and camp sites in the south, in Italy and Spain, children asleep in the warm Iberian night. He knew there were men sitting by the pool, a drink in their hand, insects flying across the light. Their wives and children are sleeping but something takes them outside, dead leaves on the surface of the pool, alert to the very fabric of things, the temperature dropping at night-time, intricate autumnal ceremonials falling into place. Knowing that this was their place in the drama that was unfolding, to be many miles away, to hear a phone ringing in the house behind him and not to answer it, to be a custodian of a hard secret, forsworn not to tell.

He switched on the Hewlett Packard on his desk and waited for it to boot. The screen the only light in the room. Hearing the little interior sounds the computer made as the systems came online. The almost imperceptible buzzes and whirrs. The byte chatter. A rigid dialectic of digital systems. Something old-fashioned and eerie the way the screen lit up the office. He imagined how his own face looked. A scribe, a monk transcriber of holy text bathed in green light. He searched the databases for the Order of the Solar Temple but the information was sparse and general. Joseph Di Mambro and Luc Jouret's names were mentioned. You read between the lines. People being tight-lipped. This was one to stay away from. You had the feeling that there was other data not entrusted to the systems. Membership lists, ledgers, records of transactions done, lists of contacts. You had the impression that there were still dossiers in existence. He knew how intelligence agencies worked. He knew how organisations like the Solar Temple could be put to use.

Masson tried Henri's mobile again and got the same message as he had received on Bennett's phone. Out on the town with his new woman. He picked up the phone again and rang the plainclothes he had sent to Henri's apartment and redirected them to the Place Vendôme with instructions to watch for any unusual activity. They were veteran cops, working towards retirement, canny and incapable of disillusion. Men that were alert to nuances. He knew they would sense his uncertainty. Masson turned his chair to look out of the window. A truth that they all knew. That out there in the night someone was hunter and someone was quarry.

Place Vendôme

11.30 p.m.

Andanson wanted to believe that they wouldn't come. That there would be no black Mercedes cutting through the late-night traffic, dropping down the gears to take the corner of the Place Vendôme and Rue Cambon, hitting the on-ramp without slowing down, accelerating westward along the Cours la Reine. Following the bank of the river, the night expressway. Andanson watching light fall along the river, watching the tourist boats borne downstream, the flat-bottomed barges. He knew that he had to keep on the move

167

to avoid drawing attention to himself. He had driven from the Place Vendôme to the Champs-Elysées and back again. He had stayed off the Champs. It was the only avenue that was busy during the month of August so the Mercedes would not go that way to be caught in traffic, surrounded by photographers. Andanson wasn't stupid. He was a user of lateral thinking in his job. When the other photographers were hanging round airports and hotels, Andanson was talking to the staff, peeling off FF100 notes from the roll in the back pocket. Gates were left open for him, door keys slipped into his hand, routes given.

Andanson knew it was the last weekend of the holidays and that was why traffic was sparse throughout the city. On Sunday the traffic would start to return from the provinces, from the south, the autoroutes jammed, backed up from the turnpikes, from the toll plazas but for tonight the city had a strange and depopulated feel and the cars that he did see were going fast, slowing but not stopping at the junctions, speeding through the great urban spaces. The drivers' expressions were grim as though they felt that this was no night to be abroad.

The Nokia was on the dashboard. It hadn't rung again. The woman had said there would be a final call to tell him when the Mercedes had left the Ritz. Andanson liked to tell people that everything in life was about timing. When he was at work he didn't shoot off rolls of film, the motor-drive whirr. You waited for the shot. You waited for the actual moment, all the grubby little frauds and evasions falling away, all the lies. And you captured the look on their face, a gratitude to it, almost glad to be found out, almost yearning for it. You held your breath and kept your finger on the shutter release and you waited for revelation.

Place Vendôme
11.40 p.m.

The Mercedes and the Range Rover that had been parked at the front of Etoile Limousines suddenly pulled away from the kerb and started to move across the Place Vendôme towards the Ritz as Furst had been told they would. Black cars approaching the hotel sound-lessly, an air of vendetta about them. The crowd of people at the front of the Ritz turned towards the cars, parted for them, trans-ferred their awe from the hotel to the cars. Furst aware that there was something strange about the crowd, that certain elements in it were withholding their attention. They were not absorbed by the texture of the scene in front of them, the two vehicles, engines on idle moving into place in front of the hotel which seemed to have transformed itself into some looming edifice of lore, a turreted folly with sinister overtones. He could see them in the crowd, their atten-tion elsewhere, following another narrative. There were two men wearing short-sleeved shirts at the back of the crowd. There were another two standing close to the front, both wearing sports jackets with collars turned up and facing each other and away from the hotel because they knew they were within range of the Ritz CCTV cameras, the pan and tilt, and did not want their faces to be cap-tured. Furst knew what they were from the way they moved, the underhand demeanours, the aspect they carried with them into the square on a warm summer's night of being conspirators, a cloaked brethren. The two at the back were British, he thought. They had fairish complexions and one of them had a badly sunburned neck which meant that they had only just arrived in France. He thought the other two were French. Furst knew that they weren't there to protect the subject. They were there to make sure that the operation went off the way it was meant to. There would be others, watching from parked cars. Strollers along the Cours de la Reine. Feeds run-ning from police CCTV being watched by operatives in empty basements. The circle spreading.

Furst could feel the adrenaline. Everything becoming heightened. He could feel the blood pumping through his body. He could feel his nervous system, the loom of impulses, proteins on the move, the neu-rotransmitters firing. To stay calm and focused he started to work his body, starting at his feet, clenching and unclenching ten times, con-centrating on each muscle group. He could visualise the webs of muscle under the skin. He could see his whole body that way like an anatomist's plate. He breathed in through his nose, out through his mouth. Bringing the respiration rate down, slowing the heart.

He thought he caught a glimpse of a face at the window of the Imperial suite. Standing back from the window and to one side so that she couldn't be photographed. In Brazzaville once an African soldier had pointed out the unlit doorway of a convent. The convent belonged to Carmelites, Belgians, the man said, an enclosed order who were allowed no contact with the outside world. Girls went in at seventeen never to come out again. Her family would come for a final visit. They would see a pale face peering through an iron grille, oathbound.

The face at the window of the Imperial suite disappeared. Furst thought about a call to evensong, a summoning to prayer in the gloom. Furst worked the muscles down his left leg and checked his watch. These were the timings. The strobe was in the right-hand pannier. In five minutes' time Furst would move to the corner of Rue Cambon. When the subjects emerged he would transfer the strobe from the pannier to his right hand. He had attached a bungy cord to the handle of the strobe with a slip knot. He would loop the cord around his wrist. He had allowed twenty seconds for this. It took two minutes to get from the Ritz Hotel to the Rue de la Reine. It took two minutes to get from there to the Place de l'Alma at 60 mph. The timings were important. You didn't have to stick to them precisely but they were part of putting structure on the night.

Furst looked at the tall hotel. It was the kind of building he hated. Ornamented, tendrilled with vine leaves. All overblown porticos and buttresses. He ran his eye over the crowd at the door. Waiting for her. The idle gawpers and hangers-on and photographers. And then there were the men and the divorce and the tapped phone calls and more men and the bulimia and the Arab who placed his brown hands on her. All the melancholy turmoil the woman brought in her wake. He knew why the other services were waiting in the Place de l'Alma. He knew his place. That an end be put to this. That there be deliverance.

Eighteen

The photographers outside had their gear ready. They were pushing
to the front of the crowd, jostling the onlookers. Harper kept losing
sight of the operatives in the crowd, unsure now as to how many of
them there were. The crowd were starting to mill, seized with some
nameless panic, turning surly when pushed. Harper watched the
Mercedes 600 and the Range Rover arrive, knowing he was missing
something. He looked around at Bennett. Bennett was pale, his
demeanour waxy and spooked, hitting the redial on his mobile over
and over again, Max not answering, Harper thought, or the network down or busy, Bennett hitting the redial as though his life
depended on it.

Grace had taken a seat at the bar. Rees-Jones and Wingfield
were sitting at a low table halfway between the bar and the door.
Henri came in and out several times. He went to the bar and the
barman poured him a drink. Grace picked up the fact that the
barman poured the drink under the counter. Henri sat down at
the table with Wingfield and Rees-Jones. He poured water into
the drink from a jug on the table. She heard him say 'pineapple
juice' loudly in English. Grace caught it straight away, the lying
voice, the bluff, dishonest timbre. The two Englishmen hadn't
noticed. The kind of stratagem she'd used herself. Ferrying the
illicit drink into social situations. She thought that the drink was
probably Pernod, the drink she started out on, Pernod and black,
a leg-opener the boys used to call it, suddenly in this place the
memory of those first drinks coming back to her, medicinal and

171

cloying, the nights in windswept beach shelters, the Pernod, the Bacardi, the Smirnoff bottle tilted, surprised that such nights could still be fixed in the mind, harbour lights on the black North Sea water, the memory hard and authentic, boys voices drifting across the shingle beds, the bone-thin Margate boys calling out to her.

'Good to see the surveillance is going well,' Harper said, sitting down beside her. 'How much do them gins cost anyhow?'

'Too much,' she said.

'Take it handy on them,' Harper said, 'I'm not sure how much trouble we're in here, but you got to be ready to move quick.'

'What are we going to do?'

'Bennett still says to stay with Spencer and the Arab and I haven't got any better ideas.'

'I'm not sure if it means anything,' she said, 'but it looks like our Henri is doing a bit of sneaky drinking on the boss's time.'

'Is that a fact?'

'I'm good at spotting it.'

'I suppose you are,' Harper said. There was a jaunty tone to her voice now. He saw she was starting the drunk's journey through the emotions, the racking trek from elation to shame.

'I wonder where the Arab got to?' Harper said.

'Stop calling him that,' Grace said.

'What? The Arab?'

'Yes. It's racist.'

'I am racist. I'm a racist and a fucking bigot as well. What's the word for somebody who hates women?'

'A misogynist.'

'I'm one of those too. Hold on, Henri's on the move.'

Henri went behind the bar. He took a phone out from under the counter.

'He's dialling nine,' Harper said, 'an internal call.'

Henri turned his back to the room as if to prevent the call being overheard but they could see his face in the mirror behind the bar, Henri being deferential, taking orders she thought, then talking fast.

'What's he up to, the slippy bastard?' Harper said.

'Talking to the boss by the look of it.'

'Selling him an idea I'd say.' Grace thought Harper was right. Henri had adopted a salesman's posture, hucksterish, making choppy hand gestures. He nodded twice quickly and put the phone down.

'Looks like it went his way,' Harper said.

Henri walked towards them, Harper turning his face away. Grace felt Henri's eyes on her, a masculine look up and down. She liked the way that Frenchmen looked at you. You felt as though you had been complimented, elevated to a higher plane of sexual being. Not like it was with Harper, his repertoire of grubby erotics, everything reduced to feeling like a car-park grope.

'Stay with me here, Grace,' she heard Harper say, 'you can drink your face off when we get out of this but for now I need you to be able to keep up.'

'First time I ever heard you say "I need you".'

'For fuck's sakes, Grace, don't get up on your high horse on me now.'

Henri sat down again beside the two bodyguards, leaning into them and talking confidentially. He could see Wingfield shaking his head.

'Whatever it is, the bodyguards don't like it,' Harper said.

Henri tried his mobile, frowned at it. He went into the lobby.

'I need to see where our Henri's gone.'

Harper followed Henri out into the foyer. He saw him go out through the front door. He walked to the window. He could see Henri talking to the driver of the Mercedes 600. Harper suspected that some chicanery was afoot. He could see Henri talking to the photographers as he came back to the hotel, taunting them. Henri came back into the hotel, crossing the foyer, stopping in the middle of the foyer and dropping to one knee to tie his right shoelace, then straightening again, snapping to his feet, a practised look to the way he did it, athletic, a honed routine.

The room phone rings and Al Fayed speaks to the hotel security man Henri Paul. Al Fayed tells Spencer that Paul has a plan to get rid of the paparazzi. She can see the way Al Fayed pits himself against the photographers. He talks to the security man about decoys, high-speed chases, outrunning the pursuit. She wants to tell him that it isn't a game. She can feel the attention rising from the Place Vendôme below, a nameless craving. Al Fayed does not see himself fixed in their feral regard. He does not know how exacting the attention can be. She knows the part that draws them. The bulimia, the *morbid hunger,* the longing, a death each time. Doctors delivering their diagnosis as though reciting from an ancient and rare document. The vernaculars of self-harm. Endocrine, dopamine, archival fragments, lost dialects, the mutter of ancient peoples lost in the shadow of history. The frowning doctors speak the words but the meaning is lost to them. Self-esteem, reflux, body image. To cut the hands. To starve the body. Rites conducted in the shadow of death. From time to time she visits a school and sees the sombre eyes of adolescent girls watching her and she wishes she was back among them because she knows that they can recite the hymnal of the corpus, that they can if they wish raise their voices in its gravesong.

Al Fayed tells her that his father has called. He has said that they should stay at the hotel but her things are at the apartment on Rue Arsène-Houssaye and she wants to go back. He talks to his father every day. They use the little baby words to each other, his father calling him by the cradle names. Dodi. Moomoo. The little caressing sounds. Egyptians. How little she knows about his family. She wonders if they carry charms with them, snake amulets, effigies of the dog god. Whispered that his uncle is an arms dealer. Khashoggi. She has seen his picture in Hello! The casbah haggler, the dealer in shadowy trades.

They take her down the back corridors of the hotel. This is her domain and realm now. The dimly lit maintenance corridors and service lifts. The hampers of soiled laundry, the flickering utility bulbs. To get away from the press she had been brought through hotel kitchens and sculleries. An underworld of exposed pipework and shredded insulation material and unpainted plasterboard. She leaves hotels and houses by the delivery bay or the underground car park. She feels herself trafficked in the shadows.

musa musa this is henri is that car there yet is that car there yet the boss is waiting is that car there

It is Henri who comes for them and leads them down the back stairs. He tells them that the chauffeur Raymond Dorneau will drive the Mercedes 600 followed by the Range Rover directly to the apartment in Rue Arsène-Houssaye as a decoy. The bodyguard Wingfield will go with them. Henri has arranged for another car, a black Mercedes S-280 to be at the rear entrance in Rue Cambon which he will drive with the couple in the back seat and Rees-Jones in the passenger seat. Henri walks in front, talking to Etoile Limousines on his mobile. She feels herself part of a patrol, four men with her, keeping her moving in the corridors, going past the boiler room, feeling the heat and rumble of the furnace and for a moment she catches a glimpse through an open door of the dull red of the furnace window and a man's dark figure bent over it as though he toiled at some insatiable maw.

These are the places where you meet the laundresses, the breakfast cooks, the chambermaids, the nightworkers, their faces lifted as you walked past the doors of their windowless rooms. She can feel their resentment following her along the corridor, that she should walk among them, white-clad and subordinate, wan goddesses of a dim-lit region.

the flower ne more doth

Henri brings them through a door and into the small rear foyer of the hotel. Wingfield leaves for the front of the hotel. Henri goes to the door to check for the Mercedes S-280 but it hasn't arrived. Rees-Jones joins him. The street is quiet. None of the photographers has yet realised the plan. Spencer sits down, lets her head fall back against the wall. Among the rooftops across the street a pigeon breaks from a ledge and flies fast through the street light and up into the darkness where she fancies there are other birds circling, hunters of night carrion, riding the shadowy updraughts.

Wingfield emerged from the rear of the foyer, walking fast, hitting the glass doors hard, crossing the pavement in front of the hotel and getting into the Range Rover. As he does so the two vehicles start moving away from the hotel. One or two flashes go off, but in a desultory way. They know this is not the real event. The photographers look for Spencer, some of the motorcycles starting to move after the Range Rover and the Mercedes 600. The onlookers are confused.

Harper stood up and walked to the concierge's desk. He pushed past the concierge. The man fell back against the luggage rack behind him. Harper scanned the bank of CCTV screens. Doorways, empty corridors, a deserted ballroom, empty streets, strange unpeopled night scenes, ill-lit, dark and troubling. At the bottom right of the display he saw the rear foyer, Spencer sitting on a low chair, Al Fayed with his arm around her shoulder.

'They're going out the back,' Harper said, 'they're going out the fucking back.'

'Where's the car?' Bennett said.

'Rue Cambon.'

'What about Grace?'

'Get her.'

Bennett went into the bar. Harper stayed by the bank of screens. The concierge stepped forward. Harper shook his head. The man moved back against the luggage rack. Harper looked at the screen which showed the front of the hotel. The Mercedes 600 and the Range Rover were gone. There were still some motorcycles at the kerb. The bystanders looked uncertain, wondering if they had somehow missed Spencer. They looked at each other uncertainly, seeming to sense that the night would be subject to gruelling perplexities. The people that Harper had identified as field officers did

176

not move. They seemed to be waiting for some signal and until then would stand sentinel.

Bennett came out of the bar with Grace. Harper looked back at the rear lobby camera. Spencer was on her feet, Al Fayed still with his arm around her. Henri was facing them, Rees-Jones was watching the door, Henri talking to them now, explaining something. The CCTV colours wrong, unsaturated, the rear lobby taking on a dank, submerged look, the edge of the images lacking definition, the timeline running across the bottom of the screen counting off the hundredths of seconds, as though some baleful deadline was upon them. Grace and Bennett joined him.

'Come on,' Bennett said, 'we got to get the car.' But Grace did not move and appeared lost in the image in front of her, the way Al Fayed leaned back against the wall, one arm around Spencer's waist. Taken back to Margate, the way the boys would lean against walls like that and hold the girls by the waist, this tenderness ceded to them, her hip against his thigh, the little proprietal gestures measured on an adolescent scale of intimacies.

Rees-Jones turned to Henri and said something. The couple started to move towards the door.

'Wake up to fuck, Harper,' Bennett said, pulling him by the arm, 'they're headed for the door.'

Harper turned towards the door. They pushed through it and walked fast down the front of the building, Harper and Bennett knowing that whoever was in the crowd, the men and women set apart by the incuriosity, would recognise them for what they were, would recognise the urgent gait, the clandestine hustle. They turned the corner, Harper pulling the car keys from his pocket, Grace losing a shoe, turning back for it. At the corner of the Rue Cambon, Harper and Bennett paused. Further down the street they could see the Mercedes S-280, Rees-Jones holding the door open.

'Paparazzi guessed it,' Bennett said. There were four photographers around the Mercedes. Spencer and Al Fayed crossing the pavement, getting into the back of the car. Harper unlocked the Renault. Grace got into the back seat. One of the paparazzi was on his mobile.

'There'll be a tribe of them here now,' Harper said, starting the

177

car. Rees-Jones got into the front seat of the Mercedes. It started to move. Harper looked at his watch.

'Sharpish, Harper,' Bennett said, 'Henri's not hanging around.' Harper putting the car into gear as the Mercedes took off at speed from the kerbside. Harper gunning the engine, the rev counter needle swinging to 8000 rpm. Harper remembering the high-speed pursuit techniques, heel-and-toeing the accelerator, feeding the clutch. They followed the Mercedes down Rue Cambon, watching it turn into Rue de Rivoli. As they passed Rue de Castiglione, several other motorcycles swung in behind them. Harper could see the round motocross headlights in his mirror, the riders low over the tanks, passing the Renault easily.

'I can't see the Mercedes,' Bennett said.

'It's too fast,' Harper said, 'I can't keep up with it.'

'There it is,' Grace said. They were out from between the buildings, into the Place de la Concorde, and Grace was aware for the first time of the spot-lit obelisk in the centre of the Place, the occult monument, decorated with hierograms, beast-carved. Grace looked at it with awe. She felt profane words spring to her lips.

'Luxor,' she said.

'What?' Bennett said.

'The obelisk,' she said, 'it came from the tomb at Luxor. There were two of them. They guarded the Valley of the Kings.'

'That's very interesting, Grace,' Bennett said, 'now would you shut the fuck up.'

'Keep the mind on the job, Grace.'

She had seen it in daylight where it seemed bland and civic. It looked different at night. You thought about the barge-borne corpses of kings carried downstream. *Uxor principas*. It seemed to be hedged about with divination. In its shadow kohl-eyed priests enacted barbarous rituals.

'She's away with the fairies,' Bennett said.

'This is some unit,' Harper said, 'this is some covert op.'

The Mercedes stopped at the traffic lights at the far side of the Place de la Concorde. Harper slowed the Renault. The motorcyclists were alongside, holding the cameras against the side windows.

'I heard the tapes,' Grace said suddenly.

'Give it a rest, Grace,' Bennett said.

'No,' Harper said, half-turning to her, 'what tapes are you talking about?'

'The calls that Spencer made to James Gilbey. The ones that were supposed to have been picked up by an amateur scanner.'

'The ones there was all that fuss about?'

'Yes. It wasn't picked up by accident. The telephone call was recorded and continuously re-broadcast until somebody picked it up.'

'Don't talk shit, Grace,' Bennett said.

'We analysed the tapes at GCHQ. There was a fifty megahertz hum. There were databursts at eleven-second intervals which would have been filtered out of a normal call. It wasn't a normal call. They re-broadcast the tapes to get the call into the public domain. They played it on a loop until some civilian picked it up.'

'So you're saying there has been covert activity going on around her all along?' Harper said.

'Why are you telling us this now?' Bennett said.

Grace said nothing.

'Watch,' Bennett said, 'he's jumping the light.' Henri pulling away from the light on red, the motorcycles caught off-guard for a moment.

'He knows how to drive that thing,' Harper said. The motorcycles streaming out behind the Mercedes, waiting for him to take the right turn into the Champs-Elysées. But Henri didn't turn.

'He's going down along the river,' Grace said.

'Gives him a straight run through,' Harper said, 'he would of hit traffic on the Champs-Elysées.'

'What speed is he doing?' Bennett said.

'Hundred and twenty kph plus,' Harper said, looking down at the speedometer.

'What's that in Her Majesty's miles?'

'About seventy miles per hour,' Grace said.

Rue Cambon Rue de Rivoli Cours la Reine

'Frogs all drive like maniacs,' Bennett said. Grace looked at him, his face white like something from an old painting, a sinner's face, pale and afraid.

'Come on, Grace,' Harper said, 'why did you tell us about her phone being monitored now?'

'I didn't think of it.'

'That don't wash with us,' Bennett said.

'Shit,' Harper said, looking in his mirror. 'It's the bike, the BMW, the one we seen at Al Fayed's apartment.'

Harper lost the BMW in the rear mirror, then picked it up in the side mirror, alongside and just behind the Renault, the rider wearing a full-face helmet. Despite the heat he wore a light-coloured balaclava underneath the helmet. He wore a blue boilersuit and heavy motorcycle gloves. Harper recognised the boilersuit as the garment to be worn then burned to destroy forensic traces. The rider was sitting upright, only his eyes visible, stony and focused, as he drew level and Grace found herself thinking of a fell rider out of history, sombre and gauntletted, bent over his mount, plague and famine in his wake. As she watched he drew level with the front of the Renault then accelerated away from them.

'What's he got on his wrist?' Bennett said. 'He's got something strapped to it.'

'Looks like a camera or something,' Harper said. Seven hundred metres ahead of them the Mercedes hit the on-ramp for the Cours la Reine, the motorcyclists behind riding the footpegs to absorb the shock. Grace staring out of the window at the river, the Seine, slow moving and vast and bearing on its oily surface the reflection of the obelisk behind them. *Uxor principas*. Its sentinel bulk.

Nineteen

The Nokia was ringing. Its arcade-game tone conjuring sinister carnivals in the Fiat, hurdy-gurdy tones. Memories going through Andanson's head. Dodgem cars. The blue grid spark of the overhead power mesh, the iron-filing smell of it. Crossing the channel in winter to spend nights in the English north coast seaside towns. Playing the slots, the fruit machines. Going on Saturday nights to the speedway, under floodlights in Milton Keynes, in Birmingham, the high-octane cinder tracks. The Saturday night roar, the kart tracks, careering into the tyre wall. James always looking for velocity. His heroes James Hunt and Barry Sheene. Blond and fleet.

James picked up the phone and heard her voice telling him that the Mercedes was right behind him. Looking behind he could see the headlights and then ahead the mouth of the Alma tunnel, the frightful maw, Belinda asking him if he could hear her, if he was listening. He placed the phone on the passenger seat, let his right hand drift on to the gear lever, knowing that the timing had to be perfect. He estimated the Mercedes was travelling at 140 kph. He dropped into third gear and watched the speedo needle move up. He needed to be moving at the same speed, car chase scenes going through his head, McQueen in Bullitt, the whitewall tyres and big-band score, McQueen relaxed, lean and iconic. The needle wavering at 145 kph. When he was sixteen he had put a photograph of McQueen on his bedroom wall. In the photograph McQueen was changing a tyre on a Ford Bronco during a 24-hour race at Daytona Beach or at Detroit, raceways somewhere in the lost industrial belts. McQueen

181

has a cigarette in his mouth and his face is covered with road dirt. He is shading his eyes with one hand and there is oil and brake fluid on his hands, the lonely perfection of this image the reason why James started to take photographs, to find and preserve each moment's lonely history, James knowing that in the hurtle and lonesome career of the asphalt tracks, some transcendence was achieved, men pitting themselves against the pell-mell raceways.

Up ahead he could see the Place de l'Alma clearly. The Mercedes stayed sixty metres behind him as though it held station there. Behind the Mercedes he could see the lights of motorcycles, moving from side to side, trying to get shots through the rear window of the Mercedes. Andanson was in control now, feeling the balance of the car. If you handled a high performance machine properly then there was much to be learned. Forgetting about Belinda now, the Order of the Solar Temple, the cultists, the covert services, the dismal plotters. He had to judge it right. The Mercedes would weigh about three tonnes, picking up momentum on the down ramp *o priory of sion*. He would have to wait to the last moment and hope that Henri's reflexes were good enough to slam on the brakes. The Mercedes S-280 was a tank. Eight-litre V-twin. It would run right over the Fiat. But Belinda had said that Henri was a pilot, that he had his night-flying licence, that he had just passed his annual medical. Henri would be feeling the same way as Andanson. Looking for the same thing in aircraft that Andanson looked for at the race tracks. To be jolted back in your seat. Feeling the turbo kick, the after-burner roar. To feel the G-forces, the wheel juddering in your hands, taking the thing to the limit in the knowledge that grace was available out on the edge of things. When the time came Andanson knew that Henri would make the right move.

Cours la Reine
12.22 a.m.

Henri doesn't talk to them. Henri is watching the motorcycles in his rear mirror. He got them at the traffic lights, taking off early. They won't catch him on the riverside carriageway and they won't get

182

alongside in the Alma tunnel with the way the road dips at the entrance, the sensation in your stomach the way you felt when you were young going over a hump in the road and you said go faster Papa then you looked out the window and saw the Mirage fighters at treetop level and you thought about duels and daring aerial combat. The way you stood at the fence of the Rochefort air base watching the pilots walk away from the aircraft holding their helmets under their arms, you could still see the altitude in their faces, seventy thousand feet, eighty thousand feet, temperatures at minus thirty, on the edge of the atmosphere, out there in the electron streams, out where the eerie cosmic winds blow.

Spencer knows the photographers have seen her looking out of the back window and have photographed her which is always a mistake letting them catch you unawares the red-eye, the cellulite, the fold of skin at the neck, *cours la reine* on the signpost going past the window. Al Fayed keeps calling her 'darling'. The little baby words. They are drawing her deathwards, her narrative in the transcripts at Langley, at GCHQ, they are poring over her calls trying to find meaning in them, the hidden meaning, the narrative of her time *with their devices with their steel they are looking* Her voice transcribed, the hearsays pored over the digital tapes *my husband* sent to vaults. Deep in the control rooms her voice is compressed. The cryptanalysts at work. The lone tech chatter, the directional microphones, the parabolics, the voice-activated, even now the disarray of her life is being ordered, cluster analysed. The archives are open to receive the digital tapes, the floppy disks, the typed transcripts. The arcana. She looks over to the river and sees the night-time barges floating past, lit fore and aft, each with a helmsman in the shadows and she catches a glimpse of a grey motorcycle coming up, a grim pilotage at hand.

Harper accelerated after the BMW, red-lining the Renault in fourth gear, but not catching up fast enough. The grey motorcycle being handled fast and expertly. This was no amateur assassin, Harper thought, or no money-hungry photographer. The BMW moved up the outside of the paparazzi motorcycles. He could hear Grace's voice in the seat behind him and realised that she was praying. Not one of the great prayers, a petition to a stern and doctrinaire Lord, but a domestic prayer, a child's grace before meals, the kindly deities and domestic angels being called on, the saints of cracked statues on childhood windowsills, the prayers murmured into the pillow at nightfall. Bennett sat without moving beside him as though he proposed some remorseless commendation of his own.

'Where is the Merc going?' Harper said.

'Into the Alma tunnel,' Bennett said, 'then he'll swing right. He has to swing right. He's heading away from the Arab's apartment. Jesus Christ, will you cut that out, Grace.'

'The tunnel,' Grace said, 'it's the tunnel.'

'What are you saying, Grace?'

'I saw the position paper.'

'You better spill it pretty damn quick,' Bennett said, 'come on, fuck you.'

'You want her to talk, don't shout at her.'

'The light,' Grace said.

'What fucking light?' Bennett said. 'The light of day? The light above the porch? The light fantastic? The fucking divine light? What light Grace?'

The Mercedes had reached the tunnel. Harper saw the BMW motorcycle draw level with it. He saw the Mercedes hit the camber and go nose-down into the tunnel. He saw the Mercedes brake lights come on at the wrong time. He saw the Mercedes brake lights stay on too long to signify an ordinary braking manoeuvre. He saw light coming from the tunnel. He took his foot from the accelerator, the revs falling away.

'Is that it?' he asked softly, 'is that the light, Grace?'

Twenty

From the office window the Seine was visible. You could see the river traffic running under navigation lights. Nightboats. Commerce without cease. You could see the shapes of men standing at the helm, the plotters of courses, the grim-faced bargees. The sirens beginning in the city, sirens rising from all quarters of the city. The sapeurs-pompiers, the ambulance service, trauma units on the move, call-outs coming into the emergency switchboards. Masson stood at the window. He heard a fax coming through on the machine behind him, an everydayness to the sound, the magneto whirr of the thing. The sheet of paper he took from it was slightly smeared and had an inky, encrypted feel. It was still warm from the printing, from the processes, and he could smell the ink, the darting printheads. After he had read it he went to his desk. He pressed the button on the intercom which connected with the cell block and asked for Max to be brought up from his cell.

When Max came in Masson told him to sit down at the desk opposite him. Max noticed that Masson was in shirt sleeves, the cuffs rolled up, an anglepoise casting light on the desk. Max had been asleep when they came for him. Max thought that this was part of the process. Sleep deprivation followed by interrogation. It was important that you were disorientated, off-guard.

'There has been a road traffic accident,' Masson said, 'involving Spencer and Al Fayed in the Alma tunnel close to the Champs-Elysées.'

'Are there injuries?'

185

'Indications are that some of the passengers are seriously hurt. The emergency services have not yet arrived.'

'Do they know what happened?'

'The cameras to the tunnel approaches were not functioning at the time of the accident. There are no cameras inside the tunnel. I want your people in here. I want to know where they were and what they saw.'

He took Max's mobile out of a desk drawer and gave it to him. Max tried it. There was no signal.

'They could be out of range,' Max said.

'Or in the tunnel. There would be no signal in the tunnel.'

Max's hands felt clammy. The fact that the cameras on the tunnel approaches were down worried him. The fact that he couldn't contact Bennett. It suggested that there were other players in the field. That other agendas were being pursued. He knew they would be monitoring the emergency frequencies. They would be controlling the flow of information. He knew that he looked untrustworthy, a wheedler, a wringer of hands. Sweating in the warm Paris night. He wondered how long it would be before he got his hands on the transcripts. He could see an injured Spencer, worth millions, literally millions. The prayers of the world. He could see her descending the hospital steps on crutches, pale, issuing a brief statement. He felt a tear come to his eyes at the thought of it. Max wasn't afraid of sentiment. The fax machine behind Masson was printing. There were lights flashing on his intercom. Time was running out.

'How much do you know about the people that you hired to follow Spencer?' Masson said.

'I told you,' Max said, 'I paid Bennett and he found the other two. Bennett is well known as an independent operative.'

'He is well known to be cheap and without scruple.'

'Why do you ask me this?'

'For a period this evening they spent time in the Ritz Hotel. A call was placed from the hotel foyer to a number in London which is known to us. I am presuming that one of your three operatives made the call.'

'I am not involved in anything untoward, Inspector.'

'You should be more careful in the people you associate with,' Masson said. Max said nothing. Masson knew nothing about the people Max did business with. He had worldwide associates, there were networks of men out there, visionary thinkers in the geopolitical sphere. Max liked to think that broader interests were at stake. Men who were out on the edge, in the frontier towns, the resource-rich wilderness areas. Men who could see the possibility in political instability, currency collapse. He'd been to the post-Soviet republics, the oil-derricks stretching to the horizon. The polluted inland seas.

Alma Tunnel

12.25

Harper stopped at the mouth of the tunnel and pulled the Renault on to the triangle of grass there. He got out of the car and stood at the top of the ramp looking down. Bennett and Grace stood either side of him. They saw the Mercedes in the tunnel below them. Harper thinking bomb, mercury tilt switch, timed charge in the wheel arch. Post-industrial carnage with body parts strewn across the road. Grace started to walk down the ramp towards the car. Bennett called out to her but she didn't stop. The horn was sounding.

'What the fuck is that?' Bennett said.

'Could be the driver,' Harper said. 'He could be lying across the steering wheel. His weight on the horn.'

There was grey smoke coming from the engine compartment of the Mercedes, oil spilling on the hot engine. The tunnel full of the smells of hot metal, the smouldering hydrocarbons. The Mercedes horn amplified by the tunnel. The sound of the horn seeming out of place here. The late-twentieth-century blare. The note of requiem. The front of the car forced into a V shape so that it looked alien to the tunnel, a downed craft of some kind. There was debris underfoot as they went down the ramp. Orange indicator glass. Tail-light fragments. Harper bent down and picked up a piece of red tail-light glass, turning it over in his hand, its machined facets with impact fractures going deep into the glass and refracting the light, something beautiful in the miniature tectonics of it. Harper bent again to pick up a piece of wing-mirror glass, part of the housing still attached.

'Fuck's sakes, Harper,' Bennett said, 'you picking daisies or something. Let me see.'

Bennett looked at the fragments in Harper's hand.

'These bits is fresh,' Bennett said, 'just broke off. The fucking Merc hit another motor going down the ramp. Must have.'

Harper put the glass into his pocket without saying anything. They continued down the ramp. Harper picked up a numberplate, laminate plastic with the numerals visible.

'I don't see the BMW,' Bennett said, 'the one that overtook us on the run in.' He bent to the ground to look at the skid marks.

'Looks like there was a motor in front of him in the right lane. Henri tries to avoid it, hits the side of it and loses his mirror, locks the wheels when he's turning left. Recovers the vehicle.'

'So it's an accident?' Harper said.

'Odd as fuck this is,' Bennett said.

'What is?'

'Right, we're here. Look where the Merc is. Old Henri, he got control of the Merc back after it struck the car, so why does he crash down there? What's his problem? We know that he's a pilot. Ex-military. The right man in a situation like this. Except that after he gets out of the first collision, straightens the motor, then he goes and drives right into one of the pillars, full fucking on. What do you reckon?'

'I don't know.'

'Fuck. You reckon she's alive?'

'We better go and see.' Harper watched Bennett walk down the ramp towards the car. Something of the operative he used to be in evidence. Harper remembered him as a scene-of-crime expert. Working out firing points, bullet trajectories from the number of strikes, from the angle at which a body had fallen, from the actual expression on the corpse's face, the degree of puzzlement. How many shooters. What direction they had escaped in. Bennett found the bullet casings dropped in wasteground, the discarded cigarette butt, finding alignments and patterns in the psychic disarray of death scenes.

Paparazzi bikes were passing the two men on the ramp now. The photographers pulling up around the car, dismounting, reaching for equipment. Looking spidery in the tunnel light. Testing light meters. Loading motor drives. Setting about their work like some debased guild. One of them opened the left-hand rear door of the Mercedes. Grace stood to the rear of the car that had struck the pillar and turned almost 180 degrees so that it was facing back the way it had come. Grace found herself counting the pillars. The car had struck the thirteenth pillar. The arcane number. She knew that her mother would seize on it. Would plot the crash site by way of ley lines, astrological histories. She would set her friends to work to find significance in the times and dates and in the ages of the crash victims. A new lease of life for them. The elderly numerologists and soothsayers, the plyers of esoteric trades.

A photographer in leathers and an open-face helmet with goggles had climbed into the back seat, spindly and black, the ovoid lenses rising and falling above the rear shelf of the car, as though to feast on some carrion there.

Harper knew there were dead and injured in the Mercedes. He knew the stillness, the sense of aftermath. He was familiar with a whole range of death, steeped in glossaries of ruin. He could see where the pillar had punched a V shape in the front of the car, the pre-designed crash features coming into play, the crumple zones, chassis members telescoping, the microsecond sequencing of crash mechanics.

When they reached the car they could see Henri's head. You didn't have to go over to him to know that he was dead. Harper had seen it before, the broken-boned sprawl, a thread of blood in the corner of the mouth, one supplicant hand extended through the broken windscreen, his head thrown back across the seat in a pose of vile abandon. Rees-Jones lay with his head on the dashboard. As they approached he lifted his head, what remained of his face a thing of bloody and defiled power, as though rituals should be

189

enacted around it, as though it should be borne aloft in depraved pageant.

'Clunk click every trip,' Bennett said, 'none of them's got the seat belt on.'

'Never mind that,' Harper said, 'what about the main party?'

There were ten or eleven photographers around the car, all using flashes. Grace could feel the sear in her eyes, a cauterising pain in the optic nerve. She thought about epileptics, aberrant brain activity brought on by flashing lights, the nerve impulses misfiring.

as the motorcycle swerved and the car lost control there was a flash of

She put her hands over her eyes. One of the photographers jostled her from behind. When she opened her eyes again she was standing by the open rear door of the Mercedes. She could see Spencer's legs and Al Fayed's distorted leg lying over Spencer's legs and understood that Al Fayed was dead though his legs held hers in a ghastly embrace, a pose beyond what might be endured. A man in T-shirt and jeans pushed past the photographers and reached into the back of the car. Grace saw *go to my love* Spencer's legs moving and knew that she was still alive. The man in jeans was talking to her now, his voice low and reassuring and Grace caught a glimpse of the blonde hair and threads of blood on the side of the face, the eyes closed, against the bloodthreads, the mar, the spoil, the vacancy, the near-to-death gape. She saw Bennett and Harper come towards her from the front of the car.

'What's the story back here,' Bennett said, 'for it's not too fucking hot in the front seat.'

'They alive?' Harper said.

'She is, as far as I can see.'

'What about the Arab?'

'Dead as a dead thing,' Bennett said, 'I bet Her Majesty will be pleased.'

'Here comes the peelers,' Harper said. A police car stopped halfway down the ramp and two policemen got out. There were bystanders, tourists in khaki shorts with video cameras, holiday-makers in ill-fitting clothes looking like a marginal people, underpass denizens, emerging uncertainly into the light. Bennett started to move towards the open rear door of the car, pushing the photographers aside. Some of them turned as if to remonstrate with him but when they saw him they turned away as though to acknowledge that his purposes there were ceremonial, black-suited and seedy, even Harper watching him thought that he looked as if a ceremonial was being enacted. The doctor who attended to Spencer did not seem to see Bennett standing at his right shoulder, Bennett looking down without expression, the photographers waiting for him to gaze his fill as though they acknowledged the court of death to have its own functionaries and emissaries, Bennett standing over the dead and the dying as though he would be called upon to carry back dispatches from this place.

The two policemen moved into the crowd around the car. In the distance Harper could hear the first sirens. He looked at his watch. Seven minutes since the Mercedes had entered the tunnel. He looked at Grace. Her lips were moving as she scanned the tunnel pillars.

'Are you all right?' he said.

'Thirteen,' she said. Cars going past in the other tunnel, the swish of tyres, the whispered cabala *finite complete and absolute*

'What?'

'It doesn't matter. What did he have on his wrist? The motorcyclist,' Grace said. Her face was pale. They were shouting over the sound of the Mercedes horn.

'Christ knows.'

'You know what a strobe is?'

'Yes, Grace, I know what a strobe is. It's a bright flashing light.'

'I saw a position paper.'

'What do you mean?'

'A position paper generated in October 1992. They were going to kill the president of the Republic of Serbia, Slobodan Milosevic. They were going to cause a strobe light to be fired into his driver's eyes when his car was going through a tunnel. The light would blind the driver and he would crash.'

'You saying that the man on the BMW had a strobe tied to his wrist? That's what you meant when you said the light?'

'The proximity of the concrete walls of the tunnel combined with

191

sufficient speed on behalf of the target vehicle should ensure fatal results.'

'You're quoting from this alleged position paper.'

'Sometimes I just remember these things. Sometimes they just come into my head.'

'Take it easy, Grace. Take her handy. Breathe deep and slow. Don't go flakey on me now.'

'We saw it, Harper. We saw the light when the car went into the tunnel.'

'We seen something, Grace, we don't know what it was.' He looked across the Mercedes. Bennett was at the pillar where the Mercedes had struck, examining the impact marks, looking back up the tunnel as though he was gauging trajectories, as though there were geometries he could draw on. Harper watched as Bennett worked his way up the tunnel margins littered with road debris, pieces of wheel trim, rubber fragments, broken sections of exhaust, the litters of the transient century. The engine of the Mercedes had started to cool but there was still smoke coming from it with the yellow tunnel lights *the leafe the bud* the two policemen trying to get the photographers away from the car, the horn of the Mercedes still going in the murk, Harper touching his face and finding sooty deposits from the oil smoke, Grace's own face smudged where her mascara had run.

'Could just have been an accident, Grace.'

'You know that it's not. You know the men that do these things.' He did know them. The artificers in the shadows. The seigneurship they exercised.

'Still and all, Grace. It's a bit far-fetched, strobe lights in the eyes. Not exactly guaranteed that you'll get the target.'

'This methodology eliminates physical evidence from the scene. That's what this paper said. They were always looking for ways to cause car crashes.'

'It means that if they miss the first time they try again.'

'Bennett says the Merc hit another car.'

Bennett was back at the Mercedes again, working his way down the passenger side of it, down on his knees in the windscreen fragments, the shards of Triplex. He stood up, brushing dirt and glass from the knees of his trousers and came over to them.

'Definitely impact with another vehicle. Fucking deffo.'

'Grace here thinks that Henri got a strobe light fired in his face from the BMW. That's what made him crash.'

'Makes sense,' Bennett said, 'he hits a car at the top of the ramp, slides along the side of it, gets control of his vehicle back again, then Bob's your uncle, our pal on the motorcycle puts the big light in his face.'

'We're in a tunnel that's going to have every cop in town in it in three minutes and we're standing here having a fucking conference,' Harper said. 'You got a minute, Bennett, then we're out of here to fuck.'

'Listen to me, Harper. We're the only people seen this.'

'We go to the Service with it,' Grace said. 'Maybe they'll give you your jobs back.'

'I don't want my fucking job back,' Harper said.

'We go to the papers,' Bennett said. 'This is it, Harper. This is the story. We go to the papers, television, you name it, me and you and Grace on the pig's back.'

'What about your principal?'

'Frogs have him. Frogs can keep him.'

'They can find this out for themselves.'

'None of them seen the BMW. None of them seen the flash of light. We can say what we seen.'

'So we're reliable witnesses now, are we?' Harper said. 'I can see them listening to us. Same people as wanted her dead.'

'That's it,' Bennett said, 'that's fucking it. She ain't dead, is she? She's in the best shape of anybody in the car far as I can see. They fucking slipped up.'

'We can't prove anything.'

'We can,' Bennett said, 'we got the numberplate.'

At the entrance to the tunnel they heard the heavy turbodiesel of a fire tender, blipping its siren as it entered the tunnel, the noise falling away into the wan registers, the air brakes' high-pressure crack and hiss making Grace jump, the sapeurs-pompiers dismounting in their silver heat-reflective helmets and smoked-glass visors looking as though they had come to deal with a chemical spill, contaminants seeping into the structure of the tunnel. Grace backed away from them as they started to open compartments, unloading two-man hydraulic expanders and angle grinders.

A SAMU ambulance followed the fire engine down the ramp, a sleek and foreign vehicle with a complex light cluster on its roof. Not like the upright ambulances she remembered, the high-sided vehicles with two-tone sirens she thought would come for Spencer and bear her away, old-fashioned and stalwart emergency vehicles coming for her out of a trusted past, out of the night streets, squad cars, Commer fire tenders, ghost fleets bringing succour, bearing her out of the tumultuous present.

'Time to get moving,' Harper said. He took hold of Grace's arm and started to walk her back up the ramp.

'What's wrong?' Bennett said.

'That cop is here, Masson,' Harper said. 'I don't trust him. I don't want him to see us here.'

Bennett looked across the Mercedes at the unmarked police car that had driven the wrong way down the tunnel. The DGSE man Masson had got out and was walking towards the Mercedes. He moved through the crowd around the Mercedes and stood looking in without expression, his hands in his overcoat pockets. He looked at each of the victims in turn, an unflinching scrutiny, even when turned on Rees-Jones's ruined face, the lower half almost torn off, a doctor working in the gristle trying to stem the blood vessels, the tongue almost severed at the root and the tongue itself visible amid the viscera *I don't remember anything after I don't remember I don't remember*. Masson looked equally at Al Fayed and Spencer but he spent longest in his scrutiny of Henri taking in the steering wheel which had crushed his sternum, moving aside the airbag to gaze on the engine block driven into Henri's thighs and crotch.

In the back seat of the police car, framed by the rear window, Bennett saw Max's face. Max looked small and unimpressive, a petty thief in the back of a squad car.

Grace wondered that Spencer should come to rest here at the end of a stretch of dual carriageway. In the tunnel's road dirt, in the flicker of utility lighting, these stretches of pocked asphalt, the loveless late-twentieth-century barrens.

Harper turned at the top of the ramp to look down on the scene below. More ambulances arriving now. The firemen were working at the Mercedes, sheering the roof pillars with long-handled cutters. Ambulance men were removing the body of Al Fayed from the car and laying it on the ground. An IV line ran into the back of the Mercedes.

'Looks like Roswell or something,' Grace said.

'Wise up, Grace,' Harper said.

'You say that,' she said, 'but you know what I mean.'

The Mercedes looking like a downed craft of some kind. The firemen working around it in advanced protective clothing. You could believe that inside the body of the car was an unknowable being, an entity with a domed forehead. The same paranoias being brought into play, the deep species anxiety. The photographers being pushed back out of the tunnel, barriers going up, calls being made to the featureless offices, the institutes with no official existence. The way her mother and her friends had talked about it. The government. The establishment. The military industrial complex. They would whisper about it and she would mock them but she thought she could feel it now. The shadowy apparatus being brought into play.

'Here comes the undertaker,' Harper said, pointing at Bennett.

Bennett didn't look as if he was part of it, walking up the ramp towards them. He looked as if he belonged to another century. He looked like a historic plotter, a whiggish radical, worn thin in pursuit of towering ideals, a man given to conspiring in lamplit rooms.

Grace realised that she was going to cry. She could feel it starting inside her gut. She knew she would give herself up to it. The great diaphragm-wrenching sobs, shoulders heaving, the wordless gutturals. Raising a child's face to them, tear-streaked and desolate.

'Get in the car, Grace,' Harper said, holding the door open. Bennett got in the other side.

Harper reversed the car off the grass. He took a slip road leading away from the tunnel entrance.

'Find a place where we can park her up,' Bennett said, 'we'll keep the old eye on things.'

'Can we just get out of here,' Grace said.

'Not yet,' Bennett said, 'find a place to park.'

195

They drove away from the tunnel. As they drove they could hear the sound of the Mercedes horn, following them into the night, the darkling plaint.

The traffic was light on the Périphérique. Scant, homeward bound. The shift workers and hotel waiters and office cleaners. You could feel the weariness hanging in the air. Andanson trying to keep pace with the broken-down Skodas and third-hand Renaults. He knew there was damage to the back of the Fiat but he couldn't stop to inspect it. He could hear bodywork rubbing against one of the rear tyres and thought he could smell burning rubber. He found himself performing repetitive gestures, wiping his mouth, rubbing his hands through his hair. Henri had kept coming. Andanson had been too far into the tunnel, the Fiat concealed by the hump in the road at the entrance. Henri hadn't been aware of him until the last second. The Mercedes filling the rear-view mirror. Andanson would be seeing it for the rest of his life. The mirror framing the front of the German car, bearing down on him like a conveyance out of old myth, songs of despair and vengeance trailing in its wake. He could see Henri's face. Henri was calm. Henri swung the wheel to the left then corrected to the right. The front wing of the Mercedes catching the rear bumper and skirting of the Fiat. Andanson moving fast, dropping his right hand to correct the lateral movement imparted by the impact of the Mercedes. The Mercedes scraped against the side of the Fiat. The wing mirror coming off cleanly. Every sound amplified by the tunnel walls. Andanson thought that the other car's wheels had locked. Andanson thinking of the races he had seen. The wheel-to-wheel duels. Rindt and Graham Hill. How they came to be alone and set apart in the race-day heat and blare. He understood now that it came down to these moments. To be deft and able in the proximity of death. In the Alma tunnel side by side with Henri for a fraction of a second. Henri keeping the power down, using the weight of the Mercedes to ease through the space between the pillars and Andanson's car. He understood the connectedness. The headlong meld of sensation. And then he could feel the Mercedes easing away. That was when he saw the grey BMW, the rider turning towards the Mercedes, standing up on the footpegs, his right hand working the throttle, the left hand pointing towards the windscreen of the Mercedes and then there was the light, the million-candela glare.

Alma Tunnel
1.05 a.m.

There were messages coming in every few seconds on the police radio. Dense bursts hanging in the warm night air. Max's French was good but he couldn't make out what was being said. The jargon-laden police traffic, thick with acronyms. He could see little of the crash scene. He asked the police driver if Spencer was dead. The driver shrugged. There were photographers standing behind barriers at the mouth of the tunnel, most of them on mobiles, talking to the agencies, to the picture desk editors. Talking big figures. We got her in the back of the car. Max astonished that there did not seem to be more urgency surrounding the crash scene. There were men in yellow emergency bibs performing humdrum tasks, talking to each other on short-wave radios. Max remembered John Kennedy getting shot, whole populations swayed with grief, people standing alone on the street with far-off and stunned expressions on their faces. People rang him and retold the events in Dealey Plaza in trembling voices. The national mood was to be grey-faced, drained. Solemn music was played on national radio stations. Here there was a man with a clipboard leaning against a fire tender and chatting to the driver. People were standing around with faces that said this was a routine call-out. Max knew that it wasn't routine. He wanted to tell them to take their hands out of their pockets, to be alert to nuances. When Masson came back to the car he could see that Masson knew this as well.

'Is she dead?' Max said.

'She is ill but alive. Al Fayed is dead, and the driver. Come with me.'

Max followed Masson back towards the crash scene. There was medical equipment strewn around the car, plastic items in primary colours, spinal support units, IV stands, portable heart monitors. Emergency equipment with a rugged, all-terrain look to it. The roof had been cut from the Mercedes. The disincarceration team were repacking their equipment. There was discoloured oil on the ground underneath it, burnt-smelling leachate. A tripod light had been set up so that it shone down into the back seat of the car. Max could hear generator hum somewhere in the tunnel. He moved closer but Spencer was concealed by the medical personnel around her.

'Is she trapped?' Max said, 'why have they not taken her to hospital?'

'SAMU procedure,' Masson said, 'they stabilise the casualty on site.' Max looked down. Al Fayed was lying on the ground at his feet.

'Shit,' Max said. In the magnesium glare of the emergency lights the body looked like a crime scene photograph from long ago, an archived chromaprint in moody black and white, Al Fayed crumpled on the ground, one hand outflung. You expected bullet casings ringed with chalk, detectives in trilbys standing around smoking cigarettes. A policeman handed Masson a short-wave radio. He took it and listened without speaking. He turned towards the tunnel exit. In silhouette Max saw a windowless police van pull up at the exit. There was riot mesh on the windscreen. There were no insignia on the exterior. Max wondered what it was doing at a crash scene. The rear doors opened and police in paramilitary uniforms started to jump down from the rear, men in combat trousers and high-laced boots. It was wrong, Max thought. Bringing the aura of repressive regimes into the tunnel. You thought dawn raids, curfew, blindfolded political activists being manhandled out of the poor quarter.

'What's going on?' He said.

'They're detaining the photographers, the motorcycle paparazzi. They pursued the Mercedes into the tunnel in an aggressive manner,

causing the driver of the Mercedes to lose control of the vehicle.'
Masson spoke in a monotone, without looking at Max, so that
Max would know that Masson did not believe this version of
events. The police were moving into the crowd of photographers.
Max could hear cursing, the police going for the cameras and camera bags first, emptying the bags on the ground and picking up the
canisters of used film. Tearing open the camera backs, film stock
spooling out, exposed and ruined. The first shots where Spencer
seems to be hunched in the footwell. The shots of Spencer with Al
Fayed's ruined legs lying across her. The shots of Spencer with
threads of blood on her face. The spoil. The mar. Developed into
contact sheets thirty-six exposures per sheet, though they didn't
know it the death-scene montage. Wide shots. Close-ups. The emulsions spoiling in the tunnel lights. Overexposed in the artificial
light. Spencer's face disappearing into the glare. You could see it in
a stop-go flicker. The body seeming to be arranged differently in
each shot, taken from different angles. Awkward positions she
seemed to have chosen for herself. Policemen ripping the film from
cameras and throwing it into the air, black coils coming to land on
the barriers in funerary swags and festoons.

'What are they doing?' Max said.

'It is a precaution,' Masson said, 'they will not be able to sell the
photographs if she dies, but we take a precaution nevertheless.'

'Quite right,' Max said, 'you have my approval for this course of
action, Inspector.' Max glanced at Masson after he spoke. He
thought he had formed the English sentence quite well. He thought
it sounded well bred. It underlined the fact that he shared certain
values with Masson. He thought it sounded like David Niven or
somebody, and wished that he could copy the Englishman's brittle
post-war charm.

The photographers were being arrested now. There were scuffles.
A motorcycle was knocked off its side stand. Max heard one man
shouting that he had been in Sarajevo. Others calling out the names
of conflict zones, presenting the names as credentials. They had
been in border conflicts. They had been pinned down in sniper
alleys. Pleading with the policeman to see that they were not simple
photographers, celebrity snappers, that through their presence in

these zones of historic terror a dark acclaim clung to them. Kabul. Beirut. San Salvador. Max in awe, hearing the names of great troubled cities being recited, the names merging into a shrill chant amplified by the tunnel, the century's vexed evensong.

After a few minutes the last of the photographers had been put into the van. The police took up position, legs apart and arms folded, facing the crowd. A SAMU crew were lifting Henri from the driving seat. His torso and crotch were black and sodden and his head fell forward as though his wounds were a void into which he gazed with odious wonder. They were lifting Henri from the car and Al Fayed was dead at Max's feet. They had put wound dressings on Rees-Jones's face and dusted his wounds with sulphamide and given him diamorphine and he made unformed sounds for he had no mouth with which to give the sounds articulation. Everywhere Max looked there seemed to be butchery.

'Try Bennett's phone,' Masson said. Max dialled the number. Bennett answered on the second ring.

'This is Max. Where are you?'

'Near the Alma tunnel. Are you still with Masson?'

'Yes. He wants you to come in. He wants you and your colleagues to give an account of the events of this evening.'

'No can do, chum. Agenda's changed a little since the last time me and you talked. Is Spencer alive? Has she drew her last mortal yet?'

'I don't think you appreciate the complexity of the situation. The lady is still alive. They are attending to her.'

'It's taking them a bit of time. Must be pretty bad.'

'The doctors are confident,' Max said.

'You're an oily old bastard, aren't you, Max? You know fuck all about doctors.'

'All Inspector Masson wants from you is to tell him what you saw.'

'I saw the light, Max. Tell him that. I saw the light.' Bennett hung up. Max put the phone back into his pocket.

'Bennett is playing for time. He is waiting to see what happens.'

'Why would he do that?'

'He must think that he has something to trade with. That he saw what happened. That he has a story he can sell.'

200

'We know what happened. Harassment by the press motorcycles caused the driver to lose concentration.'

'Yes, of course.' Max thought about what Bennett had said. I saw the light *I am washed in the blood of the Lord* He didn't think that Bennett had undergone a religious conversion. Bennett lived by his own creed. Though sometimes Max thought he did present the demeanour of a street-corner preacher, a black-suited preceptor, an evangelist of deceit.

'They should inform me of what they have seen,' Max said. 'They are working for me.'

'Not all of them are working for you,' Masson said.

'What does that mean?'

'It means that they have been infiltrated from the start.'

'By who? Which one of them?'

Masson shook his head and walked away from Max. Max trying to absorb the information.

Rue Beaubourg
1.10 a.m

'Who was that?' Harper said.

'The principal,' Bennett said.

'Mr La fucking Fontaine,' Harper said. 'What did he want?'

'He wanted us to come in to talk to Inspector Masson, tell him what we seen.'

'You said no.'

'I did.'

'Fuck's sakes, Bennett.'

'Where is she?' Grace said.

'What's that?'

'They should have taken her to hospital by now.' There was a comfort in the idea of speeding ambulances, crews tending to the injured in transit, drips being rigged, extra cc's of trauma drugs being given intravenously, estimated times of arrival tersely spoken into dashboard mikes. It was a lonely idea that Spencer should still be in the back seat of the Mercedes, the roof torn off, the body shell

201

like something you would see in a edge-of-town scrap merchants, out there in the forsaken zones.

'It's getting late,' Bennett said. 'We need to think about what we have to do.'

'We don't have to do nothing,' Harper said.

'I want you to wait here and keep an eye on what is happening, follow them to the hospital if you can.'

'There'll be security.'

'There'll be fuck all the way things are going. They didn't give her back-up before she got into the tunnel, you think there'll be back-up when she gets out of it?'

'Where are you going?'

'Henri's apartment. I'll do the door, have a little look around.'

'Henri's girlfriend might still be there,' Grace said.

'All the better. We can have a chat with her. Find out who he's been talking to tonight.'

'What about Grace?'

'I'll go with Bennett.'

'Why? You want to do a bit of forcible entry with Bennett? Not your style, Grace.'

'Following ambulances ain't her style either, Harper. She can come with me all right. Watch an operator at work. You keep the car, Harper. Me and her can get a taxi.'

Harper watched them walk away from the car. Grace smaller than Bennett, looking small and hunched-over, Bennett walking beside her, looking at her as though a deference was due, turning abruptly every few paces to see if there was a taxi approaching, his movements jerky, coat-tails swinging, capering alongside her.

Harper knew what kinds of attention were being trained on the Alma tunnel by now. The satellites turning on their geostationary axes, the landsats, high over the polar regions. He looked up. If it wasn't for the night-time haze of city lights and the atmospheric grime and accumulated fumes then you could have seen them, nudged out of orbit, converging on this place, panels deployed, riding the solar winds. Downloading images to the earth stations twenty thousand miles below.

Harper turned to look at the back seat. The numberplate wasn't

202

there. He checked under the front seats. He looked after Bennett and Grace but they had disappeared and the street was empty, the shops shuttered, although the street did not seem quite deserted, something abroad in it now that made him feel cold inside as he stared without seeing at the Paris buildings, the above-the-eyeline scape of crumbling gargoyles, the eighteenth-century grotesquerie. Harper took his mobile from the dashboard and rang a number.

Alma Tunnel
1.15 a.m.

The tunnel strip lights lead off in each direction. There is a weight in her chest. The roof of the car is gone. They have rended the roof pillars, angle grinders sparking strange constellations, flintstruck Andromedas. A motor runs somewhere nearby. There are exhaust fumes hanging in the still tunnel air. There are far-off sirens. As of distant motorcades. The white light. They are leaning into the car and speaking in French. The white light. The flash light. The burning filaments. Looking into the car wearing helmets, motorcycle helmets in bulbous carbon fibre, firemen's helmets in silver as if they are covered in foil, the back of the car the centrepiece to a futurist masque, its players coming in and out of view in elaborate, staged movements. Replaced by the faces of men who speak in French, soft voices conjoined in a murderous crooning. The backseat textures amplified by the absence of the roof. The feel of the seat covering, the nubbed leatherette against the skin of the face. The synthetic fragrances. The weight on top of you the leather and cold chrome the press and pain *their steel devices with their electric devices they are looking.*

Twenty-One

The BMW had been returned to the third floor of the all-night multi-storey car park. The spare key was gaffa-taped to the underside of the petrol tank. The handheld strobe had been dropped into the Seine from the Pont Neuf. The motorcycle helmet was locked to the bike by the chinguard and the overalls and gauntlets were in the panniers. Furst being careful about leaving fingerprints, forensic traces on the bike, wiping down the panniers, even though he knew that the bike would be destroyed. Conscious of skin fragments, discarded hair, microtraces, the cell tissue sloughing off. Furst walked from the multi-storey to the Novotel. Both buildings felt like clean space. Concrete buildings of modular construction.

In the room at the Novotel he stripped off and began wind-down exercises. Working on the abdominals, the pectorals. Re-oxygenating the dense tissue, emptying his mind. He took a set of weights from his travel case and worked with them for ten minutes, timed on the de Rietling extreme chronograph. He looked forward to getting back to the gym. Since he had left the forces he had started to run marathons and lately had started to take part in endurance events. Eighty-mile runs in the Namibian desert. Working your way into the landscape, the moistureless sand hills and gecko-haunted salt pans. The noonday temperatures rising above forty degrees. It was about defining the boundaries of pity.

He stepped into the shower. The shower was white-tiled. The fittings were chrome and stainless steel. The kind of environments he was drawn to. He was thinking of buying an apartment in a technology park that was under construction on the outskirts of Johannesburg. He had read the literature, aimed at computer graduates. He was drawn to the descriptions of the workplaces. Sterile rooms, dust-free environments. Operatives in masks and static-free garments, an otherworldly garb. Moving gracefully in benign microclimates. The brochure envisaged jogging tracks running through the park. He imagined circuit training in sparsely populated campus tracks, heavily guarded perimeter zones.

He picked up the remote and turned on the television, flicking through the late-night channels, looking for a news channel. Sky had a breaking news scroll running across the bottom of the picture. Eyewitness accounts starting to come in. Unconfirmed reports. Condition of Spencer and Al Fayed unknown. He turned the sound down and left the words moving across the bottom of the screen, news coming in in staccato sentences, bullet-pointed and ominous, interspersed with financial bulletins, the prices of metals, the cost of bonds, the reportage coming from the Alma tunnel like some other mournful commodity.

Andanson had held his nerve and stayed in lane. He had left enough room for the BMW to get through the gap between the Fiat and the Mercedes. Henri the pilot, Henri the tennis player, all the reflexes brought into play, the high-speed manoeuvre executed to perfection, the Mercedes holding station in the left lane, the car still off-balance, the energy of the manoeuvre still stored in the suspension coils in the gas-powered shocks. He remembered the look on Henri's face. Henri knew that he had made it. Turning to make eye contact with the bodyguard Rees-Jones in the passenger seat. Relief in his eyes. The close call. The hair's-breadth clearance. The Breton's thoughts already moving away from the incident. Not realising that there was no space to the left, the passenger-side front wing almost brushing the concrete pillars. Henri turned back to the road and saw the BMW as it drew alongside. Furst standing on the footpegs so that the strobe was pointed down into Henri's face.

Furst had turned his head away from the Mercedes as he pulled the trigger to avoid being blinded, looking down at his mirror instead, not expecting the light thrown back at him to be so intense, the Mercedes foregrounded against the tunnel pillars, the bleached-out scene, the tunnel pillars stark and white like colonnaded ruin, a desert city of long ago, four figures picked out in negative in the Mercedes, spectral figurines.

He hadn't expected the retinal imprint. The image still faintly visible when he shut his eyes. This was the image he would carry away with him. The inhabitants of the car like characters he had seen once in a Port au Prince backstreet processional, draped in black cloth with skeletons picked out on them, bone-people shuffling in the darkness.

He had picked up an envelope from the porters' desk. He opened it. It contained business-class tickets Roissy to Frankfurt at 7.30 a.m. There would be Johannesburg tickets waiting for him at the Lufthansa desk. He dressed in khaki trousers and a brown sports jacket. He packed, starting in the bathroom, counting the items back into a shaving bag. On the television the first eyewitness testimonies were starting to come in. Witness babble in French translated in voiceover into English. Several people speaking of the noise that the Mercedes made when it struck the pillar. Furst had been ready for it, but it still surprised him, as though some ordnance had been detonated in the tunnel. People were taken aback by the forces involved. The heavy percussive sound. Passers-by on the street above stopping and looking at each other, feeling it in the concrete beneath their feet as though there were mines there, as though extraction were taking place in some deep ore vein, dense matter being yielded up.

He counted socks and underwear into his hard-shell travel case. He folded polo shirts and trousers, working the zips and buckles and pockets of the case, each item in its place. The military count. Underwear six pair. Trousers three pair. The inspection routine that had never left him since his conscript days in the SADF. Remembering the bare creosoted huts. Standing by the bed, arms tight to your side. The smell of Guardsman boot-blacking in the air. The smell of Brasso in the night air, the barrack timbers creaking as they cooled in the savannah breezes.

When he had finished packing he employed search protocols to make sure that the room was clean. He left the room without turning off the television. It played on in the empty room. The news coming through was fragmentary, incomplete. They kept returning to the same shot of the Alma tunnel, the same fire tender parked at the entrance, its red-yellow lights turning. The repetition of the key image bringing an eerie drama to the footage. You were drawn into it, started picking out details that you had missed before. The crowd behind barriers. The dusty plane tree standing near the tunnel. A man wearing an overcoat leaning on the guard rail. Motifs of isolation emerging, of urban apartness. The mouth of the tunnel itself drawing the eye inwards and down, the mind recreating the scene, the corpse-strewn bitumen, the clandestine night scenes.

Place de la Concorde
1.20 a.m.

Bennett told her that it would be as fast to walk to Rue Cambon. Saving money on the taxi. It was strange the things that brought out meanness in him. She thought that the presence of death had done it this time, that in the face of death a certain thrift was required.

'You know me and Harper was in it in Belfast? Before you come on the scene.'

'Of course.'

'You think we can trust him?'

'Why do you say that?'

'I don't know. I just get this feeling. That he's still working for the Branch or something. He never says all that much.'

'He never did.'

'You know, about what he's been doing these last years.'

'Security work he said. Was a bit vague about it though.' Her head was sore and her limbs were heavy. The effect of the drink she had earlier in the evening. The toxins draining, the waste product channelled through the lymph nodes. She wondered if Bennett was aware that they were walking underneath the obelisk, the shadowless monument.

'Maybe he's embarrassed about it. It weren't exactly top-level stuff he was doing. After he left the force he started out doing secu-

207

rity for building sites, providing them with guard dogs, that kind of stuff.'

'No wonder he never talked too much about what he did,' Grace said.

'Play our cards right with this thing, Grace, we'll be on the fucking pig's back.'

Grace looked at him, wondering if he believed what he was saying. Bennett pale, sweating, his teeth bared in an old lewdness. She could see him in top coat and tails. A Victorian profiteer on the cadge in a foreign city.

There were still people standing outside the Ritz. She could see that they had got the news. Some of them were on phones. Others had their heads together, muttering, sunk in conference. She could see Ritz personnel gathered in the foyer, courtiers gathering to receive the news. She followed Bennett around the corner into Rue Cambon. They passed the open door of the Bar Laurent. The music had been turned off and the girls were standing at the bar watching the Sky footage of the crash scene. Some of them had their arms on each other's shoulders, or held each other around the waist with thoughtful asexual touches. Grace knowing what they knew. That these were the funeral scenes. That this was why the camera dwelt on the Alma scene, finding the elegiac vistas, the sombre night hues. Grace could see Monique standing behind the counter with a drying cloth in her hand, looking up at the screen, her face long and mournful, a sorrowing duenna from some old church. Grace could tell she knew that Henri was dead. That could be the only meaning of the image being transmitted from the tunnel. These were the obsequies, televisual observances, the bar bathed in votive tones.

'Come on, Grace,' Bennett said, 'you think the gents of the French secret services won't think of paying housecalls this evening? We got to get in and out of old Henri's double quick. You think Henri's bird's still there?'

Grace shook her head. The street window was empty, the light out. Bennett stopped at the street door. He hunched over the lock, keeping his back to her, engrossed in the practice of a dismal tradecraft, a Whitechapel lock pick, casting furtive looks up and down the empty street as he worked.

The SAMU crew had removed Spencer from the Mercedes and treatment had commenced in the back of the ambulance. Masson sat in the front passenger seat of the patrol car, talking urgently on the short wave. Max could see the interior of the ambulance. Spencer's face was obscured but he could see that there was a drip attached and that she appeared to be intubated, a coil of clear plastic inserted in the larynx. The girl they had taken from his room in Los Angeles had the same tubing inserted. The interior of the ambulance was all hard plastics, scratch-resistant surfaces. Apparatus hung in metallic swathes from the walls.

Max could see Spencer's bare feet, the jeans soiled with blood and tunnel dirt. The soles of her feet were dirty. There were small tears in her clothing, blood smears on her flesh. She looked hapless and alone.

There was a forensic team moving in a row up the slope of the tunnel. Men in disposable white boilersuits gathering debris. Skidmarks were being measured, impact points and maximum speeds being calculated. A police photographer was taking shots of the rubber tracks and the tunnel walls. Max wondered what the photographs would look like when they were developed. He knew that police photographers worked in black and white. He wondered how you made sense of them, putting them in sequence on a wall, establishing a context, narratives of empty late twentieth-century space.

He heard another engine and looked up. A street-cleaning lorry had pulled into the tunnel entrance, painted municipal yellow, looking out of place among the emergency vehicles. Max understood that this was part of the procedure. The bloodstains and tissue fragments sluiced into guttering. The glutinous arterial matter. That no staining would be left as emblem and device of what had taken place. Max was starting to wonder who was taking the decisions in relation to the crash site. If they were aware of the power of place in such matters. The way that people found these places, made them sites of visitation, followed the pilgrim ways. You couldn't wash it away.

There were three ambulances in the tunnel. The two nearest contained Rees-Jones and Spencer. The other carried the bodies of Henri and Al Fayed. Green sheeting had been placed over each man but Max could still make out the shape of their bodies underneath, the rigor starting to work on them, the bodies frozen and fixed askew. The chauffeur and the playboy, Max thought, but knew in his heart that the cadavers would no longer yield to such easy categorisation, death starting to work on them, the meat darkening, the processes at work. He found himself edging away from them. As though there were something sinewy and poised under the sheeting.

A paramedic closed the ambulance doors and it pulled off up the ramp without siren. They were closing the doors of the other two ambulances as well. He saw Masson coming towards him. A man wearing a suit walked up to Masson. He handed him a mobile phone. Masson took the phone and listened. He had the look of a man taking instruction.

'Where are they going?'

'To hospital. The Pitié-Salpêtrière. The roads have been closed. There will be no outriders so as not to draw attention to the vehicles.' Max noting again the flat way that Masson spoke. Altering the trajectory of the night's events. The night's histories reeling away into myth.

Cours Albert Premier
1.40 p.m.

Harper watched the ambulance containing the bodies of Henri and Al Fayed leaving the tunnel. The corpses, he thought, they would leave the tunnel first. The vehicle unhurried, the 2 a.m. processional of the dead begun. Harper put his phone on the dashboard. He thought that there would not be a reply to his call now. That he would have to wait until the morning. He could see the night traffic on the Seine, and as the barges bore their commerce so would the ambulances cart their mournful cargo.

There was no other traffic on the Rue Albert Premier. The road had been closed at a junction upriver, Harper thought. To allow the ambulance carrying Spencer a free run to hospital. Or to leave the way to the hospital empty and without witness.

When the second ambulance left the tunnel Harper knew that it was the one carrying Spencer. There was a motorcycle escort and two patrol cars following the ambulance, but the convoy was moving slowly. You expected outriders going ahead of the ambulance, synchronised high-speed transit, the siren's split-second tone changes. Harper expected the driver gunning it through the gears, the French ambulance low-slung and fleet, speeding through the night. Not this halting progress.

He let the ambulance pass him and pulled in behind it, staying four or five hundred yards back. She must be in bad shape, he thought. They must be trying to keep her stable. He'd followed ambulances to hospital before. Gunshot victims, bomb victims, the maimed and mutilated. He knew that an ambulance travelling slowly meant that they were trying to stabilise the victim. Trying to keep the system going. Injecting adrenaline directly into the muscle. Massaging the heart, trying to re-establish the rhythm, the dark spasm showing in the eyes. Harper began to suspect internal damage. He pictured the crash scene. The car turned to face the way it had come by the force of the impact, Spencer still facing forward. The centrifugal force acting on the internal parts, the blood-slick webbings and organ roots, the muscle wefts torn from their mountings.

The convoy moved forward with what seemed like ceremonial pace.

After a few minutes the cars stopped. Harper pulled into the side of the carriageway. He couldn't see what was happening, shadowy figures on the move around the ambulance. The street sign beside him read Jardin des Plantes. Late summer growth hanging over the wall beside him. Jacarandi, jasmines, heavy-scented and cloying. He had a policeman's wariness of parks by night. Women dragged into them, all manner of shadowy commerce undertaken, hypodermics strewn, joggers attacked. Primal memory at large in the dark shrubberies and gravel beds, stirrings in the deep brain tissue. The noise of the ambulance doors being opened and closed sounded clearly on the empty street. Voices carried in the warm night air. Harper got out of the Renault and walked a few yards up the street but he couldn't see what was happening.

The doors closed and the ambulance pulled off again. Harper followed, the ambulance not moving above five miles an hour, skirting the Jardin des Plantes, the penumbral expanse, foliage spilling on to the riverside expressway, plants he didn't recognise with vast pink night blooms, the passage along the river strangely ornamented with nocturnal exotica. Harper was finding it difficult to judge time, the ambulance seeming to be involved in a time-lag passage from accident site to hospital. When they reached the end of the Jardin des Plantes the ambulance stopped again opposite the sign for the zoological gardens. One of the motorcyclists briefly touched his siren, a single note of calamitous electronica as though a bird caged in the gardens had uttered in its sleep an alien night cry.

Jardin des Plantes
2 a.m.

Men are gathered over her but she cannot see them properly she cannot make out their faces or tell one from the other. She does not know if she will ever be able to see clearly again. The light in her eyes. She remembers from other times. The Annabels nights. The UV lights. They are readying her for a procedure she does not know what. Something is afoot. The men are foreign-sounding. Their skins are swarthy. Some cabal has come upon her and she is the subject and matter of their conclave. They have gathered about her. Cloaked figures of history, Jacobeans, foul deeds plotted. If there was more light she could see them.

There is a weight in her chest and she cannot move one side of her body. There is a history of stroke in the family. They have a tube in her throat. She failed all her exams but she remembers the suffragette ladies, the hunger-strikers force-fed, pinioned in straitjackets, gruel ladled into piping, rubberised tubing forced into the gullet. But she had read this bit *refused nourishment* ladies stripped of whalebone corsets in Holloway's damp precincts the tray of food returned, brought nude to bath, the rib slats visible. The ambulance doors open but no light comes in. She thinks she can smell flowers, fetid equatorial scents in the night air. Where have they brought her? Mrs Pankhurst says when you starve the sense of smell sharpens. Mrs Pankhurst says when you starve the hearing is the last to leave you. She thinks she hears a tropical bird, a beaked thing of toxic hue, fluttering from treetop to treetop in medicated dreams.

She thinks that they will feed her through the tube in her throat. Liquid concentrates being forced into her stomach. The things that were discussed the first time she was taken to the doctor. They told her of the danger to her organs, to the heart, to the lungs. To the womb. They discuss holding her down. They discuss glucose drips. Grim medicinal arts are brought to bear, restraints, sedation *on several occasions the patient's teeth were broken by the force necessitated* She knows the place they are bringing her. She hears the word Salpêtrière.

Henri had pointed it out to them with a laugh. Used to be the madhouse. The old hospital. She knows that it is waiting there for her. The dank bedlam. She is shaking. Spasms running through her. The palsies. They are bringing her to the asylum. She is to be brought to it along with the others, the pox-afflicted and lunatic, the ragged street preachers, the god-harried.

Rue Cambon
2.05 a.m.

Grace followed Bennett up the stairs to Henri's apartment. It seemed that Bennett just touched the apartment door and it opened.

'Wait here,' he said. She stood in the small hallway as Bennett moved through the apartment in the dark.

'There's nobody here,' he said, 'close over them shutters so we can get a light on.'

Grace closed the shutters. There were tea towels on the radiator underneath it and she used these to plug the gaps. Then she turned on the small light in the kitchenette. There were two glasses on the draining board. She could smell Henri's aftershave in the room, and a woman's perfume. Chanel, she thought, something classic, a note of fin-de-siècle decadence. The flat was plain. Grace thought of unadorned church space, the knowledge that Henri was dead bringing a rigour to the bachelor flat, its flat planes and unshaded bulbs and Formica worktops seeming bare and devotional. It always surprised her the way that men could access a frugality in themselves. There was a television and VCR against the street wall. There was a shelf of aircraft manuals. She saw Bennett pick up an Airfix model of a French air force Super Etendard. Wing markings and reg numbers picked out in enamel paint. Decals affixed. She thought of Henri working at it in the dim light, fine-brushing in the tiny writing. Henri painstaking, monkish. Bennett started to open drawers at random, running his hand along the top of the kitchenette cupboards. A man of furtive habit, he knew the hiding places, the turned-up carpet edges indicating floorboard caches, the badly flushing toilet cisterns, documents bagged and stashed in the freezer.

'Look,' Grace said. There was a woman's handbag on the coffee table, a roomy, well-used leather bag, big enough to carry a change of clothing. The clothes the woman had been wearing were folded beside it, the matelot T-shirt and jeans.

Bennett emptied the handbag on the work surface. There was a Maybelline mascara, dark-red Rimmel lipstick and black eyeliner, tissues with the imprint of lips on them where she had blotted the lipstick, kissed-on whorls and creases. Grace wondered if lip prints were unique like fingerprints. If they could identify. If they could corroborate. Bennett opened the zip pocket on the outside of the bag. He spilled out brown plastic pharmacy vials, loose capsules falling on the floor.

'We got a right fucking chemist's shop here. What the fuck is this? Permarine? Never mind. What we need is a carte d'identité, cheque book or something. Find out who this bird is.'

There were tweezers, eyelash curlers. A matchbox with Ritz Hotels on the outside. There were nail boards, wax depilation strips. There were no keys or credit cards. There were no envelopes with addresses. The bottom of the bag was coated with cosmetic residues, exemplary dusts.

'Nothing but fucking make-up in here. No fucking carte d'identié, no passport. Nothing.'

'She'll be back for the bag,' Grace said.

'You check the bedroom, keep an eye out the window for her,' Bennett said. 'Not here. The bedroom window. Keep the frigging light out, Grace.'

When Grace had gone into the bedroom Bennett phoned Harper.

Harper answered on the first ring.

'Harper.'

'It's you.'

'Course it's fucking me. Where are you?'

'Behind the ambulance, Spencer's ambulance. We're at the Jardin de Plantes.'

'Wherever the fuck that is. She's not at the hospital yet?'

'The ambulance keeps stopping. Either there's something bogey going on or they're losing her. I think they're losing her. Something's wrong anyhow.'

'Maybe they want to lose her. Grace says there's some sort of talk in the press like she's up the spout. Maybe that's something needs took care of before they get to the hospital.'

'Fuck's sakes, Bennett.' Bennett always able to make it sordid, an air of bloodstained coathangers, backstreet D and C merchants, a sinister midwifery abroad with douches and scouring solutions.

'Don't go all squeamish on me, Harper.'

'You get to Henri's?'

'Standing in his living room right now.'

'Anything?'

'I get the feeling Henri wasn't the kind of chap would leave stuff lying around. I get the feeling there was more to Henri than meets the eye.'

'What do you mean?'

'Everybody's got some secrets, Harper. But you look at this place, old Henri's got none. Clean as a fucking whistle. That's suspicious.'

'Maybe somebody got there before you. Cleaned it up.'

'Story of my life, old son. Henri's woman left her handbag here, looks like she's coming back. We'll have that chat.'

'Take it handy on her. You don't want her running to the French police.'

'Nice little chat. See if she can tell us who Henri's been talking to, who told him to take that route to the apartment. Maybe she passed the info on herself.'

'She might not be back. She might of heard the news, gone to the hospital to see Henri.'

'Not without her car keys and her purse. She'll be back.'

Bennett was holding the mobile in his left hand, using his right to search. Tumbling books to the ground in search of concealed documents. Pulling foodstuffs from the kitchen cupboards. Checking the fridge and the freezer.

Grace closed the bedroom door behind her. There was no decoration in here either. Henri's bed stood in the middle of the room. It was unmade. The room was warm and airless, rank with post-sex odours, a hormonal fug, the bottom sheet tangled, the lubricant flux, the mattress damp, items of underwear entangled in the sheets, foil discards. She closed the door behind her. A corner of the quilt touched her arm. It felt moist, fecund. There were books on Henri's bedside table. She scanned the spines. Carl Sagan. Desmond Morris. Behavioural sciences. Cosmology. She thought about Henri soul-blasted from the Alma tunnel, Henri out there in the deep cosmos, out in the plasma streams. She went through the chest of drawers beside the bed, Henri's polo shirts and slacks seeming to take on the worn-out patinas of the thrift shop, the clothing of the newly dead acquiring a winding-sheet odour. There was a flying club mascot on the bedside table. A model Ferrari. Everyday objects garnering poignant mystery to themselves in the dead man's bedroom. Grace went to the window and drew back the blind, staring down into the night-time street, a spy of sorts, she thought, a watcher in a dead man's house. The door opened and Bennett came in. He stood for a moment in the doorway, taking in the slept-in bed with one glance, the glow of the kitchen behind him, black-suited, backlit like a theatrical figure, a top-hatted mountebank bent on sexual plunder.

'Old Henri went out the right way by the look of things,' he said.

'Turn out the kitchen light and shut the door,' Grace said.

'I'm not sure if this woman is coming back.'

'She's coming back,' Grace said. 'Shut the door. Was that Harper you were talking to?'

'The very man.'

'Where is he? What's happening?'

'He's still behind the ambulance. Can you believe it, she's not even at the hospital yet.'

'Where were they?'

'Jardin de something. Jardin des Plantes.'

'The Pitié-Salpêtrière.'

'The what?'

'The hospital. That's the name of it. If they are at the Jardin des Plantes then that's the place they're bringing her to.' Grace remembering what she had read of it. *A house of wantons*. It had seemed to her haunted when she read about it. A new hospital built on to the old. A lying-in hospital for the urban poor that had become an asylum for broken-down prostitutes, and the syphilitic.

'I need to phone my mother,' she said.

'Cut it out, Grace. It's two o'clock in the morning.'

'She doesn't sleep. She can't sleep. They leave the phone beside her bed.'

'All right. If it keeps you on the straight and narrow. Go on. Go into the kitchen.'

Twenty-Two

Harper drove through the hospital gates after the ambulance. He turned to the left and parked the car in a space marked Staff Only. He walked towards the hospital, knowing that the night's events demanded an end in a building such as this. Harper knowing them as buildings he had been in before, the old hospital, the former asylum, built on and extended, growing outwards but always the dark colony at the heart of it, the windows bricked up, the cries of the forgotten echoing in distempered hallways. The place where Henri and Al Fayed await dissection. There would have been closer hospitals. But this building would have drawn the ambulance to it. Administrators and minor government officials woken from sleep to be told of the accident would know instinctively that this was the place.

After a few minutes Harper knew that he was lost. He had almost expected this. Such complexes took on shiftless metropolitan qualities, urban mystiques.

Finding himself in farflung service areas. Crossing from building to building. *Quartier Pitié*. Finding himself unable to get to the centre of things, pushed out to the periphery. Harper found himself blundering through oil tanks, rubbish skips, locked-off medical incinerator units, for the burning of waste, the human offals. As he passed windows he could see the interiors of the building. Deserted elevator lobbies, unlit laboratories. *Centre de Cardiologie*. He found himself on tree-lined side avenues. There were parks, small municipal spaces overlooked by buildings in pre-stressed concrete.

It was ten minutes before he found the Accident and Emergency entrance.

There was a small group of men standing around the ambulance. The rear doors of the vehicle were open and the interior was empty. Although Spencer had just been brought inside it looked as though the men were removing something from the hospital. Harper thought of bodysnatchers, resurrectionists, corpses exhumed by lamplight. Urban fancies going through his head. Organs removed and sold on. Shipped to the Middle East in temperature-controlled flasks.

He moved closer and saw the men under the glass and steel awning for what they were. Men in the service of the state. Civil servants, embassy staff, security service. They would know what governance would be required of them in this matter. From time to time one of them stepped to one side to make or receive a phone call. Attendant to her injury as they would be attendant unto her death. Contingencies being prepared, statements being written, positions taken, avenues of retreat opened. Harper put his head down and walked past them into Accident and Emergency, into the sanitised hospital spaces, the wide-open acreage. He could feel the glare of the strip lights bearing down on him. The radiance from which none shall hide. He knew he looked hunched-over, wary, a bearer of some grubby wound. He could feel the receptionists watching him. There were rows of orange plastic chairs with a drunk asleep on one of them. On the left-hand side the evening admissions behind curtains, the night's cubicled halt.

Walking past a row of trolleys and wheelchairs as though awaiting a legion of the maimed. It was Saturday night. Realm of the RTA victim, the attempted suicide. Harper knew that Spencer wasn't there, that she had been taken deeper into the hospital building. If she could not be stabilised here then she would have been taken to X-ray, or theatre. Through the window Harper saw two men detach from the group outside and enter the hospital. Both in their forties and trim, wearing lightweight grey suits. They seemed at home in the hospital. There was a surefootedness to the way they moved in the synthetic spaces. Harper fell in behind them. They walked fast, without speaking to each other. They crossed from the

Accident and Emergency block into the surgical block. Harper knowing they were getting closer. Padding along the non-static flooring. They moved confidently through the radiography sections, the ghost-zones of the cathode tube, the deep-tissue scans. Harper seeing the sign for Female Surgical. Harper seeing the sign for Theatre. Aware of a different atmosphere now. Theatre nurses going past, sombre, gowned. The lighting more muted. The consulting rooms and nurses stations left behind. These rooms concerned with the actual corpus, the reverie of flesh, the mechanics of anima. Surgeons scrubbed up holding their arms aloft, priestlike, adherents to the labyrinthine orthodoxies of their trade.

The two men led Harper into a corridor that had numbered operating theatres opening off each side. As they slowed a set of double doors to one of the right-hand theatres opened. A medical team emerged, darkly bloodied, pushing before them a trolley bearing Spencer, her matted hair just visible behind the mask which covered her face, the sheets of the gurney saturated with arterial spillage, with membranous substance, with clotted matter. They bore with them trolleyed oxygen tanks, saline drips, equipment clusters from which ran lines into her arms and chest, shunts and drains emptying into the gurney soakaways. There were nurses to either side. One surgeon went alongside and seemed to Harper to have his hand inside her chest, to be reaching into the cavity, the opened torso. Another surgeon came behind dressed in mask and apron. There was blood on his apparel and cap and on what could be seen of his face, so that he resembled a doctor of yore, a muttonchop sawbones. The gurney passed Harper, its green-clad accompanying corps speaking to each other in low murmurous tones. They continued down the corridor as if they transited from one uneasy precinct of the hospital's past to another. The noise of the monitors and pumps attached to the trolley faded, the digitised hubbub and magneto whirr, and Harper heard the sound of his own phone in his pocket. As he took it out he saw the surgeons guide the trolley finally into another operating theatre further down the corridor. He noticed that the two men he had followed were also speaking on phones, their faces averted, shadowed.

Harper put the phone to his ear. He listened for half a minute without speaking. He hung up and dialled Bennett's number. There was no signal. He started to walk back towards the place where he had entered the hospital. As he left the theatre block he broke into a run. He tried Bennett's phone again as he ran. There was no signal. As he went through the hospital corridors, staff stood aside to let him pass and then looked back for the pursuit, his face pale and sweating and his shirt-tails worked loose, as though he had done larceny in the hospital or absconded from authority and was now coerced to flight.

Alma Tunnel
2.45 a.m.

The sapeurs-pompiers had left the tunnel. The police forensic team had finished. Max watched the cleaning trucks move in formation down the carriageway. The Mercedes was being lifted on to the back of a police tow-truck. Blue-overalled mechanics drove planks under it then attached the planks by chain to the truck's hydraulic lift. As the car was lifted from the ground a slurry of spilled oil and engine coolant and blood became visible. A police photographer knelt to photograph the spillage and a cleaning truck detached itself from the others and moved towards it. The men worked around the Mercedes with chocks and canvas strapping to make it secure on the truck bed.

'They're going to re-open the tunnel,' Max said.

'In twenty minutes,' Masson said.

'I thought it would stay closed,' Max said.

'Why?' Masson said.

'I don't know.' Max with the feeling that events were being impelled forward by an unknown force. Masson's phone rang. He listened without speaking, then put the phone back into his pocket.

'It looks as though you have other things to worry about.'

'Why?'

'Spencer is gravely ill. They do not think she can survive.'

'What has that to do with me?'

'You hired a team to protect her.'

221

'Observe, Inspector.'

'It is now certain that your observation team was infiltrated.'

'By who, Inspector? And what harm have they done?'

'Harper and Bennett and the woman Campbell were here at the crash site.'

'You will have to forgive me, Inspector, but your own men seem eager to have the scene re-opened. More than eager. Perhaps you have something to hide in this matter.'

'All necessary forensic steps have been taken. However, there may have been interference with the crash site before we arrived. Evidence may have been removed.'

'Which one, Inspector? Which of them?'

'Wait.' Masson's phone rang again. Once more he listened without speaking.

'What is it?' Max said.

'Earlier this evening a mobile phone call was placed from Paris to a nursing home in the south of England.'

'Grace Campbell's mother is in a nursing home in the south of England. She took on the job to earn money for her upkeep.'

'Five minutes ago the nursing home placed a return call to that mobile in Paris.'

'Yes?'

'The call was received by a mobile phone located in the Hôpital Pitié-Salpêtrière. Following that a call was placed from that phone to another located in Rue Cambon.'

'Rue Cambon?'

'Henri Paul's apartment to be exact.'

'What did the calls say? Do they know what they were saying?'

'Get into the car.'

Max got into the back of the squad car. As they drove the driver put on the siren, and as if at that signal, the klaxon blare, the emergency workers converged on the area around the Mercedes, the machines erasing the oilstains, the debris trail. The Mercedes on the back of the lorry, a pressed-steel hulk, seeming to preside over the workers, corpsmen to the orphan night.

Harper reached Accident and Emergency. The foyer had filled with dark-suited men. Harper picking up the accents and the looks. French and English security services. Embassy staff. Interior ministry personnel. Diplomatic staff. Outside the foyer were lined up limousines with diplomatic plates attended by uniformed drivers. The first television satellite vans had arrived and technicians moved cables across the lawns and throughways of the hospital and Harper felt for the first time the weight of the regard that was to fall on this place and this death, which had seemed to be in the hands of a small number of people, a cadre of the shadows.

Harper went to his car. He got in and dialled Bennett's number again. Grace answered.

'Grace. Where are you?'

'In Henri Paul's apartment.'

'Where's Bennett?'

'He's in the bedroom. Watching through the window for the girl to come back. I borrowed his phone. I wanted to call my mother. Tell her the news.'

'Where's the numberplate?'

'What numberplate?'

'The numberplate that Bennett found in the tunnel. It was in the back of my car but it's gone now.'

'I don't know.'

'How was your mother?'

'What?'

'How was your mother when you called her?'

'Asleep.'

'Grace. I called the nursing home tonight.' Harper could feel the maw open in front of him.

'Yes?'

'Your mother doesn't live there any more, Grace. Your mother died five months ago.'

The line went dead. Harper started the engine. He saw that the main entrance to the hospital was blocked by a television truck. He turned left. There would be other exits from the hospital. He turned into the complex of buildings. The red brick and concrete pressed around him. He passed the morgue where Henri Paul and Al Fayed lay. A group of dark-clad men stood at its entrance.

Rue Cambon
2.55 a.m.

Grace put the phone in her pocket. She went back into the bedroom. Bennett was watching from the window of the darkened room.

'You get through to the old dear?' Bennett said. 'Taking her Complan is she? We could go two ways on this thing, Grace. Go to the papers. Tell them what we seen. I reckon this. Old Henri was told to take a certain route, go through the tunnel. Then, like you say, they block his way with another car, then a motorcyclist flashes this big light in his eyes, Henri is as blind as a bat. Fact he's in the tunnel means there's nowhere to go. He has to hit something hard, and Bob's your uncle. Mind you, Spencer looked all right but Harper says she's in a bad way. Clever, it is. They got no proof anything untoward got done. Except for two things. We got the numberplate of the blocking car. And we got this bird of Henri's, if she turns up.'

Grace let him talk. The room filled with his conniving talk, with his malign prattle. She looked at her watch. 3 a.m. She moved over beside Bennett. Standing close to him. Knowing that he could smell her. Her perfume. The old alcohol on her breath. Sweet chrism of the anointed.

'Where is the numberplate?' she said. 'What did you do with it?' He turned to her. There was sweat on his face. There was surprise at finding her standing so close. Bennett grinned, a leery thing in the dim street light, peg-toothed, opening his jacket to show the numberplate inserted in a hole in the lining, a Cheapside pickpocket's stunt.

'Me and you's got the brains to make a go of this, Grace. Harper's not talent like us. He's a fucking errand boy. He might be cock of

224

the walk on the Shankill or whatever sewer he got dragged up in, but he's used goods outside of that.'

Grace heard the key turn in the outside lock. So loud it seemed she could hear every noise, tooth and tumbler, the telemetries in miniature, muted and brassy.

'What do you think, Grace? You're a bright girl. You're respectable.'

'Give me the numberplate, Michael.'

'What are you talking about, Grace?'

'Give it to me.'

'Don't go barmy on me now, Grace. You're a level-headed girl most of the time. Think of getting a few bob for all of this. Look after that mum of yours. Bring her home to live if you wanted to.'

Bennett heard the bedroom door open. Bennett turned away from Grace. He saw Henri's woman standing in the bedroom door. Belinda taking off the wig. He saw the shaved head. The pan make-up on the face reaching only as far as the hairline.

'For fuck's sakes,' Bennett said.

'I'm sorry, Michael,' Grace said. Bennett stared at the gun in Belinda's hand. Thinking summer seasons at Blackpool, at Brighton. Danny La Rue. Henri, he thought, you dirty perv. As the transvestite came towards him, Bennett thought that he did resemble a music-hall act of sorts. A reprobate vaudevillian.

Twenty-Three

They are pressing around her. The women of the Salpêtrière. The prostitutes. The laundresses. The lunatic anciennes. She can smell the formaldehyde. The men gathered above her are speaking to each other. The heart is torn. The heart is sundered. *Cours la Reine.* They are in the body with their instruments their probes and protractors and clamps she is laid open like an anatomy plate. Strange procedures are carried out. The organs will be removed and embalmed, the body's deep contraband. She is lost in the machine clusters, the bellows pumping air into her lungs. The masked and robed figures who toil upon her. They are administering electricity to her, the immense voltages putting her back into spasm. The theatre's lights in her eyes, the pure white light. Accessing some deep memory cluster. Gymnastic classes at school. The poses they made them do. Recalled in this agony. Girls in white shorts and white singlets. Arching their backs. Walking like a crab. Light coming in through the high gym windows. The gym smelling of beeswax polish. Hearing the sound of the girls' heels hitting the ramp, vaulting up into the clean scholastic light. The embalmers are coming with their grisly potions. Girls in white shorts and white singlets *go to my love* To see the light again. The light from the tunnel, the white light, the welcoming light.

Twenty-Four

The street door to Henri's apartment was open. Harper went up the stairs. The apartment door was ajar. He went in. Masson was standing in the kitchenette.

'They have gone,' Masson said, 'they have taken Bennett with them.'

'I rang the nursing home,' Harper said, 'they told me that Grace's mother has been dead for five months.'

'The mother in the nursing home.'

'She told Bennett that her mother was in a home. That was why she took the job. To pay the nursing home charge.'

'I see.'

'What about the woman. Spencer?'

'She was pronounced dead five minutes ago. An artery to the heart was torn.'

Harper sat down in the arm of Henri's sofa. He wondered when Grace had been turned. Who she was working for. Men's motivations for treachery were usually easy to fathom. The greedy, the gamblers, the homosexuals. Women were harder to work out. There was a history of unlikely female spies in the Service, spinsters in gardening hats who passed state secrets to Eastern European governments. They were tweedy and unfathomable, users of complex dead-drop systems. He thought that Grace might belong to their ranks. She fitted the profile, alone and in her forties, living in deep cover. He found himself attracted to the perfidy of it. Masson answered his phone. He listened for a minute.

'Come with me, Mr Harper,' he said.
'Where?'
'Gare Austerlitz.'

Andanson stopped the car three miles short of his house. He got out and stood on the side of the road. He couldn't drive any more. His stomach on fire. His hands shaking. He walked around the car. The passenger-side paintwork was scraped, the wing mirror snapped off. The rear bumper and trim of the Fiat had been damaged. He saw that the numberplate was missing. He didn't know if it had been lost in the tunnel or if it had fallen off on the autoroute. One of the rear tyres was worn down to the wire where it had rubbed against the distorted bodywork.

He remembered looking to the side, seeing the Mercedes, the long black limousine alongside, seeming to emerge from a gilded pre-war narrative of privilege and repute. Andanson half-expecting a man in evening dress in the rear, a mistress in furs. He remembered the Mercedes passing him on the left so that he could see Spencer's head in the rear window. Glancing up again to see the BMW motorcycle bearing down on the Fiat, passing it and pulling in front of the Mercedes, the rider standing on the footpegs. Andanson knew that it wasn't a camera in his hand. Then the flash. Andanson feeling the fear. As though a chemical fire had ignited in the tunnel, as though a terrible process was under way. Andanson thinking he was burned. Thinking that the skin sloughed off. Andanson letting go of the steering wheel, bringing his hands up to cover his face against the light. The Fiat drifting towards the tunnel wall. He had remembered Niki Lauda rising from the cockpit of his crashed Ferrari, the fuel vapour igniting, the air around the racing driver's head shimmering with near-invisible flame, the helmet on fire, the carbon-fibre melt dripping on his overalls.

There had been a noise which he took to be the sound of the Mercedes crashing. He took his hands down from his face and steered the Fiat back into the centre of the road. He looked in his centre mirror and saw the Mercedes, spun round in the middle of the tunnel so it was facing the way it had come. The grey BMW had pulled up alongside it. Its helmeted rider looked down into the Mercedes then started to move forward again. Andanson's Fiat out of gear, barely coasting, as the BMW drew level. The rider turned his head towards Andanson. He put his left hand to his visor and saluted him. Andanson could only see the eyes and he thought that they belonged to the South African he had met although he could not be sure.

The motorcycle accelerated away. Andanson looked back at the Mercedes again. Dense oily smoke poured from the engine bay. Andanson thought of fire in the tunnel. Deadly flashovers. Roofing materials lit to combustion point. Gases wreathing, hot and toxic. He accelerated towards the tunnel mouth and out into the night.

He walked around the car again then he turned and looked back in the direction of the city. The sun had just risen but it was hot and though he was many miles away he thought that he could see the tall buildings of the city through the dust particles, something hazy and disquieting about the way they seemed to acquire definition in the late summer air. Andanson thought of ramparts of lost cities, sunbaked figments. For a moment it seemed that he gazed upon some unquiet Nineveh, eerie and lost.

Gare d'Austerlitz
4.40 a.m.

Masson's car brought them past the Gare d'Austerlitz to a bridge which crossed a disused cutting. A group of uniformed policemen and railway employees stood at the parapet of the bridge. One of the policemen beckoned to Masson. Harper followed him to the parapet and looked over. Bennett's body lay on the margin of the track below, face-up, his legs folded underneath him. His face no paler than it had been when he was alive. Harper thought that this was the right place for Bennett to die. There were scrubby plants growing between the railway sleepers. There were diesel stains on the dry earth. There was litter between the rails and beyond it a freight yard with disused shedding and rusting wagons pulled up in sidings. A place on the urban margins. Lost to dereliction. One of the hidden places of the city. A railway employee spoke to Masson.

'No,' Masson said in English, 'not a vagrant.' The man spoke again.

'A suicide,' Masson said. He looked at Harper. 'Will we designate Mr Bennett's death as a suicide? A man who jumped from a bridge? What do you think, Mr Harper? You are an expert in these things.'

'It doesn't matter what I think,' Harper said.

'No,' Masson said.

'It doesn't matter what I think, but they threw him off the bridge.'

'They are always the most effective and simple assassinations,' Masson said. 'The killing made to look like a suicide.'

'Or the killing made to look like an accident,' Harper said.

'Yes,' Masson said, 'suicide or accident.' They stared down on the body of Bennett. A recovery crew making its way across the rails to him. The body semi-concealed in the bridge girderwork and corroded signal wires and industrial piping.

                        Pas de Normandie
                        24th September

They kept Harper for three weeks. He was brought to an air base on the coast. It looked as if it had been built in the 1940s and had been closed for years. Sand from the beach blew across the cracked runways and concrete aprons. Although there were sentries he did not feel under guard. He was billeted in a wooden barrack where he took his meals. There was a portable television in the barrack and at night he watched the French news. He saw footage of Spencer and of her funeral. He saw the paparazzi taken into court. He saw still photographs of Henri. He did not understand what the commentators were saying, and he felt remote from the events in the Alma tunnel. During the day he walked on the beach, among the ruins of the coastal defences, tank traps and blockhouses. He understood the interlude that had been made available, the pensive weeks ceded to him. At night he lay awake listening to the salt-whitened hut timbers flex and crack in the onshore winds. The dune grasses rustled in stiffening westerlies. Autumnal tidal movements shifted wrackbeds and sand bars shorewards.

On the 23rd September Harper was called to the prefab which served as the camp office. Masson was waiting for him. Harper sat down on a steel-framed chair opposite him. Masson put a file on the Formica table. Harper recognised it as his own Special Branch personnel file. He knew what Masson would have found in there. There were yellowed newspaper cuttings. Photographs of Harper at rudimentary checkpoints, surrounded by men in combats with scarves covering their faces.

Masson removed a photograph of Glenn from the file. The lost boy. Masson placed a copy of the boy's statement on the table, the handwritten statement, words misspelled, scratched out. The unlined pages, still creased from Glenn's jeans pocket, the blue dye in the folds. You could almost hear the boy's voice when you looked at it, the collapsing syntax. *I was took to this big house. They done them things to me. They done them unspeakable acts.*

Masson took a typed statement from the folder and put it in front of him. Harper recognised Bennett's signature at the bottom.

'What's that?'

'It is Michael Bennett's statement detailing your involvement in the death of Glenn Annett. He accuses you of murder.'

'You don't say.'

'The boy was to appear in court.'

'They ran a boys' home. They pimped the boys to politicians and military then blackmailed them. Glenn was going to give evidence.'

'So you throw him off a ferry.'

'Where's this going?'

'The point is to make sure you know that you cannot speak about whatever you saw in Paris. There is a warrant in this file. The name on it is John Harper. The charge is murder. It can be made active at any time.'

'I've no notion of talking to anybody. Any word of Grace?'

231

'No. We don't know where she is.'

'Or who she was working for?'

'She had an interest in alternative lifestyles. She went on enlightenment courses, that kind of thing. We believe cult members made contact with her then.'

'Cult?'

'The Order of the Solar Temple. Or someone using the cult as cover.'

'Government?'

'Sometimes it is hard to tell where government ends and where other agencies begin.'

Harper wondered if there had been something awry in Grace from the beginning. If she had always been working for someone else.

'What about Bennett?'

'His body has not been claimed. The police could not find any living relations.'

Harper thought that the same end awaited him. A man without background.

'So what happens then?'

'He will be buried at the expense of the state.' Harper thought that such a process seemed apt to the man that Bennett had been. A cheap deal coffin and an unmarked grave.

Masson put the statements and photographs back into the file. He stood up.

'All that is necessary for you to know is that the accident was caused by Henri Paul. He was drunk and drove recklessly.'

'He didn't look drunk to me.'

'You wouldn't know. You weren't there,' Masson said. He opened the office door.

'Hold on,' Harper said, 'what about Max LaFontaine? What happened to him?'

'Extradition papers were served on him. He chose not to contest them. He is in custody in Geneva awaiting trial on charges of fraud. He claimed to have access to transcripts of Spencer's conversations. He was trying to sell them.'

'That's what we were doing. Protecting his investment.'

'The transcripts were bogus.'

'Far as I'm concerned you're all bogus.'

'Why do you want to know about LaFontaine?'

'He still owes me money.'

Masson looked at him. He held his eye as though he apprehended delinquent matter at the core of Harper, then turned and walked towards the camp gate where a car was waiting. Harper went back to the barrack to pack his things. When he had finished he walked to the gate where the sentry directed him to a bus stop. The bus took him to St Malo where he waited for the Paris train, the wind blowing grit along the platform, making the station canopy shiver. It was night when he boarded the train and there were few other passengers, the roads he saw from the window empty of traffic, autumn coming in, the stations going past. Dinan. Rennes. Laval. He remembered other nights on trains, coming home from the sea, from Newcastle, from Portrush, and the late-season grace that the fading light embodied then. Not this fraught light, closing from the west.

Twenty-Five

The skies above the plateau were clear except for cirro nimbus high in the jetstream. Stable high-pressure systems carried in from North Africa, the Azores, summer heat starting to build over the plateau. Over the pitted landscape. Over the scrub plant growth. There are limestone swallow holes, deep souterrains. Habitation is sparse. The military use areas of the plateau for training and exercises. There are fire zones, unexploded munitions in the undergrowth. Esoteric significance is claimed for the landscape. Ley lines are mapped out. The plateau was owned by orders of the Knights Templar and Hospitaller. Their empty guardhouses stand on karst ridges.

Andanson's car was found by a group of soldiers returning from an exercise. The Fiat Uno had been disposed of. Andanson had been driving a BMW 3 series since 1997. The soldiers had seen the smoke but the fire had almost gone out by the time they reached the car. It was parked in a clearing at the end of an unmetalled track. Portions of the car's interior and frame had been reduced to ash. The window glass had shattered, charred laminates scattered on the ground. The car frame was all that was left, grey and ash-coloured so at first the soldiers thought they were looking at a ghost car, or that a summoning had taken place in the clearing. When they got closer they could smell the vapours and toxins from the fire, the petrochemical residues. They realised that there were the remains of a man in the passenger seat.

Later it would be maintained that James Andanson had bought a jerrycan containing forty litres of petrol on his way to the Larzac. It was maintained that he had locked himself in the car and poured the petrol over himself and set light to it. One of the soldiers used the short wave to inform the local gendarmerie of what they had found. Another one noted that the keys were not in the ignition. The keys were never found. The men stood around in the clearing, some of them smoking, waiting for the police to arrive. Death by fire, the thing he feared. Andanson's body charred to the sinew. His face like a tribal carving, doleful and ancient. An evening breeze stirred the ashes and the plateau grasses. *Uxor principas.* The men could hear the sounds that the car made as it cooled. The wind rising now, a hot mistral blowing down from the hills and tarns of the Larzac, a pledge of the heat to come, of summer, whistling in the exposed shell of the silent car and in the trees, the season's lone chorale.